CONFIRMED RAKE

PARADIGM
PRESS

MARTHA KEYES

Chapter One

REBECCA

There was nothing quite so upsetting as stale bread. The buttery buns I had watched the footman clear from the dinner table a few hours ago were sitting in the kitchen downstairs. I could see them in my mind's eye, growing staler by the minute. Whether it was that thought or the excitement buzzing about in my stomach like a hive of bees keeping me awake, I was unsure.

It felt wrong to be anticipating my new life so much when I had left Grandfather alone back in Northumberland, but I couldn't help it. I had treasured my years caring for and providing company for him, and I missed him dearly, crusty temperament and all. But I would be untruthful if I pretended that, for the past few years particularly, I had not been hoping for a chance to rub shoulders with people my own age, to experience a life of balls and dinners and the theater. That opportunity was finally here, and I felt it in my bones, tasted the possibilities on my tongue as surely as I had tasted the brioche at dinner.

Tomorrow I, Rebecca Russell, would attend my first ball—in Brighton, of all places. Try as I might, I could not keep my mind from exploring all the opportunities that lay before me: the people I would meet, the friends I would make, the sights I would see, and—my stomach fluttered more forcefully than ever—the possibility of making a match. My interactions with people of the opposite sex had thus far been almost entirely restricted to Grandfather's friends, all of whom were three and sometimes four times older than I. In Brighton, though, there were bound to be younger gentlemen. Younger, unmarried, and, I dared hope, unafflicted with gout.

I threw off my covers, along with any thought of sleep. It would be a shame for those delectable rolls to become day-old buns. Besides, my sister-in-law, Diana, had made me promise that I would treat the Brighton townhouse as though it was my own, and I had become accustomed to seeking out refreshment before bed. Grandfather had always insisted on such an early dinner.

I slung my arms through my dressing gown as my stomach rumbled. If I fed its hunger, perhaps I would find it easier to calm my nerves and sleep. As things stood, there was simply too much occurring in my mind and body to allow for rest.

The August night was warm enough not to require a fire, which left me with no quick way to light the candle beside my bed. Oh well. I didn't particularly wish to draw attention to my midnight expedition. The last thing I wanted was Diana's or the servants' first impression of me to be that of a troublemaker. I had only been here a matter of hours, after all. Diana had been kind on the journey here, but I couldn't deny the awe she inspired within me.

Perhaps I would have felt less guilty traipsing about in the dark if my brother Duke had been present in the house. He had been obliged to return to his estate in north Kent post-haste after conveying me to Brighton. But even if he *had* been here, I doubted I would have felt entirely at home. I had been living in Northumberland with Grandfather ever since Father's

death—fourteen years ago now—giving me little opportunity to see my siblings. Duke had come to visit when time allowed for such a journey, but most of our interactions had been by letter.

I turned the handle as slowly as possible, opening the door to see into the darkened corridor. A bit of moonlight streamed in through a latticed window by the stairs. The unfamiliarity of it all intensified the buzz in my stomach. It had been so long since I had been somewhere unknown, somewhere I could explore and be surprised. The most exhilarating bits of life at Millbury House had been restricted to discovering what new ailment had beset Grandfather's friends on the odd occasion when he was feeling up to the task of entertaining—and it had been some time since that.

I padded across the carpeted floor and down two sets of stairs, keeping next to the carved wooden railing in an effort to prevent any creaking. My nighttime expeditions to the kitchens had taught me that the middle of the stairs was most likely to betray me by ghastly whining.

These stairs, however, made no such complaint at my presence. The house itself was utterly silent, but I could hear the sounds of the odd carriage rattling by as I made my way toward the servant stairs that led to the kitchens.

When I reached my destination, my eyes searched the stony room, adjusting slowly to the relative darkness of the lowest level of the house. My gaze passed by the hanging baskets of onions and potatoes, the wall of spices, then landed squarely upon a platter on the table, covered with a cloth. The dim but telling dome shape informed me that I had found what I was looking for.

The stone of the kitchen floor was cold even through my stockings, but they muted the pattering of my feet as I approached the table. I pulled back the cloth and smiled slightly. Bits of moonlight filtered through the two low sash windows next to the delivery door, and the buttered tops of the three buns glistened subtly, beckoning to me.

I picked one up and bit into the moist, fluffy bread. Closing my eyes, I savored the way it melted on my tongue. There was something divine about buttery brioche. Grandfather's doctor had insisted he follow a strict diet to manage his increasingly painful gout, and to make the prospect more palatable, I had offered to abide by the same regimen. The deprivation I had experienced as a result was unspeakable. I had resorted to rummaging through the kitchens in the late evenings to appease my hunger, but there had never been anything like these buns awaiting me.

I took another bite, sighing with contentment and leaning against the table, feeling calmer than I had in weeks. My brother's letter inviting me to stay with Diana in Brighton had produced a constant frenzy of anticipation inside me. But for now, I felt content, and stray bits of a nursery rhyme floated about in my mind.

O Mistress mine, where are you roaming?
O stay and hear, your true love's coming,
That can sing both high and low.

The melody diverged from the one I knew, and I paused my chewing, my brow furrowing as the singing grew nearer.

Trip no further, pretty sweeting.
Journeys end in lovers' meeting,
Every wise man's son doth know.

My nose wrinkled at the discordant warbling. It was *not* in my head after all. The singing was muffled, coming from somewhere outside and drawing nearer each moment. Whoever was singing was either not a particularly good singer, or they did not know the correct tune.

Taking another quick bite, I went over to the sash window nearest the door, wondering if I might glimpse whoever was serenading the town at such an hour. Based on how much louder the singing had become since it had started, the crooner must be passing by.

Putting my hands on the cool glass of the window, I stared out into the dark moonlit night, where a staircase led up to the pavement and the street. My ears strained to hear more of the melody as a carriage passed by, and my eyes searched the darkness, trying to make sense of the shapes of an unfamiliar place.

A face appeared on the other side of the window, and I leapt back, my scream muffled by a mouthful of brioche as my pulse sprang to life.

Chapter Two

REBECCA

I was not the only surprised one. The sound of my heart thudding was drowned out by a clattering outside as the form stumbled backward and into the empty crates at the bottom of the staircase.

My hand went to my mouth. The fall looked painful, as did the subsequent tumbling of the crates onto his form. But the man—for I could see now that he was, indeed, a man—seemed largely unfazed by it. He pushed away the crates, scrambled up to his feet ungracefully, and left the mess behind him without a second thought.

With my heart thudding hard enough to crack my ribs, I took in his appearance. His cravat was undone and his waistcoat unbuttoned, but he wore the unmistakable clothes of a gentleman. He brushed off his sleeves and began to sing again as though nothing had happened.

What is love, 'tis not hereafter,
Present mirth, hath present laughter:

Again, the melody differed from the one I knew, and it sat ill with me. I stood transfixed as he approached the window again.

It would be locked, of course, but my heart knocked wildly in my chest regardless.

The man put his hands to the sash and tried to open it. It creaked as it opened slightly, and my eyes widened in horror. The lock must be broken.

I debated for the merest fraction of a second before hurrying to the window and pressing down on the frame to close it. I could not allow a thief into my brother's home, be he dressed as a gentleman or not.

The window shut with a soft thud, and the man looked back at me, blinking as though he had forgotten my presence already. I almost feared he would fall back into the crates again with the way he swayed. Certainly, he would deserve such a fate for trying to force his way inside someone's home.

With his dark brow furrowed, he put his hands back on the sash.

"If you try again, I shall scream for the housekeeper," I said, hoping he could hear me as easily as I had heard him through the closed window. My chest rose and fell under my thin chemise and dressing gown, and my hands trembled on the wooden sash. Truthfully, I was likely to scream even if he *didn't* attempt to open the window again. Life at Millbury House had not accustomed me to this sort of occurrence. Perhaps living with Grandfather had aged me prematurely. I didn't think my heart could sustain such excitement much longer if this was what it meant to live in town.

The man's mouth turned up into a charming but crooked smile. "I wish you luck. Mrs. Groves sleeps all the way down the corridor." His speech was both muffled by the window and slurred, but his familiarity with the housekeeper's name gave me pause. What sort of gentleman forced his way into the kitchens of a home where he knew the location of the housekeeper's room?

"I am Valentine Donovan," he said, answering my unasked question, "and I mean to enter."

I frowned. Valentine Donovan? That was the name of Diana's brother, I was nearly certain. But what in heaven's name was he doing entering the kitchens? And through a window, no less? "If that is true, why not use the front door?"

My question amused him. "Have you ever woken my sister at night?" His words still slurred together. He swayed slightly and, after regaining his balance, he leaned his forehead against the window, as though he needed to rest against something solid. Instinctively, I took a step back. There was still a pane of glass between us, but with his face so near, I could see a cut on his cheek. It looked fresh, a stark red against his skin. It must have happened when he had fallen into the crates.

Guilt and misgiving assailed me. I had caused him injury—inadvertently, perhaps—and was refusing him entry into his own sister's home. He had as much right to be here as I did.

"Why not use that door, then?" I gestured to the one a few feet from me.

Head still against the pane, he put a hand out, inviting me to try it as he hummed the nursery rhyme. I moved over to the door and tried the handle. It had been locked by key.

"I tried it last night. This window"—he placed a hand on it—"is the only way in at this time of night."

I hesitated, feeling more and more convinced he was who he claimed to be. But it would be well to make certain. "If you *are* Valentine Donovan, what is the name of your sister's husband?"

He banged his head against the pane once, as though my question was unbearably stupid. "Marmaduke Russell, though any number of people could have answered that question."

My mouth twisted to the side. Undoubtedly he was right, but a man with ill intentions surely would not have pointed that out. That was certainly a point in his favor.

I sighed, content that he was indeed who he said he was.

Shifting back to the window, I waited for him to pull his head away from the glass, then I pushed up on the sash. It gave way to my efforts, only to stop halfway. Mr. Donovan gave it a shove, sliding it the remainder of the way, and I stepped back, allowing him space to climb through.

But it was not a smooth entry, and I stabilized him as he brought one leg and then another through the window. Being so near him, I was assailed with the smell of alcohol, and I recoiled, putting a hand to my nose. "You smell."

I pulled my lips in, realizing how uncivil my remark was, true as it might be. I had never been particularly adept at controlling the impulse to say what I was thinking.

"Thank you." He slipped down from the window, faltering in his step and stumbling toward me. He caught himself on the nearest table, but not before our faces nearly touched.

I stilled, stunned by the sudden proximity.

His head wobbled slightly. "You also smell," he said.

My brow wrinkled, and I turned my head to the side, sniffing my shoulder and hoping to discover what unpleasant scent I had been unknowingly trailing about with me all day—or longer, perhaps.

He shut his eyes and inhaled. "Butter." He pulled back, his lids heavy as he sang.

What's to come, is still unsure.

In delay there lies no plenty.

He paused, those dark, lazy eyes regarding me, raking over my face unevenly. The lines that followed played in my mind.

Then come kiss me sweet and twenty:

Youth's a stuff will not endure.

My heart flipped and leapt as the thought of kissing presented itself to me. The fact that he had declined to sing the song's end made me wonder if his thoughts were in the same place. Now that he was inside, I had the chance to survey him more thoroughly, though the dim light made my eyes strain. His hair looked almost black and was cropped short, and his jaw was shaded by stubble. He was the most handsome gentleman I had ever seen. Not that I had seen very many.

But any appeal the thought of being kissed might have held was overwhelmed by the smell of alcohol that hung about Mr. Donovan like a cloud. When I finally *did* receive a kiss, assuming that prospect lay before me, I wanted the man to choose it with his wits fully about him—and also because he loved me, not because a song and a muddled mind prescribed it.

"It is the buns," I hurried to say, hoping to change the subject.

His gaze became more alert, fixing on me. "Buns?"

I nodded. "Brioche."

He looked about the room until his eyes settled on the uncovered buns, and he walked toward them, his boots chafing on the stone with his lazy steps. Clearly, Mr. Donovan had been drinking too much, and now he meant to indulge in my precious brioche buns. If he ate as much as he had drunk, they would be gone in a trice.

"Beware of gout," I blurted.

Chapter Three

VALENTINE

My hand hovered atop a bun, and I looked over at the young woman with narrowed eyes. "Gout?" My senses were admittedly dulled from imbibing too freely, but I was fairly certain I had heard her correctly.

She nodded decisively. "All the drink you have obviously enjoyed tonight in addition to these buns . . . it is a terribly dangerous combination, sir."

I frowned, for my head hurt from trying to follow the conversation. "Just how old do you think I am?"

She lifted her shoulders. She couldn't have been more than a few years younger than I—around twenty, I guessed, though admittedly one couldn't trust one's conjecture after as much brandy and port as I had imbibed this evening—but she had a youthfulness that was evident even to my bleary vision.

"I shall take my chances, I thank you." I picked up a bun and bit into it. The softness of the bread and the savoriness of the butter was like heaven after the burning, strong drink of the last few hours. It had been some time since I had indulged in drink as I had tonight, and I was annoyed to find that it held less pleasure now than in the past. Even the numerous glasses I had allowed myself hadn't entirely dulled my feelings after the row I'd had with the Admiral yesterday morning. Neither had they lightened the weight of the debts I had saddled myself with. Indeed, the cost of what I had drunk had deprived me of the last bits of money in my possession.

The young woman watched me chew for a moment, something very much like hunger in her eyes. In a decisive movement, she walked over and took up the half-eaten bun sitting beside the last remaining whole one. She was dressed for sleep, her dark hair plaited and tied at the bottom with a little scrap of fabric that was fraying at the edges. I wished to touch it, for it looked as though it might come undone entirely at the slightest contact.

I blinked away the impulse. Drink did strange things to a man's mind. "Who *are* you, by the by—besides a fierce defender of kitchens and protector against gout?" I paused, unable to stop a little smile and a bit of provocation. "A new maid, perhaps?"

Her eyes filled with dismay. "Oh dear. Do I look like a maid?" She put a hand to her hair, as though it bore the blame for my teasing assumption. Perhaps she had noted how my gaze had dwelt on the fraying fabric.

I smiled and took another bite from the brioche, leaning against the table. Her reaction—and the fact that she had not recognized that I was teasing her—amused me. I was used to my provocation being met with either overwrought indignation or overt flirtation.

"Do not worry," I said, aware of how my words wavered yet unable to stop it. "You neither look nor speak like a maid. But when you accuse me of being in danger of an ailment that almost exclusively afflicts old men, I deserve a bit of revenge. You are a guest of my sister, I take it?"

"No," she said. "That is, yes. I am Duke's sister, but he is not here, so I suppose I am your sister's guest at present."

My chewing slowed, and I surveyed her, trying to force my

mind to focus despite the veneer of fuzziness over the room. So, this was Russell's sister. I could easily see the resemblance between them now. It was too dark and my mind too muddled to see the precise color of her eyes for certain, but they were light like his and framed similarly by dark lashes and brows. She was a becoming young woman, but she had the naive manner of a miss just out of the schoolroom.

I didn't dally with such women. Not ever. And certainly not when Duke Russell was involved. I valued my life more than that.

"You are my first acquaintance in Brighton, you know." She looked over at me as she took a hearty bite from her brioche. Her form was so unladylike, so visibly driven by hunger that I could hardly suppress my amusement.

Her words finally registered with me, dampening my smile. "How unfortunate for you."

Her brow puzzled as she chewed. "Why?"

"Your brother would not wish for you to know me, Miss Russell. And I think Diana would not approve, either." I watched as a few crumbs dropped onto her silk dressing gown. "A shame, for I suspect I would like you."

Her eyes widened. "You do?" It was endearing how surprising this was to her. "Suspect it, I mean."

"Yes," I said flatly. "But you mustn't return the favor on any account." There was no danger of that, once she learned more of me. Plenty of people would make sure of that. I turned away, intent on finding a bed to sleep in. It had been a long and unpleasant two days.

"Why mustn't I?"

I paused in my progress toward the door that led to the stairs. "You met me climbing through a window, Miss Russell. And foxed. Surely that is reason enough."

"Foxed," she repeated. "That means drunk, doesn't it?"

I turned more fully toward her. With any other young

woman, I might have thought she was being coy. But Miss Russell looked anything but that. Indeed, she seemed genuinely curious.

"You had a sensible reason for climbing through the window, though," she said. "And as for the drinking"—she shrugged—"at least you are still kind. Grandfather is most irritable when he has been foxing."

I didn't know whether to laugh at her free—and terribly incorrect—use of the word or to chastise her for it. Her brother would undoubtedly wish for the latter. She had mentioned her grandfather, too, and I had a vague memory of Russell telling me his sister lived in some far-off county with their grandfather. "You shouldn't use that word."

Her brow puckered. "But *you* did."

"Because I am irredeemably vulgar and entirely unsuitable. And now I have just taught *you* a vulgar word—likely the only one in your vocabulary. Further evidence of my point."

"No one is irredeemable." There was no pity in the words. It was a simple statement, said with all the confidence of someone who had never done anything that required redemption. They were the words of a saint.

That was what Miss Russell reminded me of: a statue in a church or abbey. A soft, feminine figure conveying and honoring innocence, something to be revered and emulated, meant as fodder for contemplation by my ilk in hopes of inspiring us with a desire to repent.

"And it is *not* the only vulgar word in my vocabulary." She shot me a significant glance.

I raised my brows. "Pray, enlighten me." I took another bite of my brioche, suddenly and absurdly curious to hear what would emerge from her mouth.

Her lips pursed slightly, but there was a quiver at the side, and my gaze fixed upon it. I found it devilishly hard to bring anything into focus, what with the combination of drink and dark, but that little quiver seemed important to me. A hint of rebellion in a saint, perhaps.

"By-blow." The words burst out of her mouth, and I stilled, blinking in surprise. That was hardly the phrase I had anticipated.

She looked abashed. "Oh dear. I have shocked you."

I couldn't help a chuckle, wry as it might be. In no imagined world could someone like Miss Russell truly shock me. "Hardly. It was unexpected, that is all."

"I should not have said it." She set down the last remaining bit of her brioche as though she had lost her appetite. "Grandfather nearly had an apoplexy when Mr. Finner said it at dinner one evening." Her gaze turned thoughtful. "Though, why men should be so hesitant to speak of their tussles in front of females, I do not understand."

My eyes narrowed. "Tussles?" I had never heard illicit affairs referred to in such a way, and to hear her speak of them with such frankness surprised me. What would she think to know that the man standing in front of her was generally assumed to be a man's by-blow?

Her gaze came up and met mine. "Yes. Opinions are strong and emotions run high, particularly amongst men, I think. It seems inevitable that they will sometimes feel obliged to settle such disagreements in a physical manner."

I squeezed my eyes shut, trying to make sense of what Miss Russell was saying. Blast the brandy.

"Your head is hurting," she stated. "And little wonder, for you are wounded. Shall I fetch a warm rag?"

I shook my head, for I was still attempting to make sense of the strange conversation. "Are you sure you do not mean the phrase *come to blows?*"

Her nose wrinkled. "Do I? Mr. Finner said he had learned of another of his grandson's by-blows. I understand the grandson is quite prone to violence, though I could not say, for I have not met him myself. Not that he would engage in such an activity in my presence, for if men cannot *talk* of such things in the presence of females, surely they must refrain from engaging in the behavior itself. Though, if he is lost to all sense of propriety, which his grandfather certainly thinks, perhaps he *would* become violent in my presence."

I used the opportunity to take the last bun, hiding my amusement from view. There was an entire lack of artifice in Miss Russell's demeanor, and I had to admit I found her innocence charming. She could not even use vulgar phrases correctly.

"*Come to blows,* you said," she continued thoughtfully. "Is that another way of saying by-blows, then?"

I forced my mouth to compose itself and brought my head up to meet her gaze. "No, it is not. But I agree with your grandfather that neither phrase should be used by you."

"Oh dear," she said with a little smile. "You must at least tell me what they mean, though, for I do hate to be ignorant, particularly if I have been assuming wrongly of Mr. Finner's grandson. Perhaps he is *not* prone to violence." Her expression brightened. "You see! It is just as I said. Everyone is redeemable."

I hesitated, unsure whether it would be more dangerous to tell Miss Russell the true offenses of Mr. Finner's grandson or to leave her in ignorance, with the distinct chance that she might at some point scold men engaging in a bout of fisticuffs for fathering illegitimate children. I had a sudden and keen desire to be present should it ever happen.

A carriage rolled by outside, pulling me from my thoughts, and I looked around. I had forgotten we were alone in a dark kitchen, eating brioche and discussing cant expressions as though it was the most natural thing in the world.

"Content yourself, Miss Russell," I said. "Though you may have been incorrect about the precise nature of the failings of Mr. Finner's grandson, his redemption is by no means assured."

I needed to go before I unwittingly acquainted Miss Russell with anything else vulgar. My mere presence was sullying her stark white reputation and innocence.

Bun in hand, I turned aside.

"But your injury," she called out.

I stopped in my tracks again, taking note of the stinging on my face for the first time. It was hardly the worst injury I had ever sustained, but she seemed to be genuinely concerned.

She came up before me, looking to a point on my cheek. "You have a cut. From the crates, I assume."

I put a finger to my cheek, and my finger came away unbloodied. "It is nothing."

She pinched her lips together. "I was the one who caused you to sustain it, and I feel a degree of responsibility for it. Small injuries can lead to dire situations, Mr. Donovan. Mr. Finner, of whom you will recall I was just speaking—" She stopped, her brows contracting. "Perhaps you do *not* recall it, for I have found Grandfather to be particularly forgetful when he has been foxing. In any case, Mr. Finner, the one with the violent grandson I mentioned, sustained a cut on his hand from his snuff-box, and he very nearly died as a result of it."

"His snuff-box?" I repeated.

She nodded, meeting my gaze with wide-eyed sincerity.

"Any man who still uses a snuff-box deserves to be cut by it. Rest easy, Miss Russell. I assure you I shan't die, and I need no treatment."

She hardly looked pleased, but she gave a nod. "As you wish. I shall see you tomorrow, then?" The thought seemed a happy one to her. Extraordinary creature, she was.

"I doubt that," I said. "It would be better for you to forget tonight altogether." It was possible I would, whether I wanted to or not.

"Oh, I couldn't possibly forget my first Brighton friend. Besides, tomorrow you shan't be foxing, and you can walk through doors quite properly instead of climbing through a window. And perhaps I can teach you the proper tune of the nursery rhyme you were singing."

I chuckled softly. Singing when in my cups was an unfortunate habit of mine—unfortunate, for the quality of my singing deteriorated with each glass.

"A gracious offer, but I think not." I let my gaze run over her face again, at the twinkle of moonlight reflecting in her eyes, at the way she looked to be on the verge of a smile. In another world, perhaps the two of us might have been friends. But this was not another world, and not even a night of drinking could persuade me that it was. "I *do* like you."

I shouldn't have said it aloud. One said a great many ill-advised things when drunk. It was true, though. I did like her, and I felt a sliver of regret that this conversation would never be repeated—and that I might not remember it at all.

But I couldn't allow another interaction like this with Miss Russell, charming as she might be. The last thing I needed was to add Diana and Russell's anger to my woes.

Miss Russell smiled widely, and her head tilted as she looked at me frankly. I had been regarded in all sorts of manners since my return from the Navy two years ago—with the utmost contempt, with a mind to seduce, with unmistakable fear—but never had I been regarded with so much frank curiosity.

"I like you, too," she said, "even if you *do* sing *Oh Mistress Mine* incorrectly"—her nose scrunched slightly, though she was smiling—"and hopelessly out of tune. And, frankly, I would like you more if you hadn't taken the last bun. I came all the way downstairs expressly for those, you know, and I have only had one. That is, I had four at dinner, but that was hours ago, and I am quite famished again, not to mention being entirely unable to sleep, which I find most often happens when my stomach is empty."

I thumbed the smooth side of the bun in my left hand, the

one I hadn't bitten into yet. I shouldn't want her to continue liking me, shouldn't be considering giving her the last bun to appease her. This young woman hadn't the slightest idea to whom she was talking, how I was regarded by Society, or the extent of my sins and misdeeds. She *shouldn't* like me.

My hand grasped the bun more tightly, the tips of my fingers digging holes in its soft crust.

"Good night, Miss Russell."

VALENTINE

Someone was simultaneously shoving me and drumming on my skull, but my limbs were weighed down, and I struggled to turn away.

"Valentine."

I winced at the loud voice and cracked my lids open enough to know that the aggressor had also brought the sun itself into my bedchamber. I hurried to shut out the brightness by closing my eyes tightly and shifting my head away, but I couldn't escape it.

"Valentine." The woman's voice was more insistent this time. "Wake *up*."

Suddenly, my pillow slid out from under me, my head dropping with a thud onto the mattress beneath. My eyes flew open in time to catch a glimpse of the pillow hurtling toward my face. It made contact with a *thump*.

"I'm awake," I growled, grasping the pillow and throwing it back toward my sister. I had done it without looking and was fairly certain it missed her entirely.

"How good of you to join the civilized world." She thrust open another set of curtains.

My eyes slowly adjusted to the light, and my head throbbed as I tried to push myself to a sitting position. I cracked an eye open, and the view that met my gaze was enough to remind me that I was in Brighton, not in Kent at Blackwick Hall. The memory of the row with the Admiral filtered through the pounding, and I frowned more deeply. We had had too many arguments and falling outs to count since my return from the Navy, but this one had been . . . different. Different enough to be bothering me two days later.

Diana threw something else at me, and I swore, reacting too slowly to keep the bundle of cloth from whipping me in the face and leaving a stinging sensation behind.

I clenched my jaw and scowled at her. "Will you stop throwing things at me for three seconds? May a man not have a moment to wake?"

She gave a little scornful laugh. "You accuse *me* of being uncivilized when you are the one who insists on sleeping like a man who cannot afford so much as a shirt? Put that on, for heaven's sake."

I reluctantly obliged, pulling the shirt she had thrown at me over my head.

She sat down in one of the two chairs near the window. "Now, what in heaven's name are you doing in one of my beds again? My housekeeper informed me you slept here last night as well."

I pulled the shirt down over my chest and stomach. I had arrived late two nights ago and, after a bit of trial and error, discovered one of the kitchen window latches to be broken. "And here I thought I had made the bed so nicely."

"Not to Mrs. Groves's standards. But enough of that. Why are you here?"

"The Admiral ordered me out."

She pursed her lips, a bit of sympathy in her eyes. "Perhaps if you called him Father like the rest of us, he would be less inclined to do such things."

I gave a scoff, but there was a grain of truth to what she said. It grated him when I referred to him by his title—undoubtedly because it was not done with the respect he felt due—and that was part of why I did it. I had so little power in my relationship with him, I had to grasp at whatever was available to me.

But that wasn't the only reason I insisted on it. It was a necessary reminder to myself that he was *not* my father. At least, I was tolerably certain he was not, and so was Society, if the gossip was heeded. And gossip was always heeded. The matter of my parentage had been an object of speculation for as long as I could remember. I had little in common with the Admiral or my three siblings in appearance, and, over the years, it had become a favorite pastime of many to speculate on the subject of my paternity.

I looked up and found Diana's intent gaze upon me. She grimaced sympathetically. "Give him a few days, and he will forget about it, as he always does."

I shook my head. Diana didn't understand. We were both headstrong, but she was the sort of headstrong the Admiral admired. I was not. And she hadn't been there for this particular quarrel. "Not this time, Di. This time was different. He demands I make changes."

She folded her arms and looked at me through narrowed eyes. "What sort of changes does he wish for?"

I shook out the twisted sleeve of my shirt. "Leading the Navy at Trafalgar, achieving captain at fourteen, never being born, amongst other things, I daresay."

"Come, Val, he is not so unreasonable as that. What are his true demands?"

I shrugged. "Evidence of reformation, of course. No more gambling. Keeping more respectable company. Marrying someone proper."

Her gaze went to my cheek. "And I take it by your injury that you have tossed that idea through the window. Come to blows with someone at the public house last night, did you?"

Come to blows. The words kindled a memory, and I strained at it for a moment, a little smirk coming to my lips as my conversation with Miss Russell came to mind. I *hadn't* forgotten it. That felt like a victory.

"Where is Duke?" I asked, refraining from answering her question.

"In Kent, seeing to matters at the estate. He expects to return in ten days or sometime thereabouts. You know, perhaps it *is* a good time to reform, Val. Every rake must do so at some point. There is something particularly revolting about a rake of advanced age, as I am sure you will agree. Besides, reformed rakes make the best husbands, they say."

I scoffed lightly. "And who, pray tell, are *they*? Whoever you are referring to apparently did not say it enough for *you* to believe such a thing, for you married the straightest of arrows."

The phrase was utter nonsense. What woman in her right mind would wish to attach herself to a scoundrel, forever wondering if his supposed reformation was genuine and lasting? And what was more, what woman could ever love such a figure to begin with?

"You might like being reformed," Diana continued. "I never thought to marry, as you well know, but I confess I have become a converted proponent of it now. There is something to be said for having a person who has sworn to love you and stay with you, no matter how terrible you are or how miserable you make them." She smiled teasingly.

I couldn't even manage to return a smile. If vowing to love someone truly meant they would love me always, I might have been tempted by marriage. Perhaps. But a vow was merely a string of words, as easily forgotten and disposed of as the scraps of yesterday's dinner. My own mother had made such vows, and it seemed as though *she* had forgotten them enough to produce *me*—and she had been a much better person than I ever would be. As for the Admiral's vows to my mother . . . well, he had certainly not stayed with her, opting for the far preferable life of sailing without her whenever possible.

"Or," I said, "you could simply lend me enough money to save me the trouble of reforming."

She was shaking her head before I had even finished my sentence. "Duke has expressly forbidden me from doing such a thing. He is convinced you need to experience the consequences of your actions."

I leaned my head back against the headboard. I couldn't fault Russell for being disobliging. I wouldn't have lent myself money if I'd had any to give. I was a poor investment, and Russell was far too wise for that.

"I could write Father and advocate for you," Diana offered.

"Don't bother." I closed my eyes, wishing my problems would disappear as easily as my lids shut out the light. "He specifically mentioned that such an act would be fruitless."

"Well, there is no harm in trying."

I shook my head. "I shall come about. I just need a place to stay in the meantime."

How I would come about, I didn't know. I needed money, and I needed it soon. The Admiral had generally rescued me from the worst of my debts. It had always been just enough to tide over the most insistent of my creditors, but never enough to offer me a clean slate. The result was that I remained under his power, which I resisted mightily—too often by accruing more debts just to anger him.

I hoped I would not be obliged to resist his power much longer, though. The prize money I was due from my time in the Navy—a tidy thousand pounds—could not stay in the Admiralty Court forever. It had already taken far more time than was usual to settle everything. In my last letter, Jones, the prize agent assigned to the case, had assured me that progress had been made and I could expect a resolution soon. Nearly a month had passed since that communication.

Diana looked at me apologetically. "You cannot stay here, Val. Duke's sister has just arrived, and I shall be busy escorting her to various engagements." She smiled and lifted her chin. "I am a respectable chaperone now."

"A chaperone, let us say," I teased. "I fail to see what your social engagements have to do with me staying here, though. Particularly when you remain in my debt from all the help I gave you with Russell."

She directed me with an impatient expression. "Rebecca is an impressionable young woman, Val. It became very clear on the journey here that she has almost no experience at all in Society. She has been under the care of their grandfather since their father's death, and as the man was somewhat of an invalid and a recluse, she was forced to be one as well. The last thing I need is your handsome and mischievous face making things any more difficult as I attempt to give her a proper start in Society."

"In one breath, you admonish me to reform, and in the next, you forbid me from keeping company with anyone respectable?"

The only acknowledgment of this she gave was a rueful smile. "I will help you in any other way."

"Any way but providing the only things I need," I countered. "Shelter and money."

She stared at me consideringly. Seeing an opportunity to press my advantage, I pressed on.

"I shall keep away from your sister-in-law," I said. "I am not in the habit of preying upon naive young women, you know. All I require is a roof over my head and a bed to sleep in. I shall even eat with the servants—or in here. Just for a few days. A week, perhaps." If I could manage to discover how soon the prize money would come into my possession, I would be in a much better position.

Diana held my gaze, weighing my words against whatever qualms she had. The length of the hesitation only underlined how I was perceived, even by the one remaining woman in my life who loved me. I was a risk, a blot on the family's reputation.

"Very well," she said. "You may stay here. But only if you promise that you will *heed me*, Valentine. You are under my power now." The threat of the last sentence was sapped by the way she smiled as she said it.

"I promise," I said, too desperate to do anything but agree. "Your wish is my command, dear sister."

I had secured shelter. It was money I now lacked. One creditor in particular had become belligerent with me, and I wouldn't put it past him to send me to debtor's prison if it came down to it. Being in Brighton would buy me some time, at least, for no one knew I was here yet.

If my older brother, Theo, hadn't been in India, I might have humbled myself enough to ask him for assistance. But as that was not an option, I was obliged to look elsewhere. I needed news of the prize money, and there was one person who might have more recent knowledge of things than I.

I dressed for the day and, with a glance down the corridor to ensure I would not break my word to my sister by running into Miss Russell, I slipped out and toward the servant staircase. If Miss Russell made a habit of spending time in the kitchens, however, my efforts might prove in vain.

She was not there, though. Perhaps the kitchen devoid of brioche buns was not a place of interest for her. The only people there were the cook and two maids, whose eyes both rounded at the sight of me. One of the maids' mouths drew up into a smile that welcomed interaction.

I gave the three of them a quick nod and slipped through the door before any of them could address me. The crates were stacked neatly again, and I took the stairs two at a time up to the pavement. What a difference sobriety and an unlocked door could make for entering and exiting a house.

I made my way on foot to the townhouse of Captain Yates, only to be disappointed upon being informed that he was out.

"Do you know when you expect him to return?" I asked the butler.

"No, sir," he replied unhelpfully. I had the sense he didn't particularly care for me, though what I could have done to instill him with such a dislike after only a few seconds, I wasn't sure.

"Perhaps you could do me the favor of informing him I will return before dinner, then." I began to turn.

"It would be a wasted effort, sir," said the butler stonily. "My master has other engagements this evening—with the esteemed Lawrenson family."

I turned back toward him slowly. The words were meant to put me in my place, I gathered. "Well," I said with a sneer, "I would hate for you to waste any effort doing anything but being disagreeable, so you needn't bother informing him of my visit."

It appeared I would be attending the Lawrensons's party tonight.

Chapter Five

REBECCA

As we rumbled along toward the Lawrensons's party, I rubbed the gauzy fabric of my overdress between my gloved fingers. I had worn this dress only a handful of times. There had been little occasion for it at Grandfather's, and yet I hadn't been able to resist when I had seen the gauze in the dressmaker's shop in the village closest to Millbury House. It had been a lavish purchase for a future I could only hope for.

That future was here, just minutes away, and my heart beat erratically as we drew nearer.

Diana smiled at me from across the carriage. "Nervous?" She looked a vision in salmon-colored silk, and so entirely at ease.

"Excited," I replied. I *was* nervous, but it wasn't the dreading sort of nervous. It was all anticipation.

"I am glad to hear it. I hope the evening will be enjoyable. And I vow not to suffocate you as your chaperone. I am here to help you, you know. To assist you in meeting new people, including a few gentlemen, I hope"—she raised her brows enigmatically at me—"and to protect you from the rakes and rogues who will be so overset by your beauty that they may forget themselves."

I gave a little laugh, finding it difficult to imagine such a situation—or how precisely Diana would handle it. I had no doubt she would know just what to do. She seemed a paragon of wisdom and elegance to me, which was why I declined to ask her the question buzzing about in my mind: what exactly *was* a rake?

I had heard the term, of course, and knew rakes were frowned upon, but no one had ever provided a definition. They never did. People simply bandied words about, expecting that everyone would implicitly understand them. On the few occasions where I had asked Grandfather to explain a particular word to me, he had frowned deeply and told me not to bother my head about it. I had come to find that I could often guess at the definitions instead of providing evidence of my ignorance, and thus far, that had served me fairly well. But *rake* was one of those hazy concepts I had never been able to understand.

I peered through the carriage window as we slowed to a stop in front of the Lawrenson house. It was lit up like a beacon in the night, each of the orderly windows lining the red-brick façade displaying a trio of candles. I had never seen anything so lovely or inviting.

Our own carriage was one of many lined up to let passengers down, and as more were waiting behind ours, Diana hurried us out and onto the pavement. A pair of footmen in light blue livery welcomed us through the front door, and immediately the buzz of chatter hummed in my ears. I had never heard such a glorious sound. So many voices blending together, punctuated by laughter, and all to a background of violins and a cello.

My pulse raced at the prospects before me. Who might I meet this evening? When I laid down my head to sleep in a few hours, whose faces and names might accompany me there and into my dreams?

Diana smiled at me, as though remarking my awe, and

guided us toward the drawing room, from which the music was coming. I yielded to the pull of her arm on mine, allowing my eyes to travel about the corridor, taking in the silks, the taffetas, the waistcoats, the feathers, and the beads. It was everything I had ever hoped it would be, but I would need a week to appreciate it all.

I was hardly aware of our quick interaction with the host and hostess, so distracted was I by the grandeur of the affair, and before I knew it, we had passed into the drawing room. My gaze was immediately drawn to the people gathered in the middle of the ballroom. Seeing people standing up for a set should not have affected me so, and yet it sent a shiver of pleasure through me.

Diana observed the direction of my gaze, and her expression took on a hint of apprehension. "You can dance, can you not? I should have asked before bringing you."

"Yes," I replied enthusiastically.

A year ago, I had managed to persuade Grandfather to hire a dancing master. Not even the fact that Mr. Abbot hadn't taught a lesson in two decades or that he was five-and-seventy had dampened my excitement, neither had the slow tempo we were obliged to keep as a result of his rapidly advancing age. I had made no complaint, merely practicing on my own at a quicker tempo after he had left each week, an imagined young gentleman guiding me about, or, on one or two occasions, one of the maids, though that had never gone terribly well.

But tonight, I wouldn't need to imagine a partner or ask a maid to assist me. I would finally be able to put my learning to use.

"Perhaps we can find a bit of refreshment as we get our bearings," Diana suggested, nodding at the tables in the corner. "I do love it when the refreshments are presented this way. When the servants bring them about, they never seem to pass by me when

I most want them to. Besides, I am starving, and it is much less awkward to fill a plate than to take five pieces from a footman's platter. Shall we?"

Happy for any opportunity to take in more of the surroundings, I readily assented, hoping it would help me to find my way. Besides, I, too, was hungry, and supper would not be for some time.

The refreshment tables were spread with platters of small sweetmeats and savory sandwiches, with large crystalline bowls at either end, offering drinks for parched throats after vigorous dancing.

A liveried servant ladled the offered beverage into two cups, and I took mine with thanks, sipping it gingerly. It was sweet and fruity, and the feel of it washing down my throat and into my stomach made me realize how thirsty I was. I drank it eagerly, savoring the taste of something besides the tea I almost exclusively drank. Of course, a hot cup of chocolate in the mornings before Grandfather woke had also been a guilty pleasure of mine—a secret between the cook and me.

Before I well knew it, my cup was empty. After a moment of hesitation, I set it down on an empty platter and glanced at Diana. She had a small plate in hand and was adding items to it. She was quick, easily selecting an option from each plate amongst the array of offerings.

I followed suit, taking up my own plate and looking at the spread before me. I was uncertain what most of the dishes were, and a few of them looked downright questionable. My hand hovered as I glanced at Diana's plate, noting how full it was.

I swallowed. What if I chose something that did not agree with me?

Dithering between two platters full of things I didn't recognize, I glanced up, hoping to see if Diana had truly selected one of everything. If so, was it because she was hungry, or because she felt it polite to do so?

Her back was to me, though, as she spoke with an older man. I looked around at the other people selecting refreshments. Two women stood at the other end of the table by the beverage bowls. One sipped from her glass, and a sour look pinched her face.

"Ratafia," her friend commented. "Dreadful stuff, is it not?"

The other woman nodded, and, setting the nearly-full glasses down, they moved away from the table.

I looked back at my own empty glass, suddenly questioning my enjoyment of the drink. A twinge of overwhelm tainted my excitement. The sheer number of unfamiliar people around me was equally exciting and unnerving. On the rare occasion when Grandfather had welcomed guests to Millbury House, there had never been more than ten sitting to dinner, and none of them had been under the age of forty.

To my left, a gentleman emerged from the door leading off the drawing room, and my heart gave a little stutter. Mr. Donovan had been handsome in the darkness, but in the light of the drawing room, I found myself staring for a moment. Unlike Diana, his features were dark, accentuated further by the furrow on his brow as he stopped before the drinks. The cut he had sustained from the crates last night was still visible on his cheek, but it did not detract from his handsomeness.

He inspected the contents in the glasses, and his frown deepened, as though he, too, was suspicious of the beverage. He took one from the footman and lifted it to his lips.

Relieved to see one familiar face in a sea of strangers, I flitted over to him. "Mr. Donovan."

His head came up, and his gaze settled on me for a moment before recognition lit his eyes and lessened the furrow in his brow. "Miss Russell." He gave a little bow, then looked around. His eyes settled on his sister, still engaged in conversation.

Remembering myself, I executed a small curtsy. "How very good it is to see a friendly face."

His eyes narrowed for a moment. "Indeed." He looked as though he might turn away.

"I am sure you are rather busy," I said, "but would you mind telling me what these are?" I stepped back toward the platters which had given me hesitation.

Mr. Donovan looked at me for a moment, glanced at his sister again, then joined me.

I pointed to the food in question. "I am quite hungry, and of course I wish to give a fair chance to the refreshments the hosts have so kindly provided, but I admit to feeling a bit of doubt over these two in particular."

"Licorice and marzipan," Mr. Donovan said, pointing to them in turn. "But you are under no obligation to eat anything, Miss Russell, however kind the hosts may be. In fact, I would urge you not to eat either of those."

"But I wouldn't wish to give offense." I glanced around the room, wondering where the hosts were—and *who.* I had met them but could not even remember what they looked like. "Who *are* the hosts, if you please? I met them when we first entered, but I was so taken up admiring everything that I do not remember their faces."

A little half-smile appeared on his lips. "Over there, by the orchestra."

My gaze moved to the place indicated, and I took in the sight of a middle-aged woman in a scarlet gown and feathered head-dress and a man in a well-tailored black suit and gold-buckled shoes that glinted in the candlelight.

"Thank you ever so much," I said, relieved. I did recognize them faintly now that he had pointed them out. In fact, Mrs. Lawrenson's enormous feathers had been what had distracted me from their faces when we had met. "And you are certain that I shan't be considered rude for not trying *all* the refreshments?"

"I am certain of it, Miss Russell."

I glanced once more at the licorice, then up to Mr. Donovan. "I imagine that must be preferred over the possibility of me choking on them or spitting them out."

His amusement grew, though the frown upon his brow continued to be a fixture. "Undoubtedly. Though an argument could be made for the latter instance."

My brows went up. "Could it?" I couldn't imagine how.

"It would be a valuable commentary for the Lawrensons, providing them with food for thought on the selection of refreshments offered here. Perhaps I will make it a point to choke on the ratafia, which is unfit for human consumption." He regarded the glass he held with aversion.

"Oh." I bit my lip with an abashed smile. "It seems I have very poor taste, for I quite like it. I already finished my glass."

"Then you should have another," he said without hesitation. "You needn't apologize for your tastes, Miss Russell, or be so concerned with what other people like and dislike. That is the path to unhappiness."

"Perhaps you are right," I replied. "I do so wish to make a good impression, though."

His eyes searched mine with an unreadable expression. But it was a relief to admit such a thing, and there was no trace of disgust in his eyes.

I leaned closer to him, lowering my voice. "The truth is, Mr. Donovan, I have been looking forward to precisely this sort of party for years, but now that I am here, I am realizing that I haven't the slightest idea how to go on in such a place." I looked at him, hoping to gauge his reaction. I tried to smile. "Each minute, I feel certain that I will embarrass both myself and your sister by the end of the night."

His gaze still rested on me, his dark brown eyes scrutinizing but not uncomfortably so. "I promise you, Miss Russell, that you could do nothing which would embarrass my family more than we are entirely capable of managing on our own. Cease thinking of such a thing and enjoy yourself." He offered me his glass. "If you want another cup of ratafia, you should drink it, devil take my opinion and the opinions of everyone in the room."

I hesitated for a moment, then took the glass from him. A trace of a smile graced his lips, as though in approval of my acceptance of the drink. "Good evening, Miss Russell." With a slight bow, he turned and walked away.

I watched him disappear through the door from where he had come, wishing I could so easily set aside the opinions of the scores of people here as Mr. Donovan did. Perhaps that was what was meant by a rake—someone who paid no heed to the opinion of Society. If so, I would give much to be just such a rake just now.

With a glance around the ballroom, I took a sip from the drink he had given me, feeling a little thrill at the act of raking. But when yet another pair of women looked at the bowl in disappointment, I set the rest of it down as inconspicuously as possible. Taking up my plate instead, I began selecting items from the platters that interested me, forgoing the ones Mr. Donovan had warned me against, hoping dearly that he had been correct about not offending the Lawrensons.

"Still choosing, are you?" Diana came up beside me. "Forgive me for not introducing you to Mr. Gamblin, with whom I was just speaking. It was an intentional oversight on my part, for I rather thought you would prefer *not* to know him." Her nose scrunched in distaste. "He is a widower who thinks he is thirty rather than twice that, and I imagine you would find his assertiveness off-putting. I know I do. But come, let me intro-duce you to the Bradleys. They are the most charming young women."

With plate in hand, I allowed her to lead me to a group of three women standing by the curtained windows lining one side of the room. After a quick greeting with the woman I assumed to be the mother of the younger two, Diana urged me forward.

"Allow me to introduce you to my sister-in-law, Miss Russell. Rebecca, this is Miss Bradley and Miss Maria Bradley. I just met them the other day and immediately thought to introduce them to you when you arrived." She turned her attention to the young women. "Miss Russell came just yesterday from Northumberland."

The Bradley daughters smiled at me and curtsied. Feeling hopeful at the prospect of adding two more faces to the ones I would recognize, I returned my own curtsy, doing my best to be a credit to Diana.

She and Mrs. Bradley began discussing my brother's whereabouts, and the daughters stepped toward me, the older of them taking me by the arm.

"Miss Russell, how glad I am that your sister-in-law thought to make an introduction. Maria and I were admiring you not five minutes ago as you stood by the refreshment table."

"Oh," I said, wondering if they had seen me drinking the ratafia and what their opinions on it were. "That is very kind of you to say. I, too, am glad for the introduction, for I know not a soul here aside from Diana."

The sisters exchanged glances.

"But you know Mr. Valentine Donovan," Miss Bradley said.

"I should say so," said Miss Maria with a twinkle. "Enough so that he gave you his own drink."

A little flush crept into my cheeks at the tone of their comments. "Well, he is my sister-in-law's brother, you know."

"What has that to say to it?" Miss Bradley quipped, her eyes gently teasing me.

"He was merely being kind," I said, hoping my cheeks weren't as red as the heat in them had me imagining.

"But that is just it, isn't it?" said Miss Maria. "He is not the type of man to be kind."

My gaze flitted toward the door he had disappeared through earlier, and I felt a bit of defensiveness on his behalf. My interactions with him were limited so far, but aside from his defiantly taking the last brioche, he had done nothing to make me think him unkind.

"Perhaps the reputation is unjustly bestowed," I said.

The sisters shared glances again, though the meaning in them was unclear to me. I felt an unexpected bit of envy for the relationship they had, the way they could communicate with one another without saying anything at all. I had always wished for a sister of my own, or a bosom friend, at least. Perhaps—just perhaps—I would find that in the Bradley sisters. They had embraced conversing with me so readily, after all, and that was a kindness I would not soon forget. Diana was a more natural option, of course, for she was my actual sister-in-law, but she was so far above me in every way that she felt more like a mentor than the sort of intimate feminine connection I had hoped for.

"Well, it is a shame if he is not a suitor of yours," Miss Maria said. "What a thing it should be if he was! A confirmed rake is nearly as much of a catch as a titled gentleman."

There was that word again: *rake*. And a confirmed one, at that. Whatever that meant.

"Have you any other suitors?" asked Miss Bradley.

I thought of my time at Grandfather's house, wondering if there was anyone during my time there that might qualify as a suitor. But by no stretch of the imagination could I claim such a thing. "I am afraid not," I said with a sheepish laugh. "Have you?"

"Of course," Miss Bradley said it so matter-of-factly.

"Mr. McGrory asked Grace to dance two sets last week," Miss Maria said. "He is just over there. The one with the blue waistcoat. And just behind him is Mr. Kinsley." The little smile she wore told me that he was *her* suitor. "He is the son of a baronet."

"A second son," Miss Bradley clarified.

"Yes, but son of a baronet all the same, and the eldest brother is not at all in good health, so there is reason to hope." Miss Maria admired him for another moment, then turned her attention back to me. "We must find a suitor for *you*, Miss Russell."

"Every young woman must have one if she wishes for a successful Season," said Miss Bradley. "There is nothing more certain to attract a score of other suitors. Men do love a competition."

"Oh," I said, wondering what things besides suitors I was deficient in—and how I could acquire one without delay. I had so many questions for the Bradley sisters, but I kept them inside, unwilling to give further evidence of my ignorance for fear they might deem me unfit for association.

They were good for their word, though. Between Diana's and their efforts, I was soon introduced to no less than five young gentlemen, all of them agreeable, one of whom asked me to dance.

Performing a country dance in a set of people my own age under the blaze of a chandelier full of candles was unlike anything I had ever done. My staid lessons with Mr. Abbot had not prepared me for the exhilaration of it, or for the way the energy of those around me added to my own. And while my own partner was not the most enthusiastic of dancers, the other gentlemen with whom I shared passing figures more than made up for that. I ended the set breathless and my cheeks aching from smiling.

As promised, Diana as a chaperone was helpful but not over-bearing. When I was not engaged on the ballroom floor, she kept near enough to be on hand, but far enough to offer me the opportunity to engage in conversation.

It was a night of wonder and elation, almost dreamlike as I went from conversing to dancing on the ballroom floor to wondering at the opulence of the house, with its black-and-white checkered floor, ornate plasterwork ceiling, and intricately carved wood trim.

But the night was not to proceed in untainted magnificence.

Chapter Six

VALENTINE

If I had harbored some hope that my stay at the Lawrenson dinner party would be short, I was disappointed. Captain Yates seemed intent on avoiding me, dancing every set as he did, without an opportunity for me to have even a moment's word with him between.

I took refuge in the card room, observing other gentlemen at play who were fortunate enough to have money to lose. I certainly did not. Not yet, at least. Once I received my prize money, I would be in a position to discharge my debts and still have some money to spare. The Admiral would then cease to hold power over me.

Every ten or so minutes, I slipped into the drawing room with the hope of catching a glimpse of Captain Yates unengaged. The first three times, my only reward had been a brief interaction with Miss Russell at the refreshment table and, later, a group of giggling young women asking me if I meant to dance. I hadn't said a word in response but rather stared broodily until they had run off together in another fit of nervous giggles.

I emerged a fourth time, seeking out the captain amongst the skipping dancers, the onlookers, and the small groups of people standing in huddled conversation wherever they could find a space for it. My gaze alighted on a dancing Miss Russell, her cheeks becomingly flushed, her face wreathed in a smile of genuine joy, and bits of her hair surrendering to the vibrancy of her dancing by coming loose from her coiffure. She was the picture of innocent and unaffected pleasure; it was a sight not often seen amongst all the jaded people in attendance tonight.

In a few weeks, she would become like the others, dancing less for the joy of it and more for the game of cat and mouse that drew the crowd in attendance. It was a shame, really, for her smile was charming and guileless.

She made a fault in the figures of the dance, and my muscles tensed as I watched for the resulting embarrassment. This was what she had been speaking of earlier, I assumed—her fear of embarrassing herself and my sister.

If *I* let what people thought of me affect me, I wouldn't survive. Someone like Miss Russell could afford to do so, for she was beginning here with a clean slate, a reputation untainted.

But she merely laughed at the mistake in a way it was impossible to find anything but endearing. I was glad for her sake to see her unfazed by the error, apparently unworried by what her partner or the audience thought of it.

"Received any inspiration?" Diana came up beside me, trying to follow the direction of my gaze.

I folded my arms and turned my attention back to Captain Yates. "Aside from a renewed determination never to again attend such an event?"

"And yet here you are," she said with a significant glance. "What I *meant* was have any fine young ladies caught your eye and instilled you with a desire to reform?"

"I hate to disappoint you, Diana dearest, but I imagine you are well accustomed to it by now. Much as it may surprise you, I did not come for such a purpose. I came to speak to Captain Yates."

"So you say," she said, cocking an eyebrow at me. "But there must be some young woman here you have watched with more interest than the others."

I hardly managed to suppress a roll of the eyes. "I changed my mind. I *have* been inspired this evening—by the vividness of your imagination. If you'll excuse me, I'm for the card room again."

Diana sighed, but she made no move to stop me, and I threaded my way through the people who stood between me and my refuge. Once inside, I surveyed the tables that had been set up, deciding which game would be most interesting to observe.

I felt eyes on me, and my gaze stopped at the corner table where two middle-aged men played. The one looking at me had hair like salt and pepper, though his brows remained a solid black. It was Lord Newham, a baron of substance and a surly countenance. Society might all have their own views on to whom I owed my parentage, but I had instinctively felt that Lord Newham was the man from the first moment I had seen him.

His gaze dropped back to his cards, just as it always did when we happened to catch eyes, which had been an oft-repeated occurrence since my resignation from the Navy and frequenting of Brighton Society. More than once, I had considered speaking to him, but I had never actually done so. I wasn't sure I truly wanted to. If the man was my father, he certainly didn't wish for it to be known. And I had had enough of unwilling father figures.

I settled in to watch a game of piquet, sipping a glass of port as I did so. My patience was finally rewarded a quarter of an hour later when Captain Yates appeared in the doorway. His eyes searched the room and, once they had settled on me, he made his way toward me.

"Donovan," he said with a breathless smile. Undoubtedly, he had just finished yet another lively country dance.

"Your appetite for dancing is unmatched, Yates." If the Admiral had heard me addressing the captain without his title, he would have had a fit.

Yates undid the buttons of his coat, as though ready to settle in to a less formal environment. "Just making up for your lack of such an appetite."

"My sincerest thanks," I said drily, pouring him a glass.

"What is it, then? Your sister said you were looking for me."

I made a mental note to thank Diana for saving me. Heaven only knew how many more sets I would have been obliged to wait out. I handed him his glass and led the way to two couches near the unlit fire, where he flipped out his coat tails as he sat down.

I took a seat, stretching out my legs and crossing my ankles. "I have a few creditors—one in particular—who are becoming bothersome. Perhaps you know the type."

"Decidedly," he answered with a chuckle, taking a sip from his glass. Somehow I imagined he *didn't* quite know. We both came from money, but Captain Yates had two distinct advantages over me: firstly, he was his father's heir, and secondly, his father was nothing like mine. If he was truly in financial distress, his father wouldn't hesitate to pay his debts. He couldn't know how it felt to be constantly threatened with the sponging house.

"I thought I would ask you if you had heard any recent developments with the prize money. The last I had heard from Jones was that he expected things to be finishing up soon."

Yates frowned. "I haven't heard from him in a fortnight or so, I think. These things can take a devilish amount of time, you know. And our case has taken far longer than normal."

I gritted my teeth. "I am aware of that." After my resignation from the Navy, Captain Yates had been in command when he had taken yet another prize ship. The money from that venture had already been paid out.

"I'd lend you the money myself, Donovan, but I happen to be in a bit of a difficult position myself."

I swore, setting down my drink on the side table beside my chair. "I am not asking you for money, Yates."

"No," he said, tossing back the rest of his port. "But I would still give it to you if I had it. Now if you'll excuse me, I've promised the next set to Miss Robles."

"Of course you have," I said.

He flashed me a smile and set down his glass with a clank. I watched him go, suppressing a sigh. An entire night wasted.

I finished off my drink and rose from my chair, wishing I had the prospect of a game of faro or *ving-et-un* to take my mind from my troubles. I watched Yates bow to Miss Robles and lead her to the ballroom floor. Miss Russell did not form part of the set, and I looked to the refreshment table, wondering if she had decided she wished for another glass of ratafia.

She was not there, though, so I glanced to my side and found her just a dozen feet away from me, with indeed another glass in hand. She was turned with her profile to me, admiring a set of ornate, porcelain vases on the mantel before her. True to form, Diana was nearby but engaged in conversation.

Miss Russell glanced over at me, and her mouth drew up into a smile. She was rosy-cheeked, the joy of the evening written in the lift of her expression.

"Mr. Donovan," she said, summoning me over with a hand.

After a moment of indecision, I walked over to her.

"Have you seen these vases?" she asked. "They are exquisite."

I had seen a hundred such vases over the course of my life, but with her wide, awe-filled eyes looking at me expectantly, as though a treasure awaited me if only I would take a few steps nearer, I found myself stepping closer, albeit reluctantly.

"Look at the detail." She brought her face a mere few inches from one of them. The vase was supported by a set of porcelain claw feet with gold nails.

My lips drew up in disgust. I had told Miss Russell not to worry about how her tastes differed from those of other people, but I repented of that comment now. "It is hideous."

"Positively grotesque," she replied, flooding me with relief on her behalf. "But that makes the attention to detail all the more fascinating, doesn't it? To spend so much time and effort and money on something so . . ."

"Ghastly."

"Precisely," she said reverently, turning her head to the side as though in awed admiration. Her eyes narrowed in a squint. "I find it fascinating, for instance, that the artist—"

"A generous description."

"—managed to make the most delicate of gold leaves, and yet this creature set atop it is impossible to identify." Her nose scrunched. "Is it a pig? A cow?" She put a hand to it.

"Careful, Miss—"

The vase teetered on its clawed feet, and both of us rushed to stabilize it.

Neither succeeded. It slipped from its place and fell to the floor, shattering into a hundred pieces of gold leafing and painted white porcelain. The crash was resounding, echoing throughout the high-ceilinged drawing room and putting an end to music, dancing, and conversation as all eyes searched for the source of the commotion, landing squarely upon us.

I glanced at Miss Russell, who had hopped away to avoid the shards scattered about our feet. Her eyes were wide, her expression stricken, her body motionless, as though she had been frozen in time—and horror.

The silence was stunning in its starkness, contrasted against the cacophony of sounds present just moments before.

"Oh dear!" Mrs. Lawrenson came rushing through the crowds, holding her skirts up to the side, her dismayed gaze taking in the scene of destruction. "My precious *Sèvres!*" She bent over and picked up one of the clawed feet, from which one of the nails had broken off.

I knew an overwhelming desire to laugh at the ridiculous spectacle of her cradling the repulsive fragment in her hands. But Miss Russell betrayed no such desire. Her cheeks swiftly shifted from a colorless pigment, much like the white porcelain, to a splotchy red. I thought of her words from earlier—how long she had anticipated this night, her fear of bungling it. The way she stared at the remnants of the vase, it was as though the broken pieces signified the ruins of her reputation, the lost chances at a successful entrance into Society.

Mrs. Lawrenson's gaze had been scouring the wreckage, but it flicked up to me.

"How did this happen?" Her eyes shifted between me and Miss Russell.

This was Miss Russell's worst nightmare come true, and I didn't think I could watch it unravel, watch *her* unravel. She had been so vivacious, so vibrant just two minutes ago.

I took a small step forward, bringing the attention firmly onto myself. "So clumsy of me."

Chapter Seven

REBECCA

My jaw went slack, and I stood stock still. Mr. Donovan was taking the blame?

His words acted like water over the heads of the audience and the silence gave way to hushed chatter.

"He is *smiling*," said a nearby voice, hardly bothering to whisper.

"Probably drunk," said another. "He usually is, you know."

I glanced over at Mr. Donovan, my brow furrowing. I hadn't noticed any signs of drunkenness from him, certainly nothing like last night. Something flashed in his eyes, and a muscle in his jaw jumped. His lids suddenly drooped ever-so-slightly. Picking up a small fragment by his feet, he offered it to Mrs. Lawrenson with a little stumble.

"Those go together, I imagine." His words slurred slightly as he tried to reattach whatever he was holding—the clawed nail, apparently—to the foot. It tumbled into Mrs. Lawrenson's hand.

What in the world was he doing?

Mrs. Lawrenson's mouth pressed into a thin line. "This vase"—her voice shook with restrained anger—"cost fifteen guineas."

My eyes widened. I had broken fifteen guineas. Shattered them to bits. It was a staggering price, and for something so . . . monstrous.

"Then you grossly overpaid, Madam."

Mrs. Lawrenson's body shook with fury. "It was part of a set —a one-of-a-kind set. It must be replaced."

Diana came up by my side, taking my arm in hers. I closed my open mouth, blinking as though I had been in a trance until now. Diana's eyes were intent, fixed upon her brother, who spoke.

"If it is, as you say, one of a kind—I think we may thank the powers that be for that fact—how could it possibly be replaced?"

Her gaze turned stony. "With money, Mr. Donovan. Your money."

She expected him to pay. To pay for *my* error, for I had been the one to reach for the figurine on top, and Mr. Donovan had attempted to warn me. I glanced around the room at the scores of eyes watching us. How I wished I could shrink back into the curtains and disappear. But I couldn't allow Mr. Donovan to take the blame on my behalf.

I stepped forward, gathering my courage. "If you please—"

"Of course, Mrs. Lawrenson," Mr. Donovan said, cutting me off unceremoniously. "Only send over the bill." He blinked lazily and glanced at Diana. "To the Russell residence."

"It shall be done immediately," Mrs. Lawrenson said.

I made to speak again, but Mr. Donovan flashed me a warning glance I didn't dare ignore. Its lucidity reconfirmed my suspicion that he was only *acting* drunk.

Two footmen appeared, one with a broom and the other with a bin, and Diana ushered me away to make room for the sweeping. I felt sick as I followed her, my gaze seeking Mr. Donovan. But he was already gone.

"I am feeling a bit under the weather," Diana said. "Would you mind terribly if we went home?"

My throat constricted. "Of course not. It is undoubtedly for the best."

She instructed a nearby servant to have our carriage brought around.

"Nonsense," she said as we made our way back to the house's entrance. "It has nothing to do with that silly vase and everything to do with the fact that I don't sleep terribly well when Duke is away, which means I am a bit tired. Valentine," Diana called out as we emerged into the lamplit street.

He was a few yards ahead of us, apparently intending to walk home, but at the sound of his sister's voice, he paused. His erect posture shifted to a looser one as he turned toward us.

"You can ride with us," Diana said.

"I am walking," he said with a quick glance at me under his drooping lids.

My chest tightened. Was he angry with me? For being so reckless? For being such a coward that I hadn't spoken up immediately, as I should have?

Diana's lips tilted up in amusement as our carriage rolled to a stop in front of the house. "I cannot possibly let my brother wander the dangerous streets of Brighton in such a state. Get in, Valentine."

He looked as though he might resist—a jaw so rigid was not the result of a submissive man—but after a moment of silence, he relented. Shuffling his feet, he approached the carriage as Diana and I descended the steps toward it.

"The door," Diana said, and Mr. Donovan paused mid-motion, backing out of the carriage door and standing to the side to assist both of us up the sole step. I tried to catch his eye, but it was no use. His veiled gaze avoided mine.

Sighing, I chose a seat beside Diana while Mr. Donovan took

his seat across from us, sliding into the corner and resting his elbow on the small lip of the window.

Diana rapped a fist against the ceiling, and the carriage lurched forward. We drove in silence for a moment. Mr. Donovan closed his eyes, and his head slumped onto his supporting hand.

"Enough with the act," Diana said. "If you think I cannot tell when you are well and truly bosky, you do me an injustice. And I am glad that you are not, for I need to speak with you."

Mr. Donovan's gaze shifted to me for a moment.

I, too, needed to speak with him. I needed him to know how grateful I was for his intervention—and that I meant to pay back every penny of the cost of the vase. But that conversation would have to wait.

"I had a letter from Father today," Diana said.

Mr. Donovan made to rise. "Now I *am* walking."

Diana put up a hand to stop him. "No, you are not. This is important."

His jaw tightened, and he leaned back against the squabs.

"He has guessed, of course, that you came to me after . . . everything. He wishes for me to send weekly reports to him on your progress."

Mr. Donovan turned his head to the side and gave a little snort.

"You may scoff all you want, but you need him. I would hazard a guess that you haven't fifteen guineas to offer Mrs. Lawrenson, to say nothing of the other debts troubling you."

My guilt-stricken conscience reared its head, urging me to speak. "*I* shall be paying the fifteen guineas."

"No," he said firmly.

Diana sat silent for a moment, her gaze shifting between the two of us. "Whatever the case, I urge you to strongly reconsider your approach to Father's demands. I think with a bit of effort on your behalf—a few drives in the park with eligible women, making appearances at more parties like tonight's, being seen in the presence of respectable young ladies—he might relent enough to pay some of your more imperative—"

"*Enough.*" Mr. Donovan's voice was as tense as his expression, any trace of pretended intoxication long gone.

Diana pinched her lips together, holding his gaze for a moment before turning to me. "Forgive us for speaking so freely, Rebecca. I hope you will excuse it, as we are family now. I know we may rely upon your discretion."

"There is nothing to forgive, of course," I hurried to reply. "And I shouldn't dream of . . . that is, yes, you may indeed count upon my discretion—and my assistance, if I can lend any." I glanced at Mr. Donovan, hoping he would understand how eager I was to repay his kindness.

Diana smiled at me gratefully. "It is very good of you." She turned her attention back to her brother. "We may speak of this more tomorrow when you have had time to consider things."

"No consideration is required," he shot back at her. "If he thinks I may simply begin frequenting the company of the prudish set, he is more obtuse than I had thought. Now, let us drive in silence."

I thought Diana might ignore his request—or had it been a demand?—but she kept her mouth primly shut. As for my part, my stomach was a bundle of knots. Mr. Donovan had not only taken the blame for my blunder, he had done it from already difficult financial straits. He seemed, too, to be at odds with his father. I couldn't imagine that would be easy, though I hardly harbored any memories of my own father now.

When the carriage came to a stop, Mr. Donovan hopped down from it, helping Diana down, then me. Once my feet were firmly planted on the ground, I stood still, looking up at him and the deep frown he wore. "I *shall* pay for the vase, Mr. Donovan." I tried to infuse my voice with as much stubbornness as I could muster.

"You shall do no such thing," he replied, shutting the door soundly.

His resistance awoke a flame of determination in me. "I shall."

He met my gaze, and my heart stuttered slightly at the fierceness in his eyes. "You shall not. End of discussion."

"I cannot let you take the blame for *my* mistake."

He began walking toward the door. "It was not your mistake. I knocked the vase over."

I skipped to keep pace with him. "That is false, and you know it."

He turned to me again once we were inside. "I know that you set it off balance. But it was my attempt to right it that sent it to the ground." He removed his gloves and handed them to the footman.

"Assuredly not," I replied.

He let out a frustrated sigh. "We can continue to speculate, Miss Russell, but the fact remains that I gave Mrs. Lawrenson my word that I would pay for the vase, and I intend to do just that. Do not meddle in the affair, if you please."

His words were cutting, but as he was insisting on taking responsibility for the public humiliation *I* had caused, they lost their sting.

My mouth twisted to the side. "If only those wretched vases hadn't been so eye-catchingly ill-favored, this all could have been avoided." A little smile crept onto my lips unbidden as the image came to mind of Mrs. Lawrenson holding one of the feet like she might an injured bird. It had not been amusing at the time, but in retrospect, I couldn't help finding it so.

Mr. Donovan's brow knit. "What?"

A little bubble of laughter escaped me despite my best attempts to stifle it. "I should not laugh, for it is a serious thing, but"—I pulled my lips between my teeth—"I do think the world is a better place without that vase."

The corner of his mouth ticked up at the edge. "Unfortunately, the other half of the pair is still intact."

I sighed, and a movement nearby caught my eye. Diana stood at the base of the staircase, watching us with a thoughtful expression. She must have been unaware that her brother had accepted responsibility that was not his.

Mr. Donovan took note of her as well and hurried to shrug out of his coat, giving it to the footman and proceeding out of the entry hall and into the wider area at the base of the staircase, effectively ending our conversation.

"I shall repay *you*, then," I said.

"I do not want your money, Miss Russell," he said as he hurried up the stairs and disappeared toward his bedchamber.

I pinched my lips together in frustration.

"He is impossible," Diana said with a little smile. "Better to just leave things be than to waste your energy."

I sighed. "But I cannot in good conscience allow him to do this. You mustn't listen to what he says, Diana, for it is very much my fault the vase broke, and I should have said as much immediately, but I was a coward at the sight of so many eyes upon me. I simply froze."

She smiled at me and gestured for me to walk up the stairs beside her. "Quite understandable, particularly given how Mrs. Lawrenson reacted."

I shook my head as we reached the top of the red-carpeted staircase. "I must find a way to repay him. Can he not be persuaded to allow it?"

Diana grimaced. "Valentine is quite the most stubborn man you will ever meet, Rebecca. I'm afraid it is a family trait. But you needn't worry your head over this. He has much more vital troubles to set his mind to than a ludicrous vase." She covered her mouth with a hand, yawning. "Now, if you will excuse me, I am feeling rather tired. I should imagine the same is true of you after the day you have had."

I nodded with a smile, and we parted ways, my own mind and heart still troubled by the issue.

My maid was eagerly waiting in my bedchamber to help me prepare for bed. She was not, properly, *my* maid, for the one who had assisted me at Grandfather's had stayed at Millbury House. Rather, Dorothea was one of Diana's servants, and she had kindly offered to see to my needs, for which I was very grateful. She was a spritely thing, short and thin, with mousy brown hair, but I had latched onto her immediately, eager for a friend, and she had been more than willing.

She asked me about the night's occurrences, and I took the opportunity to bemoan my social failures, to confess the mortifying situation I had brought about, and to recount how Mr. Donovan had accepted the blame.

"Mr. Donovan?" she said in her thick accent, staring at me in the mirror with wide eyes as she removed the pins from my hair. "Took the blame, he did?"

"Yes," I said slowly, caught off guard by her reaction. Was it wrong of me to have told her? "What? Why do you say it like that?"

"Only that it's so romantic, miss," she said. "I don't know him so well myself, but he has all the other maids' hearts aflutter. And to have him come to your rescue in such a way . . ." She blinked as though the mere thought made her dizzy. "It would have made me weak in the knees, I reckon."

I frowned, saying nothing. There had been nothing romantic about the gesture—or about how he had spoken of it afterward. On the contrary, he seemed to be eager to be done speaking of it. But Dorothea's words settled in my mind, impressing upon me how little I understood things. I wasn't even certain I would recognize a romantic gesture if it *did* occur.

The long and short of tonight's lesson was that I was ill-equipped for Society. I could listen sympathetically as elderly men complained of their ailments, I could play a staid game of cribbage with them, I could ensure the proper distance of the chairs from the fire to avoid overheating or, heaven forbid, a chill, but I hadn't the slightest idea how to conduct myself around gentlemen my own age. That made my hopes of making a match seem very improbable indeed.

What I needed was someone who could provide me with guidance—to tell me in a straightforward manner the things everyone would assume I already understood.

I also needed to find a way to repay Mr. Donovan for his sacrifice on my behalf. Diana said not to concern myself over it because of the other pressing matters occupying him, but that was precisely *why* I needed to find a way. And Diana's words to her brother had given me a fair idea of what would be of help to him, if only he could be convinced to receive it.

VALENTINE

I woke in the morning with a headache, my night haunted with dreams of creatures that were half-pig, half-cow, dripping in gold, with monstrous claws that crumbled, only to be replaced in a matter of seconds by even longer ones.

I rubbed my eyes, dispelling the image. That dashed vase wouldn't leave me alone, and now I had to find fifteen guineas to pay for it. It would have been better to knock the second one to the floor so that it couldn't be used in the creation of a replica.

What had possessed me to take responsibility for the shattering of the vase, I didn't know. I was not one for gallant gestures—an understatement if there ever was one—and I hadn't even two shillings to rub together, much less fifteen guineas.

But what was done was done, and at least now Miss Russell's night wasn't overshadowed by the occurrence. It was not her fault, really. The supposed artist who created the vase would undoubtedly have given it a sturdier base if he had wanted it to survive.

I rose from my bed, wincing as my head pounded more

unbearably with the action. I hadn't drunk nearly enough for that to be responsible. I could only think the aching a result of the worries pressing in on me.

I reached for the bell pull to summon one of the footmen. My stomach was rumbling, and a bit of food might help with the pain in my head, as well. A brioche bun wouldn't be unwelcome, in truth.

The footman helped me dress for the day, though what I was to *do* with my day, I wasn't at all sure. I had promised Diana I would make myself scarce, and yet, where would I go? A man with no money to spend had few palatable options in a place like Brighton.

Another footman appeared just as we were finishing. He carried a silver salver, upon which sat two letters. I looked at them with misgiving.

"Two pieces come for you, sir." Parry held the salver out toward me.

Reluctantly, I took the papers and dismissed both of the servants, breaking the seal on the first letter unceremoniously. It slipped open easily, though, as though it hadn't been sealed properly. It was a short letter from Waudby, my bootmaker, phrased civilly but laced with implied threats about what the result would be if my account was not promptly settled.

I swore under my breath. How had he found me so quickly? I had barely arrived in Brighton.

I flipped the letters over and broke the second seal. My teeth clenched as I recognized the Admiral's neat but harsh script. The communication was even less welcome than the previous one—and its threats less veiled.

I think you will appreciate my forwarding of the bill from Waudby, as it seems an urgent matter.

I glanced at the back of the other letter, tightening my jaw. The Admiral had undoubtedly opened it, accounting for the weak seal. The man was unbearable. I felt a sliver of guilt for leaving my brother Phineas with him. Save for a comment here and there about his reclusive reading habits, the Admiral generally left him alone, but that was only because the Admiral's attention had been enough occupied by me during my time at Blackwick Hall. I had no shortage of flaws for him to criticize.

I took the liberty, too, of informing Waudby of your new direction in Brighton. It pleases me that you have taken up residence with your sister, for it shows a promising determination to seek out the best of Society and mend your ways. There are many eligible young women in Brighton at this auspicious time of year, and I trust you will take the opportunity to come to know them so that you may choose a proper bride for yourself—one who will exercise a positive influence over you.

I look forward to Diana's reports of the progress you are making. If the first one is favorable, Waudby will be pleased to find that your account there has been settled.

I crumpled up the letter and threw it into the fireplace, where it tumbled for a moment in the grate, then back out and onto the floorboards. Fitting. No matter what I did, I could not rid myself of the Admiral or how beholden I was to his supposed generosity. The very word was laughable. It was not charity that prompted him to pay my debts; it was the search for dominance and control.

It was not the only financial hold he had over me, either. My mother had left me a bequest at her death—somewhere in the region of eight hundred pounds—but the Admiral had thus far withheld it, maintaining that she would not wish for it to be squandered on brandy, lightskirts, and cards. My hopes to purchase a modest estate with the inheritance had thus come to naught, and I had accepted that I would likely never see the money, leaving me with the predicament of how to make my way in the world when the only training I had was in the Navy— a profession I would die rather than return to, if only to spite the Admiral.

I shut my eyes, pressing my fingers to my temples. I needed

food. Food always set the world aright. But that was another problem all its own.

Diana wished for me to keep out of sight—of Miss Russell, I presumed. That, I could manage. But I hadn't been ignorant of the intrigued gazes of the maids since my arrival. Yesterday morning, one had entered my bedchamber when I was wearing nothing but my shirt—a miracle in and of itself, as I often forwent even that when I slept. After a gaze that lasted far longer than necessary to inform her that I was not yet decent, she had tittered something about not realizing the room was occupied, then beat a not-so-hasty retreat, eyes still on me.

So, would Diana prefer that I scramble for food in the kitchens amongst the maids? Or eat at the breakfast table with Miss Russell? Or perhaps Miss Russell, too, would be in the kitchens. It wasn't clear to me whether she made a habit of spending time there or if I had simply caught her at just the right time.

I could always order my food to be brought to my room, of course, but I needed to get out—and I hated having crumbs in my bed. This room was coming to feel quite cramped already.

I settled for ordering my breakfast to be taken out to the terrace behind the house. Unconventional, perhaps, and slightly chilly, but preferable to the alternative. I checked the corridor for any sign of Miss Russell before stepping out of my bedchamber. Satisfied she was nowhere in sight, I paused at the top of the staircase to listen for movement below.

It was ridiculous that I needed to exercise so much caution, like a common thief in my sister's home. In my experience, chaperonage was just as necessary to keep the behavior of the women in line as it was to safeguard against the conduct of the men. As Miss Russell did not strike me as the type to throw herself at a man, however, I found these precautions burdensome.

"There you are!"

I stopped mid-stride on the landing, turning my head to find Miss Russell looking at me from the doorway to the breakfast room. She smiled broadly at the sight of me. She was far too cheery for the early hour.

"Do you always rise so late?" she asked.

I frowned. "It is only half-past eight."

"Precisely. *I* have been awake since six o'clock. Grandfather always insisted on beginning the day early. And ending it early, for that matter. I have been drawing out my own breakfast for the last hour in hopes of talking to you, but one can only drink so many cups of chocolate before feeling positively sick. I believe four is the magic number. Or opposite of magic, perhaps, for there is nothing magical about feeling sick, which is the result a drop more than four cups is bound to produce."

"Four cups?" I asked, incredulous. She had drunk four cups of chocolate while waiting to converse with me?

She nodded, her nose wrinkling slightly. "The first is always the best." She motioned for me to follow her in.

I hesitated. I could refuse, but it would give offense, and I was strangely reluctant to see the stricken look upon Miss Russell's face if I did so. Her humor had already sustained a significant blow after, apparently, four cups of chocolate.

I glanced up the stairs, looking for any sign of my sister, but Diana was not an early riser. Evidently, Miss Russell kept the same hours as the Admiral.

"A cup of chocolate will do you good," she said. "I like to add a bit of cream and cinnamon in mine. I can do that for you if you like. I shan't take much of your time, either, but I do wish to speak with you."

I could guess that the reason was last night's occurrence with the vase, and I had little desire to discuss it further, but I was admittedly intrigued by the cinnamon. I had never thought to put such a thing into chocolate.

"I fear a few minutes is all I can spare." It was a lie, of

course, for I had a great deal of time and little to occupy it. "Certainly not enough time to test the four-cup theory."

Her mouth stretched into an appreciative smile. "A few minutes will suffice. You can test my theory another day." She turned and led the way.

The breakfast room was a small, cream-papered room with little besides a mahogany table, a collection of chairs with upholstered seats, and a small sideboard. "How in the world did you manage to spend an hour in here?"

"Oh, quite easily," she said, taking up the pot of chocolate. "I sat over there." She pointed to the little window alcove that faced the street. "It is astonishing how many carriages passed by over the course of the hour—and so early in the day, too. Such a bustling city, isn't it? Quite different from Millbury House, for it was always so exciting when a carriage arrived there." She set down the pot and took up the one with cream, pouring it with a little flourish that made my brows knit. She finished by sprinkling a hint of cinnamon from a small porcelain bowl.

"Here." She handed it to me.

"Thank you," I murmured. It occurred to me that it might prove awkward if I disliked the concoction. I didn't much like chocolate normally.

I glanced at the liquid, one of my eyebrows raising. Against the rich brown of the chocolate, the white cream stood out, formed into two drops and a curved line beneath. I looked up at Miss Russell, who was watching me with a bit of anticipation.

"Everyone should begin the day with a bit of happiness," she said.

The corner of my mouth twitched. It was such a silly and strange thing, after all, but the smiling face *did* lighten my mood a bit, and after a morning of unwelcome news, that was something, certainly. "My day did not begin that way," I said, "but perhaps there is hope yet."

"Oh dear. Is something amiss?"

"Naught but a headache." I didn't wish to tell her the whole of it.

"I find that chocolate is a wonderful cure for the headache," she said. "In fact, if I do not have it in the morning, I am quite sure to *have* a headache by noon."

I chuckled softly. It was difficult to stay in a sour mood when Miss Russell said such ridiculous things. And there *was* something about the cream face . . . . Perhaps Miss Russell was so cheery because she had seen four of them this morning.

I began to lift the cup to my mouth, only to pause. My lips turned down at the sides. "It shall be ruined if I drink it."

"Oh, you needn't worry over that," she said, finally taking a seat. "If you leave it another minute or two, it will no longer be a happy face. In fact, it turns into something a bit frightful when left too long, and it is much better to remember it as a happy face."

She was right, I could see. The curved line of the mouth was forming more and more into a blob with each passing second. I took a sip.

A burst of flavors filled my mouth. Rich chocolate, tempered by just the right amount of cream, followed by a little prick of cinnamon. It was the most delicious beverage I had ever drunk —and I had drunk more than my fair share of beverages.

"You had four of these?" I asked.

She nodded. "Grandfather was obliged to take rather extreme measures in his diet due to the gout, and while I tried to support him by adhering to the same regimen, I . . . was not strong enough." The amount of guilt in her expression was ludicrous. "I took to drinking this before he woke in the mornings." There was a pause. "And rummaging through the kitchens once the house was asleep."

"Quite understandable." I took another sip of the chocolate. "I take it that your offering this to me is evidence that you have ceased worrying over the state of *my* health. Or perhaps you dislike me and are trying to hurry me toward my gouty future."

Her eyes widened. "The former, certainly, for I like you exceedingly. And any fear I had over your health the other night was, I have since decided, a result of the foxing. The way you stumbled about made me wonder if you were already suffering from a mild case of gout. But I quite see from your athletic figure and unremarkable way of walking that you are in your prime."

I did not often suffer from the desire to smile, but just now, it was all I could do to stifle it. Miss Russell's frank way of speaking, of somehow simultaneously insulting and complimenting was something I had not yet encountered. "I am glad to hear it." I took another sip.

"Do you like it?" she asked.

I set the cup down and nodded. "I do. You are onto something, I think."

"Sometimes I slip in a lump of sugar," she blurted. Her eyes flitted to the sugar bowl.

I raised my brows and, as she met my gaze, I used the tongs to slip a small lump of sugar into my own drink. The happy face was entirely unrecognizable now, and as I stirred it, it disappeared entirely, blending with the thick, dark chocolate and turning it a brown more like Miss Russell's hair.

"Was it the chocolate you wished to speak with me about?" I didn't particularly relish the thought of Diana walking in on this unplanned—on my part, at least—meal Miss Russell and I were having.

"No," she said. "It is something quite different." She seemed slightly hesitant now that the time had come for the discussion she had called me in for.

I felt a sudden unease.

"I hope you are not angry with me for hearing what you and

Diana were discussing on the way home from the party last night . . ."

"It is not as though you could have done anything to avoid hearing it." I took a sip of the chocolate. It was sweeter now, like a dessert one might have been offered at one of Prinny's parties. His creaking stays would likely burst at the mere description of this creation.

"I suppose I could have covered my ears," she said. "The proper thing would, no doubt, be to pretend I did *not* hear it, but I have been thinking on it since, and I have a proposal."

It was not common for me to be surprised, but Miss Russell seemed to have a knack for it. I hid it behind another sip of chocolate, taking my time to respond. "What sort of proposal?"

"A way for me to repay you for last night's kindness."

I set down the cup and looked at her squarely. "It was not a kindness, Miss Russell. If you knew me better, you would know that I have made it something of a habit to do things which fly in the face of what most people would think sensible or suitable."

Her brow puckered. "Why is that?"

"We have been over this, if memory serves. Because I am irredeemably vulgar and unsuitable."

"We *have* been over this," she replied. "No one is irredeemable. But that is all beside the point." She began stirring the empty cup of chocolate before her, and the small spoon clanked softly against the porcelain. "Whatever your motives, you did me a great service, and I mean to repay you for it."

"I will not accept your money, Miss Russell."

"I believe you, and that is why that is not what I am offering."

"And just what *are* you offering?" I took the final sip of my chocolate.

"To be one of your respectable young ladies."

Chapter Nine

VALENTINE

I stared at her. She was still smiling, but there was a hint of anxiety in it as she watched my reaction.

"I do not know why Diana says you must be seen with respectable young ladies or how that will help mend things with your father, but that is none of my business. I simply wish to help you, for I like you."

Those final words produced a little twinge in my chest. I couldn't remember the last person who had told me they liked me, and this was the second time Miss Russell had said it in the past five minutes. But I could imagine she would find a reason to like the devil himself.

"Miss Russell," I said, resettling myself in my chair. "It is very generous of you to offer yourself, but I am afraid I must decline."

"Must you?"

"I must."

"Why?" It was an obstinate question, demanding a solid reason.

I took a moment before responding. "It is precisely *because* you do not understand why Diana suggested such things that you should not offer to do them." Miss Russell had no idea that she was volunteering her assistance to a rake or how it would affect her to do so.

"Then tell me," she said, "for then you may be content."

I clenched my teeth together. For someone so cheerful, Miss Russell was surprisingly stubborn.

"Let me put it this way," she said. "Do you believe being seen with me would help accomplish what you need to accomplish?"

I didn't answer immediately. Instead, I took to doing the same thing Miss Russell was doing—mixing the nonexistent liquid in my cup of chocolate.

What *did* I need to accomplish? I needed money, and with the delay of my prize money, things with the Admiral were quickly coming to a head. Without his goodwill and favor, I was likely to end in the sponging house. Being seen in Brighton with Miss Russell was certain to offer some level of appeasement to the Admiral, for no one who had spent so much as two minutes in her company would doubt her character.

Which made her appearing with me entirely wrong. "I believe," I said slowly, "that being seen with you would do more damage to *you* than it would help *me*."

"In what way?" she asked, visibly confused by my comment.

There was no way around it. I would have to be direct with Miss Russell if she was to comprehend just what she was offering.

"Being seen frequently in my company would ruin your reputation."

She laughed lightly. "You must do better than *that*, Mr. Donovan. I do not believe it for a second. In fact, if I am being quite honest, this scheme of mine is not entirely selfless, for it would benefit me as well." Her color was a bit heightened as she continued. "The Bradley sisters assured me that being seen having you as a suitor would draw the attention of many other suitors."

"The devil they did." I pinched my lips together. "Forgive my language. It is just that . . . I am a rake, Miss Russell. To associate in such a way with me would be to do irreparable damage to your reputation."

She had ceased stirring her empty cup and now played with the edge of the tablecloth, a frown on her brow. "A rake, you say."

I tightened my jaw. "Just so." I had often been called such, but it was a different thing entirely to label *myself* as one. And to Miss Russell, no less.

She looked up suddenly, decidedly. "Mr. Donovan, what *is* a rake?"

My jaw slipped open.

She hurried to speak. "It is only that, well, it is a word I have heard many times, but no one has ever taken the time to explain it. They merely say it in hushed voices, as though their tone of voice alone will communicate the definition. And yet, still I am in the dark." Her eyes pleaded with me. "Please. Put an end to my ignorance and tell me: what exactly is a rake?"

I was at a loss for words. And as Miss Russell looked at me, waiting for me to provide the definition, the seconds ticked by on the mantel clock and carriages passed by out on the street. "I am hardly the person to explain such a thing to you."

"You are precisely the person to do it, for who better to tell me what a rake is than a real rake?" Her eyes narrowed for a moment, her head tilting to the side as she considered me. "What sort of a rake are you?"

"What sort of rake am I?" I repeated, for I could think of nothing else to say to such a bizarre question.

"You wouldn't happen to be an *affirmed* rake, would you? Grace and Maria Bradley assured me that having an affirmed rake as a suitor is almost as good as a titled gentleman."

"Confirmed. It is a *confirmed* rake. And a confirmed rake and a titled gentleman are not mutually exclusive things by any means. But believe me when I say that you do not wish for a rake, whatever sort he may be. On no account should you heed such nonsense."

"It is not nonsense, for Grace told me that Bessie Nicholas had the attentions of one for two weeks, and she is now the most courted woman in Brighton. Apparently, she had not a suitor to speak of for the last two Seasons!" She held my gaze significantly, as though such evidence ought to weigh heavily with me.

"Bessie Nicholas was not courted by a rake," I said. I happened to know the man who had courted her, and he was a flirt, certainly, but not a rake.

"But what *is* a rake?" she said in exasperation. "And what is a confirmed one?"

When I made no response, she stood and walked over to the window. She stared through it, sighing. "It is very embarrassing to be ignorant in a world of seasoned men and women." She spoke softly, and against my will, I felt a bit of sympathy for her.

I knew how unkind the world could be to those who were naive in their understanding of its workings. I had seen it first-hand in the Navy, for the more shrewd sailors were quick to take advantage of the green ones, humiliating them for amusement.

I sighed. "A rake, Miss Russell"—she whirled toward me, listening intently—"is a man who cares for nothing but his own pleasure, be it amongst cards, drink, or women." The last word was the most difficult to say, though all of it made my stomach feel tight and unsettled. It was strange to hear such a description of myself from my own tongue. It didn't *feel* like an accurate description—or at least not a comprehensive one—but I had certainly acted the rake.

I knew a rare flash of regret, of disappointment in myself. Upon my resignation from the Navy, I had thrown myself into dissolution, partly as a way to cope with the death of my mother. I had done it equally, though, as a sort of vengeance upon the Admiral, who had browbeat me into the Navy and manipulated me to stay in it longer than we had agreed upon. In the process, he had deprived me of being present at my mother's deathbed.

And what did I have to show for my choices now? All my efforts to revenge myself upon the Admiral had turned against me, putting me even more at his mercy and ruining my reputation in the meantime. I had been so busy punishing him for the past that I had spoiled my own future.

There had been moments of pleasure over the past two years, certainly. But by and large, my ventures with cards, women, and drink had brought me a great deal of trouble and very little relief. The pleasures were fleeting, and when they were gone, there was nothing to cover the gaping hole I had used them to fill.

"Oh," Miss Russell said simply. "And are you still . . . doing those things?"

"Yes. No. That is—" I stopped myself, frustrated at my fumbling. Why did I want so badly to say no? And why was she asking such a question? She had seen me drunk the other night, after all, and I had *told* her I was a rake. "The important thing is that I have done them enough to be a rake. A confirmed one, even."

"But surely what one is doing *now* and what one does in the future are of more importance than what one has done in the past."

"Not to Society," I said. "Besides, my sins are recent enough, I assure you."

She looked at me thoughtfully. "And your father demands you stop your . . . raking?"

My lip twitched in spite of myself. "He does. He demands I become respectable."

She nodded. "And am I not respectable enough to assist you in that?"

"Miss Russell," I said, frowning deeply, "I—"

The door opened, and Diana walked in, slowing as her gaze took in the scene. I watched for the telltale pinching of her lips that would show her anger, for I had gone against her demand to stay away from Miss Russell.

But there was no anger. After a short pause of surveyal, she even smiled. "Good morning, the two of you."

"Diana," I said, seizing the opportunity for someone else to explain to Miss Russell why her idea was entirely unsuitable. "Perhaps you can speak some sense to Miss Russell."

"Oh?" She took a seat across from me, her brows raised. "What are we discussing?"

"You mustn't be angry with me, Diana," Miss Russell rushed to say, coming over to the table and sitting on the edge of the chair beside my sister. "It is only that I had set my mind to your brother's predicament as well as to my wish to do what I can to make my time in Brighton successful—I was a grave disappointment at the party last night—and it occurred to me that there might be a solution to both problems."

Diana poured herself some chocolate. "Go on."

Miss Russell situated herself in the chair so that she was fully facing Diana. "Your brother needs to demonstrate to your father that he has ceased his raking"—I glanced at Diana, whose brow quirked at the phrasing as she finished pouring—"and *I* could benefit from being seen in the company of someone widely admired."

Diana's gaze snapped to me, and I grimaced. "You see why your good sense is so desperately needed. Nothing I have said to Miss Russell seems to have persuaded her of how ill-advised such a plan is. Or that I am *not* widely admired."

Miss Russell looked at me, her head cocked to the side. "I cannot force you, Mr. Donovan, but it is a very good plan, I think. If you are so set against it, perhaps you could introduce me to one of your rakish friends, and *they* could help me instead."

"My rakish friends?"

She looked at me frankly. "Do you not have such friends? People with similar interests generally band together, so I assume you do. It wouldn't be for long, you know, and of course they could resume their raking afterward—perhaps even during."

I shot a harried look at Diana, who was staring at Miss Russell thoughtfully. After a moment, she turned back to her chocolate. "*I* think it is a very good plan, Rebecca."

Miss Russell looked at me with a victorious smile. "You see?"

But I could not see, for I was busy staring at my sister. What the devil was she saying? "Diana *dearest*," I said through clenched teeth. "Might I have a word with you by the window?"

She held up a finger as she took a sip of her chocolate, then set the cup down and patted her mouth with a napkin. "Of course."

"If you will excuse us, Miss Russell," I said, my nostrils flaring. I rose from my chair and strode over to the window, waiting for my sister.

"What the devil, Di?" I hissed as she faced me. "Are you mad?"

"Very likely," she said. "All of us Donovans are, I imagine."

"No imagining is necessary in your case," I replied. "One moment you demand I stay away from Miss Russell, the next you're telling me to carry on a ruse of a flirtation with her?"

"Yes, a bit of reflection can do wonders, can it not?"

"Two seconds' worth? For that is as long as you've known of this plan to reflect upon it."

"*I* changed my mind about my demands of you last night. And the only failing in the plan is that I did not come up with it myself, but I cannot fault Rebecca for that." She looked to Miss Russell, who was at the table, pouring herself another cup of chocolate. She would be sick. Or inordinately happy. Both, perhaps.

"In any case," Diana said, "I think it will serve quite well."

"Serve to ruin her reputation," I said.

"Nonsense. I am still her chaperone, and as you are the brother of her sister-in-law, there will naturally be an element of protection to her in the connection between you. It is expected that you would spend time in her company now that she is living with me. It is just enough for safety but not enough to stop interest in the possibilities of the connection. The perfect recipe, in fact."

I looked away, scrubbing a hand over my jaw in exasperation. I should have known Diana would throw her lot in with Miss Russell. She always had the very worst ideas.

"Valentine," she said, more subdued than before. "You are in a difficult situation, and this could be the answer—temporarily, at least—to your problems. If people have reason to think you have begun to reform, it is not only Father who will soften, but your creditors as well." She took my hand in hers, waiting to speak until I met her gaze. "You cannot waste your entire life spiting Father."

I shook my head and looked through the window. It was as Miss Russell had said. The city was full of constant traffic: equestrian, pedestrian, vehicular. I had come here to escape, but escape was beginning to seem impossible. If the Admiral was intent that my debts follow me, he could ensure that happened no matter where I went. Not that I had the money to go anywhere else.

"Besides," Diana said, "you are a guest in my house now, and as such, I expect you to help me make Rebecca's time in Brighton enjoyable and memorable, which means attending events with us, of course, or taking her out for a drive when I cannot entertain her."

I opened my mouth to speak, but she put up a hand.

"And in return," she said, "I shall send favorable reports to Father. And I assure you that I shan't let any harm come to Rebecca. If I sense that is occurring, I shall naturally end things without delay. But I do *not* fear that."

I ground my teeth together, unable to deny the sense in what she was saying. I found it dashedly difficult to say no to Diana, or to women in general, for that matter. It was not the Admiral's threats, after all, which had kept me in the Navy; it was my mother's pleading not to do anything that might tear the family apart.

This was precisely why I only kept company with women who never asked anything of me. My interactions with them were business, the expectations clear from the beginning. I needed it that way, for the more I gave, the more I cared, and I hated nothing more than caring.

But this was a business arrangement, too. I could put a little shine on my blackened reputation, and Miss Russell could become of greater interest to Society. It would keep the creditors at bay until the blasted prize money came through, and stop the Admiral breathing down my neck.

It was temporary. And once I *did* have my prize money, the Admiral would come to see that his plans for me had been foiled yet again—and he could no longer force me to comply.

"Very well," I said. "I will do it."

Chapter Ten

REBECCA

I felt much more at peace with things, knowing I would be able to assist Mr. Donovan in some way. He did not seem enthusiastic about the plan, of course, but I wasn't certain Mr. Donovan was the sort of man to be enthusiastic about anything. He appeared to be the type to resist accepting help, and thankfully, I was used to that, for Grandfather had been the same way. Some men needed to be cajoled into what was good for them, and I hoped he would see the benefits in time.

After all, it seemed fitting that I should help him with his reputation after he had preserved mine. The thought would undoubtedly seem a mite dramatic to some, but I couldn't help but think that it would have made a great, black mark upon my entrance into Society to have my first impression be one of clumsiness—and breaking something so precious as a *Sèvres* vase, however hideous I thought it. Ornately ugly things must take just as much time to produce as ornately beautiful ones. Perhaps more.

Either way, whatever his intentions had been, what Mr. Donovan had done had been a service for which I would be forever grateful.

He had an engagement with his friend Captain Yates in the afternoon, and Diana and I had an engagement in the evening, so I did not see him until the following morning as I was finishing breakfast.

He paused in the doorway when he saw I was the sole occupant of the room, his brows contracting slightly. It was a curious thing, for it seemed they were *always* poised in a sort of frown. I wouldn't have thought them capable of frowning further, and yet they never failed to do so. It was impressive, really, particularly as it did not detract from his handsomeness. Indeed, I had never met anyone with so unhappy a countenance, and yet, I found that rather than putting me off, it intrigued me. What could cause a man to look so serious, so somber all the time?

"Good morning, Mr. Donovan," I said. "Would you care for a cup of chocolate?"

He stepped into the room. "I would. But you needn't trouble yourself. I can make it."

I raised my brows. "Can you? I think you will find the happy face a greater challenge than you realize. I have had a great deal of practice, you know, and likely made it look deceptively easy."

He took a seat across from me. "With four cups of chocolate a day, you will have had a great deal of practice indeed."

"Oh, I only drink four cups when I am particularly nervous."

"And you are not nervous today?"

I shook my head and rose to my feet to pour from the pot. "I am full of anticipation, in fact."

"Have you been here for an hour again?"

"No, for I am trying to accustom myself to town hours. I found it difficult to sleep past six with the noises on the street. Sugar, sir? If you mean to have some, I shall put it in now so that it does not spoil the happy face." He looked as though he could use a happy face. Or four.

"Yes, please."

I slipped a lump of sugar into the thick liquid. "Diana says you offered to take me out in the carriage today and give me a tour of Brighton. It is very kind, for I have been so anxious to become better acquainted with the town."

There was that deep frown again. "Yes, Diana is very generous with my time."

I hesitated with the cream pot in hand, my cheeks growing a bit warm. "Oh. Did you *not* make such an offer? There is no need—"

"I did." The muscles in his jaw flexed, as though it cost him dearly to say such a thing. Was it a lie? "I would be honored if you would accompany me this afternoon for a ride in town, Miss Russell."

I kept my gaze on him for a moment, deciding how to take such an unenthusiastic invitation. "Thank you, Mr. Donovan." I poured the cream, making the smile more than usually dramatic before letting out two drops for the eyes. After sprinkling a bit of cinnamon on top, I handed it to him. I would make him smile today if it was the only thing I managed to do.

M r. Donovan gave me his assistance as I stepped up into the phaeton, keeping a folded piece of paper in my other hand. He was looking grim, as usual. Hardly a promising omen, but I was determined to make the ride enjoyable. There was so much to see in Brighton, and I was eager to feel at home in its streets, to recognize its buildings. And perhaps, for Mr. Donovan, looking grim was the equivalent of what in others would be a pleasant expression.

"You remind me of Mr. Philpotts, you know," I said as he stepped up and took his place beside me.

He took the reins in hand. "Mr. Philpotts?"

I nodded. "When I first met him, he was very churlish. But it wasn't long before he insisted on sitting beside me whenever he came over for dinner, acquainting me with all his latest ailments."

Mr. Donovan gave a nod, and the groom stepped away from the horses' heads. Mr. Donovan gave a flick of the reins, and the phaeton pulled forward.

"And just how old is Mr. Philpotts?"

"Three-and-seventy, I believe."

"Gouty?"

"Oh no," I replied. "Mr. Philpotts's struggles run more in the vein of rheumatism."

"I see," he said grimly. "Your insistence on comparing me to men nearing their deathbeds is not particularly flattering, Miss Russell."

I looked over at him beside me. It was a good opportunity to admire his profile, which was decidedly handsome. He looked a bit less severe from this angle. "I do not do it to give offense. It is merely that they are the only men I *have* to compare you to, sir."

I clenched my hands into fists as we passed by another carriage with mere inches to spare. Mr. Donovan gave no indication the close call had fazed him in the least.

"Surely you had other friends back in . . ." He shot a questioning glance at me.

"Northumberland. And no, not exactly. Our parish was a haven for the aged. The most exciting occurrences were the frequent funerals. Any younger people were either merely passing through, attending one of said funerals, or not the sort with whom Grandfather wished me to associate. He finds it hard to leave the house due to his gout, so my interactions were generally limited to those occasions on which he had the energy to entertain his friends."

"At exhilarating parties of dancing and revelry?"

I laughed. "Only in my dreams!"

"And what sort of entertainment *is* to be found amongst men riddled with gout and rheumatism?"

"Dinners of plain food which start promptly at four-thirty and last until everyone has shared their latest complaints."

"Good gracious. And what time is that, in general?"

I lifted a shoulder. "Half-past seven. Though two or three times, Grandfather had to insist people leave at a quarter after eight. When it rains, Mr. Philpotts's rheumatism is particularly bothersome, you know."

"No," he said. "Thankfully I do *not* know. You poor girl."

I smiled nostalgically. "I did not mind so much, for it was a deviation from my usual routine. Indeed, I find I miss Mr. Philpotts. And Grandfather, of course. But you see now why I am at such a loss for how to behave in settings like the Lawrensons's party—and why I need your help to know how to go on in Brighton."

"My help?" He laughed a bit, giving me a glimpse of what a smile from him might be like. But it was gone as soon as it came. "A rake is not the best guide for proper conduct in Society, Miss Russell."

An open carriage approached, and I recognized someone I had met at the party the other night. I gave a little smile and a wave. My muscles tightened as we passed the carriage again, for there was barely room for the two equipages, and I entirely expected our wheels to lock. But they did not.

I let out a relieved breath. I would become accustomed to it in time. "I trust you to tell me the truth, for you are not the sort to tie a bow around things, are you? And that is just what I need —someone who will tell me when I am making a *faux pas* and answer my questions directly and honestly. Can you do that for me?"

He looked over at me, his dark eyes considering. They were lovely eyes—brown like the creamy chocolate once the happy face had been stirred in. Perhaps there was happiness some-where in those depths, too.

He gave a curt nod.

I grasped his arm with my hands. "You will? Thank you ever so much."

His gaze flicked down to my hold on his arm, then away again.

"Oh," I said, letting go. "Was that wrong of me? If so, you must tell me, for that is precisely what I need."

His lips pressed together. "I did not mind it, but other men might find it an . . . invitation of sorts."

I laughed nervously. "Oh dear. All my impulses seem wrong. How grateful I am that you are good enough to let me make my mistakes with you. You do not think too badly of me, do you?"

"I do not," he said, his gaze fixed on the road ahead. "What is that?" He nodded at my hand.

I looked down at the paper I held. I had forgotten all about it. "Oh, yes. I thought we might discuss a few things while we have a moment."

He glanced at it again warily. "What sort of things?"

I unfolded the paper. "I wrote down a few things you might do to make people believe you are enamored of me."

"Make people b—" The carriage jolted as the wheel hit the raised pavement. He clamped his mouth shut. "Is that what I am meant to do?"

I blinked. "Well, yes. That is the point, isn't it? For your father to believe you to be directing your efforts at a respectable young woman, and for Society to be amazed that the new Miss Russell seems to have captured the elusive heart of Mr. Valentine Donovan?"

He looked more grim than ever. "What is on this list of yours?"

"I jotted down a few things that came to mind this morn-ing." I straightened the paper and cleared my throat. "First, take me on a drive, which I suppose we may cross off the list now, though perhaps a second drive would be even more effective than a first. Second, look at me with eyes that twinkle longingly. Third, twist one of my curls around your finger. Fourth, wear a ring with a locket of my hair. Fifth, fervently kiss my hand, then look up at me through your lashes. Sixth, dance two sets with me. Seventh, fight a duel over me."

He snatched the paper from my hand, holding it in front of his face. His eyes darted between the road and the words I had written, and his expression contorted with disgust. "Where the devil did you come up with such a list?"

I shrugged. "From my observations at the party."

He handed the paper back to me. "You observed a duel at the party?"

"No," I admitted. "That was one I came up with from a conversation I heard at Grandfather's one evening."

"Amongst men who grew up in the age when dueling was the fashion," Mr. Donovan replied caustically. "And legal."

I looked at the paper, doubt filling my chest. "Is it a bad list? Do these things not convey that a man is enamored of a woman?"

He gave a little scoff. "If he is a coxcomb, perhaps." He glanced over at me, becoming more serious. "I do not think it wise for us to pretend to be in love, Miss Russell."

"Oh, I wouldn't be pretending to be in love with *you*," I reassured him. "You would be in love with me, and I would merely be flirting."

"I see," he said drily. "Be that as it may, I wouldn't wish to . . ." His lips shut tightly, as though he was hesitant to continue speaking what he was thinking.

"Go on," I said. "You promised you would speak plainly with me, after all. And though I may not be the most experienced young woman, my feelings are not easily hurt, I assure you. I could hardly have survived life with Grandfather if they were."

He blew out a puff of air from his nose. "Very well, then. In short, I would not wish for the line between ruse and reality to become blurred."

I was silent for a moment, considering his words. "You mean you worry that I would begin to think you were well and truly in love with me—or I with you."

He gave a nod, and I could see the reluctance in his eyes, as though he still feared how his words might affect me despite my assurances.

I smiled. "It is very thoughtful of you, Mr. Donovan. But you need not fear that. You are very handsome, of course, but I rather think when I fall in love, it will be with someone who does not hate it when I smile."

He reared back slightly. "I do not hate it when you smile. You have a . . . very lovely smile."

"Thank you," I replied, displaying just such a smile. "Then it is not others smiling which you detest but smiling yourself."

"I do not detest smiling," he replied.

"And I do not believe you," I replied, waving at a passing carriage. "For I have yet to see you do so, which is very unfortunate, as I think this carriage ride would be more helpful to my reputation if you did not look as though you hated it."

"I do not hate it," he said, apparently troubled by my words. There was a little pause. He stretched his mouth so that I could see his teeth.

"Oh heavens," I said, drawing away slightly. "Does it hurt?"

He shot me a glower and elbowed my arm. It was a playful gesture, and it sent a little wave of pleasure through me.

"I am only teasing," I said. "We can practice, of course. It is like anything else—it becomes easier the more you do it. I find it helps to think of things in your life that make you happy."

"And in the absence of such things?"

"That is impossible. Everyone has things in life that make them happy, if only they will recognize them. I could frown like you if I chose, for I have known sadness in my life, and *you* have things for which to be grateful that I haven't."

"Such as?"

I hesitated a moment. But I was feeling a bit daring just now. I hoped to help Mr. Donovan and his father come to a reconciliation, didn't I? "A living father."

He gave a little snort, shaking his head. "An ironic choice, Miss Russell. Whatever father figure you are imagining, the Admiral is not it, I assure you."

"Who is the Admiral?" I asked, baffled.

"The man people assume to be my father."

I glanced over at him, surprised by his strange choice of words. "Assume?"

"Assume." His mouth was drawn up in a smile, but it was an ironic one. "Did you know, Miss Russell, that you have the doubtful pleasure of being in the company of not only a rake but, to use a phrase you may now better appreciate, a man's by-blow?"

I stared at him, the wheels in my head turning. "*That* is what it means? An illegitimate child?"

"Yes," he said flatly.

"Oh dear," I said, my eyes wide.

He glanced over at me, and I thought I saw a flash of disappointment there. It was quickly veiled—or perhaps imagined in the first place. "Yes, indeed. You see now why I tried to warn you against this plan of yours—and against me."

"No, no," I said. "It is not that. I was merely thinking of Mr. Finner's grandson. He is *not* violent, then."

Mr. Donovan chuckled. "Are people only allowed one flaw? If so, I am very exceptional, indeed, for I have a whole quiver full."

"That is not what I meant. Only that I had inadvertently ascribed to his grandson a fault that he is not guilty of."

"Unless he is."

"Yes," I said. "But I think it better to assume the best of people, do you not?"

He looked at me strangely.

I took in a breath and folded up the list I had made. "Well, enough of Mr. Finner's grandson. We were speaking of *you*, and two fathers is surely a reason to smile, for it is one more than most have. I believe anything can be looked at as a blessing if one looks at it in the right way."

"Really?" We rounded a corner onto the street that ran parallel with the sea. "Let us try your philosophy. How about a mountain of gaming debts?"

I lifted my chin, thinking for a moment. "Evidence of many nights spent in the company of friends."

He laughed, though this time it was not caustic. "Not always accurate, but I see what you mean. What about a ruined reputation?"

I thought for a moment. "An opportunity for redemption."

His lip lifted at the corner. "A broken vase."

"An unlikely friendship."

He glanced at me, and I offered him a little smile, though my heart was pattering in my chest. I hoped he would think of me as his friend, for I wished to think of him as mine.

"It is your turn to try now," I said. "A brooding companion."

He didn't respond while slowing the horses as a cart crossed in front of us, and I wondered if he meant to ignore me. The cart moved out of the way, and he gave a flick of the reins. "A man concerned with the task of keeping you safe."

I smiled. "See? You are a natural." My heart skipped at the sight of the Bradleys walking on the pavement ahead. I glanced beside me at Mr. Donovan, who still wore his usual somber expression. "Can you not try to look just a *bit* more pleased to be with me? No one will believe you to be enjoying yourself if you refuse to smile or wave."

"On the contrary, Miss Russell. People would begin to worry over me if I *did* smile or wave."

I greeted the Bradley sisters with an enthusiastic wave of my own, taking pleasure in the way their gazes moved between me and Mr. Donovan.

"You are showing enough enthusiasm for both of us, I think," he said.

My eyes widened as a grand, cream-colored building came into view, with eight pillars and three times as many windows. I had been so focused on conversing with Mr. Donovan, I had forgotten the purpose of our drive. "We seem to have neglected the tour part of this drive."

"So we have," he said. "Well, that is rectified easily enough. That oddity looming before us is Prinny's Marine Pavilion. In front of us is the Steyne. And over there is St. James's Street."

"What a grand tour you give, Mr. Donovan," I said ironically, "but no matter. We will do it properly on our next drive. Oh dear. Is that Mrs. Lawrenson approaching us?"

"I believe so," he said coolly.

I tried to be as calm as he was as we drew nearer, arranging my mouth in a polite smile and waiting for Mrs. Lawrenson to greet us. But though she looked straight at us, there was no greeting to be had. She looked away purposefully until our equipages had passed one another.

I let out a gasp of offense. "She cut us!" I hardly knew whether to laugh or cry. When in doubt, though, I always chose the former. And as I let myself smile, the hilarity of the situation pressed itself upon me, and the laugh built and built. "She cut us." I struggled to get out the words. "Over the most hideous vase!" I put a hand to my stomach, doubling over.

Mr. Donovan looked over at me for a moment, then smiled reluctantly. "I am glad you find it amusing, Miss Russell. Welcome to the first taste of what to expect from keeping company with me. It is an unusual day indeed if I am not cut once at least."

I took in deep breaths, blinking to dispel the tears of laughter as I composed myself. "I cannot blame her entirely. How frustrating it must have been to have her lovely party—and her favorite vase—ruined by us."

Mr. Donovan was silent for a moment. "Do you always believe the best of people, then?"

"I try to." I wiped at the corners of my eyes, determined to compose myself. "It is a bit selfish, perhaps, but I find it makes me happier to do so." I looked at him again. It wasn't difficult to believe the best of Mr. Donovan, whatever he might say or think of himself. He had a sort of charm about him, for all his brooding and his straightforward manner of speaking. In fact, if I squinted, I could almost imagine him smiling.

His brows drew together, making it more difficult for me to pretend such a thing. "What are you doing?" he asked.

"Imagining you smiling," I said. "I have an ambition to see you wearing an ear-splitting grin."

He directed his eyes forward. "Temper your ambitions, Miss Russell."

I continued looking at him, and he sent me a few quick frowning glances. "How long does it take you to imagine a smile?"

"I am not imagining a smile anymore," I said. "I am admiring your profile. It is so . . . young and free of wrinkles."

He grimaced.

Chapter Eleven

VALENTINE

L ike Miss Russell's grandfather, I needed to drink less port, though perhaps for different reasons. My morning cup of hot chocolate with a sprinkle of cinnamon, a lump of sugar, and just enough cream to make a happy face, was becoming my consolation for abstaining. Apparently, I was not so different from the gouty old gentleman as I would have liked to think myself. Miss Russell had said my face was less wrinkly, at least, so there was that. More consolation.

Since our drive, I had only been required to attend church with her and my sister, then escort them for a walk along the beach. Diana had invited a friend of hers to join us on the latter occasion, leaving Miss Russell and me to converse—and for me to hold the collection of seashells Miss Russell insisted on acquiring.

I was not one for polite conversation, but I was quickly discovering that neither was Miss Russell. She was more likely to ask me a forthright question about some cant phrase she had heard than to remark upon the weather. Though, when she *did* comment on the weather, it was hardly a mundane affair. Having never before been to the sea, she was thrilled with the amount of sunshine Brighton received—and the sunset in particular.

She seemed to trust me implicitly—a trust I had done nothing to deserve, but which I was oddly hesitant to break. It was as though she relied upon me, and that was a new experience which made me feel unsure. I had made a point of being unreliable before now.

A week after my arrival in Brighton, Diana yanked open my bed hangings and informed me that we were to attend an outdoor ball that evening.

"Surely you do not require my attendance." I covered my face with a pillow as I had come to do. This was not the first time Diana had burst in on me in such a way. She was not generally one to wake early, but whenever she did, she seemed to come straight for me.

"I do require it. And as I shall be sending my weekly report to Father in the morning, the timing is fortunate. Think how it will be to tell him that you have attended not one but *two* balls in the space of a sennight."

I pulled the hangings closed on the side where Diana was, then slipped out of bed on the opposite side and reached for the clothing one of the footmen had set out. "Perhaps you shouldn't mention the first one. I doubt the Admiral will be thrilled when he discovers I drunkenly broke a vase." I pulled off the shirt I had slept in and tossed it onto the nearest chair, then slipped into my pantaloons. "By the by, have you seen the bill from Mrs. Lawrenson?" She had promised to send it over immediately, but I had not yet received it.

"I have," she replied. "And I paid it."

"What?" I pulled on a new shirt and stepped out from the privacy of the bed, staring at her.

"You needn't worry. She believes it came from you, so there is no harm done."

"No harm done? That was a debt of honor." I frowned and

pulled the braces hanging from my pantaloons over my shoulders. "And you promised Russell you wouldn't pay my debts. I will repay you."

"Do not be ridiculous, Val. It was Rebecca who broke the vase, and as she is under my care, Duke would expect me to pay for it. Now, please, let us stop talking of it, for I am sick to death of that ridiculous vase. As for the plans tonight, we shall dine here at half-past seven and leave at nine."

I was too relieved to make any further fuss about the ball *or* the vase, for I hadn't had any idea how I would come up with fifteen guineas. I had even paid a visit to a Brighton moneylender, only to be thoroughly humiliated when he refused my request. Whether my reputation preceded me, or the Admiral and my creditors had warned people against me, I couldn't say.

———

Diana and Miss Russell had already begun eating when I stepped into the dining room at a quarter to eight. I checked for a moment on the threshold as my eyes settled on Miss Russell. The sage green gown she wore might have been dyed for the express purpose of bringing out the color of her eyes, and her hair was becomingly piled on the crown of her head, with two cream ribbons encircling the coiffure.

She smiled at me. "How very handsome you look."

I proceeded into the room and glanced at my sister, who was piercing green beans with her fork rather than looking at me. I had rather hoped she would spare me the necessity of replying by intervening, but she did not.

"Thank you," I said a bit stiffly. "You look—"

Miss Russell put up a hand to stop me. "Oh, you needn't compliment me just now. I would rather you did so at the ball."

Diana *did* look up at that, her mouth pulling into an amused smile as she ate. "Very wise."

I was strangely nervous as we made our way to the ball an hour later. Thus far, my dealings with Miss Russell had been such that they could be looked upon by Society as slight aberrations from my usual behavior. But tonight was bound to change that. As Diana had said, two balls in the space of a week was unheard of for me, and it would not go unnoticed.

Would people believe I was changing? And, if so, would they begin to expect things of me? That was what unsettled me most. It was far less painful to confirm people's bad opinions than to disappoint their good ones.

The ball was being held on the back lawn of Peckley House, and I escorted both Diana and Miss Russell on the path that looped around the side of the house toward the rear.

No expense had been spared for the occasion, it seemed. A makeshift ballroom floor had been constructed and surrounded on three sides with wooden posts. Green garlands draped between them, while ornate oil lamps rested atop, lighting the scene. A small orchestra played from their position on the stone terrace. Liveried footmen with silver platters dotted the scene, ready to refresh the guests with food and drink. Past the ballroom floor, a path ran toward the manicured gardens, which were surrounded by hedges low enough that a few stone benches were visible at various points. Oil lamps illuminated the paths, precluding any thought someone might have of a clandestine encounter in the darkness.

"How glorious," Miss Russell said in a hushed whisper. She smiled and leaned closer to me. "And not a vase in sight, so you may rest easy. Though I would not be surprised if I knocked over one of those lovely lamps."

Her pleasantry relaxed me a bit and reminded me that I was not the only one nervous about this evening. Miss Russell would be wanting to make the best impression possible after the last party, and she was relying on me to ensure that happened. I was also to compliment her appearance at some point during the night, ostensibly in a way that would allow others to overhear.

What *had* I been thinking, agreeing to this? I could not remember the last time I had offered someone a compliment. Provoking a duel was a far more natural request.

Already a number of gazes had paused upon us. I ignored them, reminding myself what I was doing here—saving myself from debtor's prison and helping Miss Russell.

The orchestra struck up the prelude to a reel, and couples began gathering on the ballroom floor.

"You haven't yet asked me to dance, Mr. Donovan," Miss Russell said.

"I could hardly have done so given the fact that we only just arrived. Besides, I am not a dancer."

"He is a very good dancer," Diana said. "He simply chooses not to do it to be disobliging. Until tonight." She smiled at me, her meaning clear. This was part of what I was expected to do, and she would not take no for an answer, particularly if I wished for her to send a good report to the Admiral in the morning.

The bill from Waudby sitting in my bedchamber came to mind. I gritted my teeth for a moment, cursing the situation that denied me what I prized most in life: ignoring the wishes of others in favor of what suited me.

Swallowing my pride with as much ease as I might swallow a fire poker, I put out my hand, my jaw still tight. "Would you care to dance, Miss Russell?"

She smiled broadly, as though my lackluster tone bothered her not at all. Setting her gloved hand on mine, she gave a little curtsy. "I would like it above all things."

I led the way to the ballroom floor, and we took our places amongst the set. My heart was hammering and my chest was tight in a way I hadn't experienced in years. Miss Russell, on the other hand, switched between looking at me with anticipation and looking around cheerily at the couples in the set. She couldn't have appeared more pleased to be there.

The figures of the dance began, and I was glad to feel that despite not having danced much in the past two years, memory was strong enough to assist me.

"You did not like my list," Miss Russell said as we came together, "but you never told me what things you *would* recommend to convince people that you are falling victim to my manifold charms." Her smile twinkled at me, as though the idea was a silly one. And it *was* for me, but I could see how easily another man might do just such a thing, for Miss Russell was full of vivacious and unaffected charm. She was a rarity in a place like this.

I had struck down her list of ideas, but as a matter of fact, I had no alternatives to offer. I was not in the practice of doing or saying things to woo respectable women. In my dealings with the opposite sex, I had garnered a reputation for being cold and aloof. There were some women of looser morals who disliked that and preferred men to shower them with vapid compliments and whispered words of love. I had never been able to do such things, for they seemed hollow, and I had always been afraid of leading any of those women to think I felt more for them than I did—or perhaps equally afraid of beginning to truly feel such things for *them*. I needed a connection that was as easily broken as a strand of a spider's web.

"Perhaps we can speak of that later," I said.

"Very well," she said. "Let us just enjoy this dance, then."

Miss Russell was not a perfect dancer by any means. Indeed, she made more than a few mistakes, but as she only laughed and maintained an impressive level of gaiety despite it, I found myself enjoying the experience to a surprising degree. I even laughed once, an oversight I regretted when I saw the wide eyes of the spectators. I may as well have announced my intention of becoming a monk.

"We needn't dance the second one," Miss Russell said a bit breathlessly as the reel ended.

I straightened my coat as I tried to catch my breath. "I asked you to dance for the set."

"Yes, but it is most fair for us to dance one of the dances and then do something *you* enjoy during the second one. Come."

I didn't argue further, for I was too relieved. I didn't dislike dancing, but I disliked being observed while doing so.

"What do you wish to do, then, with the time allotted you, Mr. Donovan?" Miss Russell wrapped her arm through mine in a way that was as familiar as it was artless.

"How many options do we truly have?"

She shrugged. "We could eat refreshments, of course, though I think they are serving ratafia, which you detest. We could watch the dancing, but I would rather not do that, if you do not mind, for I think people might assume you couldn't bring yourself to dance with me anymore if we simply stood as spectators."

"Content yourself, Miss Russell. I have no desire to be a spectator."

"We could walk the gardens—oh! Perhaps that is what we should do. It would give us the opportunity to observe other couples and find a few ideas to replace the ones on my list of which you disapproved."

I nearly said no, but I was eager enough to distance myself from the prying eyes of those who had observed my momentary lapse in austerity, and I could never say no to fewer people nearby. Besides, I knew what a bit of curiosity over what the couples in the garden were doing might teach us. Perhaps Miss Russell's list had not been so far off the mark as I thought.

We informed Diana of our intentions, and the way she coolly reacted had me narrowing my eyes at her for a moment. It was almost as though we were doing precisely what she wished for us to do and she was trying not to betray that fact to us. Or perhaps I was simply too suspicious.

I acquired a glass of ratafia for Miss Russell from one of the footmen as we made our way into the low-lying hedges. She had not observed me taking it, so when I handed it to her, she looked from it to me in surprise. "How very thoughtful of you."

My insides wriggled a bit. She was quick to praise me for attributes I did not possess. It had been easy enough to take the drink from the passing tray.

She sipped contentedly on it, looking all around us, including up. "You can see a few stars," she said with a smile.

I glanced up to a sky of deep blue, a number of scattered gray clouds, and a peppering of stars. The sight of the small pricks of light stirred something in me. Nostalgia, perhaps. I had often stared out at the ocean as a midshipman, thinking how small I was in such a vast expanse of deep waters. But the night sky was more vast still, its heights less explored, less understood even than the depths of the sea.

"What are you thinking?" Miss Russell asked in her frank way.

I shook my head and pulled my gaze back down to earth. "Just that I haven't looked at the stars in some time."

In the middle of the gardens we reached a small, gurgling fountain, and Miss Russell took a seat on the stone edge, lifting her gaze back to the sky. "I like to look at them often—whenever the clouds oblige, at least. I find them . . . comforting."

I frowned. I hadn't ever thought to use such a word about the stars. "Why?" If she could ask frank questions, so could I. I hesitated for a moment, then took a seat beside her.

"My own problems don't seem quite so large when I see them. They remind me that there is light in the darkest of skies, even when they are masked by the clouds." She looked to me. "Do you not find them a comfort?"

I looked up, pinpointing the North Star and trying to decide just how I felt about it and its fellows.

"You must have seen them often as a sailor."

"Yes. You cannot avoid them on a ship, for they surround you. At night, they are the only thing that delineates a horizon at all. Otherwise, the world around is just a massive expanse of inky black. Sources of light are difficult to come by on a ship, so seeing a blanket of stars spanning from horizon to horizon is . . ."

"Breathtaking." Her eyes were on me, but it was clear that she was trying to imagine what I was telling her. If anyone could appreciate such a sight, it would be Miss Russell.

"I don't think I ever grew accustomed to it," I said. "On cloudless nights, I was always in awe." What she had said about the stars being comforting . . . I *had* felt that. No matter how much the Admiral had humiliated me in front of the other sailors, no matter how miserable the day had been, I felt a little less angry, a little less overwhelmed under the stars.

A little splash of water sounded, and I brought my gaze down. Miss Russell had a hand in the water of the fountain.

"What are you doing?" Had she dropped something?

She pulled her hand out and shook it gently. "I wanted to know if it was warm."

I regarded her with amusement. It never would have occurred to me to do such a thing.

"It is a shame to only *see* things when they can be smelled, touched, heard, tasted."

I raised my brows. "Do you intend to taste the water, then? Or smell it?"

She laughed, but the passing of a nearby couple drew her attention away. She tilted her head to the side as she watched them, her eyes narrowing slightly.

"I do not think *they* are in love," she said. I followed her gaze to the man and woman walking. They had as much distance between them as the path between the hedges would allow.

"No," I said. "I think you are right."

"He is so very stiff." She turned to me, regarding me for a moment. "He reminds me a bit of you."

My brows contracted. "I am not stiff."

"Are you not? Then what do you call this?" She rose to her feet and with a theatrically rigid motion, put out a bent arm as far away from her body as she could manage, as though I were a woman and she was offering me to take it.

"That is not what I did," I complained.

"Oh, but it is."

"Forgive me for not offering you my arm in the proper way. I did not know there *was* one."

"Well, there isn't . . . *if* you mean for everyone to think you dislike the person you are escorting to the ballroom floor, which is entirely opposite of what we are trying to convey."

"If you disliked it so much, you might have said something then."

"I did not wish to trouble you or say something unwelcome."

"And when has that ever stopped you?" I clamped my mouth shut, waiting for her expression to change when I realized how hurtful what I had said had been.

But she merely bit her lip, her smile still visible. "Very true. Do you dislike me terribly for it?"

"Strangely, no." I let out a relieved breath, for I wasn't certain what I would have done if I had wounded her feelings. Just the thought of it made me feel uncomfortable. "In any case, I am sorry for disappointing you with the shape of my arm."

"It is not just the shape." She set down her drink on the edge of the fountain. "Come. I shall demonstrate the proper way."

I stayed where I was, shooting her a look meant to communicate what I thought of such an idea.

"How very grumpy you are." She took me by the hand, and I

rose to my feet reluctantly. She put a hand on my forearm and the other on my upper arm, forcing my elbow to bend. "A man who is anxious to be close to the woman he is escorting will offer an arm"—she arranged my bent arm so that it was extended in invitation—"and then, once it has been accepted"—she set her hand gently upon mine—"he will draw it back near his body, thusly, bringing the young woman nearer him."

I looked over at her beside me, reluctantly amused.

"Yes, you have the way of it now. And if you truly wish to be convincing, you should look at me frequently, as though you cannot help it." Her mouth twisted to the side as she regarded me. "Ideally, though, you would look longingly rather than on the verge of laughing at me."

I did indeed laugh. "Undoubtedly I would be so overcome by the mere sight of you, I would be moved to tears."

Her lips turned down in consideration. "I think that would be a bit excessive. And knowing you, people might be more inclined to think you were crying for boredom rather than due to inspiration."

The fact that she had truly considered my teasing suggestion made me shake my head in amusement. "How have you come by such wisdom when you have spent your life surrounded by people with one foot in the grave?"

"It is common sense," she said plainly. "Another way to be convincing would be a covert squeezing of my hand."

"Covert enough to appear secretive but obvious enough for others to see it?"

She smiled widely. "See? You *do* understand! And here I thought *you* were meant to be the expert in love."

"It is not love which rakes are known for, Miss Russell."

"Ah, yes. Your rakery. I had forgotten about that."

I laughed softly. She had forgotten I was a rake. No one *forgot* I was a rake. It was central to what most people knew of me—that, and that I was a bastard.

Her brow knit, and she picked up her drink, taking a sip. "Why *are* you a rake?"

I blinked. "What?"

"Why are you a rake?" She looked at me, and her expression grew suddenly wary. "Am I not supposed to ask that?"

"I do not know about *supposed*, only that people generally *do not* ask it."

"Why not? Everyone has reasons for doing what they do. I would like to know yours."

The water in the fountain trickling behind us and the strains of muted orchestral music filled the silence. No one had ever asked me why I was a rake.

She looked at me still, waiting for a response.

I shrugged, unsure what to say.

"You must find joy in raking," she said, "otherwise, you wouldn't do it."

I considered her words. Did I find joy in being a rake? Precious little. "Joy, no."

Her brow puckered. "Then why do it? Why do or be something that is not making you happy?"

I pulled my gaze away from hers. Sometimes the certainty and familiarity of unhappiness were easier than the risks of pursuing happiness.

Captain Yates emerged from around the nearest hedge, accompanied by a man named Mattock. I didn't know much of him, but by the dandified manner of dress he had adopted, I was certain I would not like him. His collar was so starched, it might have been made of marble, and his hair had been swept forward and pomaded into oblivion, so that I feared it might crumble if touched.

"Oh," Miss Russell whispered urgently to me. "Now would be the perfect time to compliment me."

"Compliment you?"

She slipped her arm into mine again. "Yes. Something about my eyes. Or my slippers. Surely you know how to compliment."

I opened my mouth to protest, but I was too late.

"There you are, Donovan," Yates said. "Your sister said we would find the two of you here. Will you not introduce us to your charming companion?" I could see the interest in Yates's eyes and the intentness in Mattock's as their gazes moved to Miss Russell.

"No," I said unapologetically.

Miss Russell gave a little laugh. "Mr. Donovan is intent on monopolizing me this evening. He has been filling my head with compliments. The last one was particularly flattering." She looked to me, blinking like an innocent. "What was it again?"

I clenched my teeth, and my gaze flicked to Yates, whose eyebrows were both raised. He looked at me, all patient expectation—and a hint of amusement that made me wish to throw a fist into his face.

Miss Russell nudged me with her elbow.

"Your eyes and slippers," I said, my nostrils flared and my jaw tight.

There was silence, but I made no attempt to fill it.

Mattock cleared his throat. "No doubt something about how you are a vision, from your eyes down to your slippers. Though, if it had been me, I would certainly have included your hair in that, for I doubt I have ever seen anything so becoming."

My hold tightened on Miss Russell's arm.

Mattock took a step toward us. "At the risk of seeming forward . . . I am Henry Mattock, Miss Russell, and I was wondering if you would join me for the next set."

Miss Russell smiled broadly and attempted to extract her arm from mine, a task made somewhat difficult due to my efforts to prevent it. I was still attempting to take stock of Mattock and decide what sort of man he was. Miss Russell's innocence might easily be taken advantage of.

She looked at me for a moment, as though unsure whether I was playing a part or in earnest. Yates cleared his throat significantly, and I loosened my hold.

Pulling her eyes away from me, Miss Russell handed me her glass of ratafia and smiled at Mr. Mattock. "I would be delighted."

He offered her his arm, and as she took it, he pulled it close to his body. Miss Russell's gaze flitted to me, full of meaning. I raised a brow as a sliver of annoyance lodged itself under my skin.

I watched the two of them walk off into the lamp-lit hedge rows and toward the ballroom floor. Yates turned to me, giving me an enigmatic look. "Since when have you danced a reel and dallied in the gardens, Donovan?"

I looked down at the nearly empty ratafia glass in my hand and threw back the last of it, cringing at the taste. "Probably about the same time you started acting as chaperone to Mattock. Will you take to wearing caps to complete the role?"

He chuckled. "It simply happened that I was asking your sister after you at the same time that he was asking after Miss Russell. She is a taking thing, isn't she?"

"Did you have something particular to say to me, Yates?" I started walking in the direction of the house.

"Things are more serious than I thought, then," he said. "Jealous of Mattock, are you?"

"Merely wondering when you intend to tell me why you sought me out. If you mean to ask me to dance, the answer is no."

He hurried up beside me. "And yet you danced with Miss Russell."

"Your powers of observation never cease to amaze," I said drily. "What do you want, Yates?"

"Can a man not seek out his friend for company?"

"Certainly." I heard the sound of Miss Russell's laugh and

glanced at the ballroom floor where she skipped along the set joyfully. I pulled my gaze away and swiped a tart from the nearest footman's tray. "But if he is as annoying as you are being, he cannot expect the company to persist."

"Well, aren't you just delightful? I came to ask if you wished to accompany me to the club, but I repent of my intention."

I stopped, turning toward him. I didn't particularly wish to spend the remainder of the evening watching Miss Russell dance. I had done what I came to do; I had fulfilled my duty. "Yes."

"Yes what?"

"I will come with you."

"The devil you will. Not if you mean to be unpleasant."

I took in a deep breath. "I shan't be."

Yates targeted me with a raised brow of skepticism.

"Fine," I conceded. "No more unpleasant than usual."

He smiled and clapped me on the shoulder. "Good man."

Chapter Twelve

REBECCA

F eeling it a victory, I had jumped at the invitation to dance with Mr. Mattock, for we had been introduced at the last ball, but he had not asked me to dance then. He was a fine dancer, though he seemed more focused on what the spectators thought of his dancing than of carrying on a conversation with me.

Despite that, I thoroughly enjoyed myself, though I preferred Mr. Donovan's staid dancing, for at least he had spoken to me throughout the set. He had also been reliable in those moments when I had mistaken the figures, ready to help me. At the end of the set, Mr. Mattock left me in the charge of Diana and immediately moved to the nearest young woman to request the approaching dance.

"He is determined to dance each set," Diana explained, following my gaze.

"Yes, I can see that," I said. It was a bit less flattering to have been invited to dance by Mr. Mattock now that I had experienced it and knew that every young woman in proximity to him would too.

"He *did* go out of his way to seek you out, though," Diana said, watching me.

I took in a breath and smiled at her. "I am glad for it, for dancing cannot help but make me happy."

My mind went to the conversation I had been having with Mr. Donovan. I searched the area for any sign of him. Had it been rude of me to leave when we had been discussing something as important as happiness? I had an ambition to better understand Mr. Donovan, and it seemed as though I had been a bit nearer to that before Mr. Mattock had appeared.

Arm in arm, the Bradley girls approached, cutting off my search. It was difficult to see anyone amongst the hordes in attendance, particularly if they had a mind to avoid the crowds, which I could imagine was true of Mr. Donovan.

"Miss Russell," Miss Bradley said. "We were hoping to find you in attendance this evening. Have you had any refreshment yet?"

"A bit." My brow furrowed slightly. I had left Mr. Donovan with my glass of ratafia. I hadn't even thought before forcing the glass upon him, and I felt a twinge of guilt for it, hoping it hadn't felt dismissive. In retrospect, I would have preferred remaining with him in the garden to dancing with Mr. Mattock.

"Come, then." Miss Maria offered me her arm. "One of the footmen is carrying a tray with some very good butterscotch."

I looked to Diana, who gave me a smiling nod, and I accepted their proposal. I was flattered that they had wished for my presence here, and I was eager to solidify my friendship with them.

Once we had found the footman in question—and a few others—Maria expressed a desire for drink, her gaze fixed on the footman carrying a platter of glasses.

The elder Miss Bradley's lips turned down in distaste. "I believe all they have left is ratafia."

Miss Maria sighed.

I had been meaning to take a glass from the approaching

platter, but I paused. It seemed I was the only person who had any liking for ratafia—I and the people who hosted such parties, for it seemed to be frequently offered.

We moved toward one of the wrought-iron benches that sat beneath the wispy strands of a willow tree.

"Now," Miss Maria said, "you must tell us everything, Miss Russell. I thought you said Mr. Donovan was *not* a suitor of yours, and yet we find him not only taking you out for a drive, but also *dancing* with you, of all things."

"Yes," Miss Bradley said, "I had never even seen Mr. Donovan dance before tonight. I must say, it only increases his attractions, for he is unexpectedly skilled."

I felt a strange possessiveness course through me and brushed it aside. "Yes, he is, isn't he?"

"And he even laughed. Who knew he had such a handsome smile? It sent my heart fluttering just watching! How did you persuade him to dance?"

Miss Maria sent an elbow into her sister's side. "Grace," she chastised. "It is not civil to assume she was obliged to *persuade* him. I am sure he asked her because he could not resist with how lovely she looks tonight."

I managed an uneasy smile, remembering how Diana had all but required her brother to ask me for the dance.

"I did not mean it uncivilly." Miss Bradley adjusted the thumb of her glove. "It was just such a surprise to see him dancing—and then to see him escort you to the gardens." She cocked a brow at me.

"Indeed," Miss Maria said significantly. "I can tell you that it was not only *our* eyes upon the two of you. Did we not tell you that claiming Valentine Donovan as a suitor would be a victory?"

"You did," I said, my voice a bit thin. He was *not* a suitor of mine. Not really. But the whole purpose of this was to make people think he was, so I could not follow my impulse to confess that to them.

It was nice to be admired too. I couldn't deny that. And all my longings for a sister felt a bit less hopeless with the Bradleys seeking me out as they had tonight, inviting me to share refreshments together.

"I wonder if he shall ask you for a second set," Miss Maria said.

"I highly doubt that," Miss Bradley said. "That would be something indeed."

"There *was* some discussion of a second set," I said. That was a bit of a stretch, really. I was the one who had mentioned a second set, and it had never been a serious suggestion. Perhaps in time Mr. Donovan would come to dislike dancing less, but until then, one dance of one set would have to do.

Miss Maria and her sister exchanged impressed glances. "A second set! Then we should not be concealing you here under this willow. What if he has been looking for you and cannot find you? We shall accompany you to him and make our apologies for keeping you out of sight." She rose, and I followed suit, my stomach twisting at the thought of what Mr. Donovan would do when we approached him with the expectation to dance a second set. I didn't know whether to quake in my slippers or laugh at the inevitable reaction he would have.

We made our way back to the crowds surrounding the ball-room floor, and I wished I had taken the glass of ratafia after all, for my throat felt dry and my hands clammy beneath my gloves. I knew Mr. Donovan well enough to know he would not humil-iate me by refusing to dance a second set together, but I would certainly be obliged to apologize profusely to him later—and do something else to make reparations.

But Mr. Donovan was nowhere in sight. Perhaps he was hiding under a different willow tree. When we caught sight of

Diana, Miss Bradley suggested we ask her if she had seen him anywhere.

"Oh," Diana replied, an apology in her eyes. "I am afraid I saw him leaving with Captain Yates some time ago."

My stomach clenched, and I felt the Bradley sisters' gazes turn to me.

I gave a little laugh. "Oh, yes. That is right. He had warned me that if the captain came, we would not be able to dance the second set."

Diana looked at me intently. She saw through my excuse, and I knew it, but she smiled after a moment. "Yes, well, no doubt he will be eager for that second set next time. In the meantime, there is someone I would like to introduce you to . . ."

I allowed her to guide me to the gentleman in question, and I did my best to be kind and civil and to make conversation with him. But my mind was elsewhere. Mr. Donovan had left, and he had done so without telling me. It was not out of character, of course; he had never wished to attend this ball.

And yet, it hurt me a bit, all the same.

Chapter Thirteen

VALENTINE

The Brighton Club wasn't far from the outdoor ball, which meant it required only ten minutes for Yates and me to walk there together. I had spent a great deal of time there in the past—before the river of my finances had run dry—but I felt a tingling of nerves as we approached the front steps. Would I be strong enough to withstand the temptations there? If I cared for my future, I would need to. The short amount of time I was staying would, I hoped, aid me in that determination. I needed to return to the ball in time to escort Diana and Miss Russell home.

"Everyone will be thrilled to see you," Yates said as the liveried doorman pulled open the blue door with a large brass knocker.

"Will they?" I said drily. I had lost plenty of money at the tables there, most often to Colin Sutcliffe. The thought of him had me gritting my teeth.

The decor inside the Brighton Club was what one would expect of a gentlemen's domain, with the dark, rich hues of mahogany, gold, and deep blue prevailing throughout. It felt familiar and yet simultaneously foreign now that I was entering with no intention of playing. We passed into the main room, which was set up with a sideboard spread with sweetmeats, savory pies, and drink. There were primarily men there, but one or two women were present—hardly the type I would introduce to Miss Russell. There were a few new faces in the room I did not recognize, evidence of the amount of time I had been away —months, in fact. I doubted Diana would be thrilled to know I was here, let alone that I had left the ball without informing her.

Guilt niggled at me, and I clenched my teeth. It was not an emotion I allowed myself to play host to. It was too dangerous. Guilt prompted change, and I didn't wish to change. I wished for the Admiral to *believe* I had changed, only to find himself suddenly bereft of control over me.

Thankfully, I had found that the more I ignored the guilt, the less I felt it.

"Donovan!" Mr. Duffy, who had been observing a game of cards, left his place to come greet me. "We had given you up for dead—or worse."

"Worse?" I shook his hand.

He looked at me significantly. "Wondered if you had decided to go to that new club Gilby is trying to start."

"You are offensive," I replied as he clapped me on the back. "The truth is much less controversial. I have merely been done up." My gaze skimmed the room, settling for a moment on Lord Newham who sat in a wingback chair on the opposite side of the room, one hand on his cane.

He was looking at me, and I held his gaze, curious and wary. Miss Russell's words about how fortunate I was to have two fathers repeated in my mind. How I knew this man was my true father, I couldn't say precisely; it was simply something I felt innately. I had never told anyone of my suspicion, however. It was no one's business, and what difference did it make?

"Took refuge at your father's, did you?" Duffy asked knowingly.

"Call him the Admiral," Yates said, "or Donovan shan't know of whom you speak."

My eyes stayed fixed on Lord Newham, watching for any hint of his thoughts on the conversation.

"We all have our own theories about who really deserves that epithet," one of the other gentlemen joked. "My money is on old Clarkson."

My heartbeat sped as laughter broke out. Lord Newham held my gaze for a moment, then rose and, leaning heavily on his cane, left the room.

What to make of that, I didn't know.

"Come, then, Donovan," said Duffy. "It has been too long since we played. I believe you will find that my skill is equal to yours now. Or perhaps greater."

"He can play with you after he plays with me." Colin Sutcliffe had emerged from the rear door through which Lord Newham had just disappeared.

Our gazes met, and my lip pulled up into a sneer at the sight of a face I had come to know better than I had ever wished to— the blonde hair in perfect disarray, the lazy blue eyes, the ever-present self-satisfied expression. I might be a rake, but I was an irritable one, which meant there were plenty of women who disliked me. But Sutcliffe . . . he was all charm, with plenty of money, too. It was a deadly combination.

I had not fared well the last time I had played cards with Sutcliffe, and I wanted nothing more than to amend the ending of that story. Risking money at cards had made me feel alive in a way nothing else had since my mother's death. But paying my debts to him had deprived me of the last bits of capital I had. I had nothing to wager except the probability of my ending in debtor's prison. It wasn't the Admiral's insistence that I refrain from my gaming that kept me from wagering my pocket watch; it was my promise to Diana and Miss Russell.

"Not tonight," I said. "I am merely here to observe—and escape a ball."

"That is a shame," Sutcliffe said. "I have so missed our . . . *enlivening* games, Donovan."

I wanted to slap the sneering smile off of his lips—and win all my money back from him. But tonight was not the night for it, so I merely turned away and stationed myself where I could watch Yates play.

When I played cards, time slipped by in large chunks. Tonight, it crept by. Whether that was because I was merely watching or because I knew I should have been at the ball, I didn't know, but tonight's guilt was like a pesky fly, no sooner swatted away than it returned, demanding my attention. The image of Miss Russell dancing with Mr. Mattock continued presenting itself to my mind, but surely that was evidence of why I *needn't* feel guilty. She was occupied and well-entertained, whereas I had been feeling suffocated by all the eyes upon me. If the goal was to help attract other suitors for her, I couldn't stay with her at all times.

I glanced up and my eyes fixed on the woman walking through the door. The last time I had seen Nellie White had been months ago, when we had enjoyed a prolonged association. She was as beautiful as ever, her rich blonde hair piled atop her head, her lips and cheeks accentuated with rouge. The gaudiness of her apparel, however, detracted somewhat from her beauty. In my absence from Brighton, it seemed she had found the company of a different gentleman—one generous enough to provide her with the rubies hanging around her neck.

Her gaze fixed on me, her eyes lighting with curiosity. She made her way over, her hips swaying under the sheer fabrics of her crimson and black dress.

"Valentine," she said as she approached. "I cannot decide whether to kiss you or slap you." Her words were teasing, but there was an undercurrent of resentment beneath them. I had left Brighton without a word on my last visit, eager to avoid my creditors. Apparently, she had not appreciated that.

She came in close, wrapping an arm about my waist and bringing her face close to mine. I turned my head away, and she stilled.

Yates looked up, his gaze shifting between us as I gently pulled her arm from around me. I could not afford—and not just literally—to become mixed up with Nellie at the moment. Or any other woman, for that matter.

"A great deal has passed since you last saw Donovan, Nellie," Yates said. "He has met someone. A captivating little thing by the name of Miss Russell."

I nearly kicked Yates. It was an awkward position to be in, feeling inclined to deny what he was saying but being unable to. The entire purpose of what Miss Russell and I were doing was for appearances, after all.

Nellie looked at me, trying to force me to meet her gaze.

"No cards?" said Mr. Duffy. "Rebuffing Nellie? Do we have a reformed rake in our midst, gentlemen?"

A chorus of laughter greeted this, and Nellie smiled, gliding a few soft fingers across my cheek. "Once a rake . . ." She left the other part of the phrase unfinished, but *always a rake* echoed in my mind like the touch of her hand. "Let me know when you have abandoned the act." She turned away, though she looked back at me over her shoulder. "I find reform boring, and it would be a shame for Valentine Donovan to bore me."

I watched her walk away, frowning as she made her way over to Sutcliffe.

"Once you left, she found her place in Sutcliffe's pocket," Yates explained, as if the way she sat on his lap wasn't enough evidence of that. Sutcliffe looked up at me, the sparkle of mingled victory and challenge in his eyes.

"I can see that," I said, turning my gaze away. That explained the finery she was wearing.

"No need to pout, Donovan," said Mr. Duffy. "We all know she prefers you."

"But *he* prefers Miss Russell," Yates said, shooting me a teasing look.

I had had enough of such comments, and as they only continued during the game I was observing, I rose to leave, hoping I would be able to slip back into the ball with my absence unnoticed.

"He cannot stand to be away from the infamous Miss Russell a moment longer," quipped Sutcliffe as I made my way toward the door. Laughter spread through the room, and, gritting my teeth, I left.

My escape to the Brighton Club had not been nearly the reprieve I was hoping for, and I almost regretted having left the ball at all. At least there, I would have been spared Sutcliffe's sneer or Nellie's remarks.

I slipped past the footmen at the entrance and took the path around the side of the house, stopping where I had a view of the ballroom. My eyes searched the scene for any sign of my sister or Miss Russell. They were not easy to find, and I began to wonder if they had left without me. I wouldn't have blamed them.

Finally, my eyes settled on the two of them together, seated in the area surrounding the makeshift ballroom floor. Miss Russell was watching the dancing, but the expression she wore was the most somber one I had yet seen.

Diana looked over, her gaze finding me as though she had sensed my return—or had been waiting for it. I swore softly. She knew I had left, and she rose from her seat, making some excuse to Miss Russell.

I heaved a sigh, staying where I was so she didn't think I was attempting an escape. I couldn't have made one even if I had wished to, for she kept her gaze fixed on me.

"Did you have an enjoyable interlude?" she asked. "I assume

you went to the club?" She brought her head nearer, smelling me—for alcohol, I assumed.

I pulled away, but she seemed satisfied enough by her investigation. "No," I replied. "And yes."

"It serves you right," she said. "Did it not occur to you to tell me or Rebecca that you were leaving?"

"I did not think it would matter so much." My eyes moved back to Miss Russell. Her hands were folded in her lap, her gaze fixed on the dancers, but there seemed to be a distant look in her eyes, as though she was not really seeing them. "Why is Miss Russell not dancing?"

"An astute question," my sister responded. "Once you left, so did the invitations to dance, it seems. And then, ever since discovering your departure, she has been less enthusiastic on the whole."

Guilt reared its head again as I watched her. Why did it matter to Miss Russell whether or not I was in attendance when she had been occupied with a different partner?

"And you could not manage to find her other partners?" I said incredulously. "You know every person here, Di."

"Rebecca is not a simpleton, Val. She wants to be asked to dance, not to have dances arranged for her. And even if that were not the case, she asked me specifically not to do so, as she was feeling a bit under the weather." She pressed her lips together to show me what she thought of this excuse. "I tried to persuade her we should leave, but she was worried about how you would find a way home." Her expression told me she thought me entirely undeserving of Miss Russell's solicitude.

I didn't say a word, leaving Diana to make my way toward Miss Russell. Silently, I sat beside her. She looked over at me with a bit of surprise in her eyes.

"Oh," she said. "It is you."

"It is I," I confirmed, feeling my insides twist more than ever at the mixture of emotion on her face. It was as though she was trying to look happy at my arrival but couldn't entirely mask her lingering feelings of disappointment.

It made me feel a wretch. "I am sorry for leaving. I did not . . . I thought you well-occupied."

She smiled and shook her head. "You needn't apologize. I am sure you have a hundred things you would rather be doing than playing the suitor to me." She let out a laugh that sounded as valiant as it did forced.

I felt a need to see her laugh genuinely again, to put a smile back on her face. "Shall we dance?" It was difficult to get out the words, but I managed it. "We can slip into the second dance of the set, for there is a bit of space at the end there."

She shook her head, a rueful smile on her face. "No, I shan't ask that of you. I am feeling rather tired. Unless you have a desire to stay, I would prefer to return home." She made to rise from her seat, but I took her by the hand.

"Miss Russell, I am not practiced with apologies, but I can see that I have ruined your evening, and that was not my intention."

"You haven't." Her soberness disappeared in an urgency to set me aright. "It was I who did that."

I frowned.

She bit the edge of her lip. "It was selfish and vain of me, but I told the Bradleys you had asked me to dance a second set, and they insisted on coming with me to find you. But . . ."

"I was gone."

She nodded, settling that unconvincing smile on me again. "Somewhere more enjoyable, I hope."

"Not in the least." I was a cur, for I had humiliated her in front of people she wished to impress. Why she cared for the opinions of Grace and Maria Bradley, I didn't know, but that did not change the fact that she did. If I had only told her I was leaving, I might have spared her the embarrassment. It had been cowardly to slip out as I had.

"It is not too late for that second set," I said. "We can wait for the next one and station ourselves right in front of the Bradleys. I will even attempt to smile most of the time."

"Not the smile from the carriage, I hope. Besides, the Bradleys left ten minutes ago. But it is of no account." She met my eyes. "Truly. Let us go home. I think Diana wishes to, as well."

And so we did. But I promised myself I would make up for tonight to Miss Russell somehow, if only to hear that genuine laugh again.

Chapter Fourteen

REBECCA

Despite what Mr. Donovan seemed to think, I had never been angry with him for his disappearance. I had merely been . . . sad. I thought a great deal about why as I fell asleep that night, and I realized that it was because I had come to care for him, for what he thought of me. I considered Mr. Donovan my valued friend. The Bradley sisters were friends, too, but my friendship with them felt different. I had to be more guarded in front of them to prevent doing or saying anything to make them rethink our association.

In any case, Mr. Donovan's unnoticed departure from the ball somehow felt like evidence that he did not value our friendship equally. That was my fault, no doubt, for I had enjoyed so little of the sort of friendships that I enjoyed now in Brighton that I was overly eager to think more of what I had than was merited.

It didn't help that my personality was the sort to quickly embrace whoever I was confronted with. I was not particularly adept at reining in my enthusiasm to converse with anyone who had such an inclination. But I needed to adapt to my new situation. I was not at Grandfather's anymore; I was in Brighton Society, and things were different here. Restraint was the order of the day, and I needed to try harder to demonstrate it.

I made just such an effort when I stepped into the breakfast room the next morning. Mr. Donovan was there, holding a plate at the sideboard, giving me to think he had only just arrived. Diana was one to take breakfast later, I had discovered.

Mr. Donovan looked up at me, the trace of a smile pulling up the corner of his mouth. "Good morning."

His smile did strange things to me, but taking in a breath and remembering my plan, I gave a tempered smile in return. "Good morning." See? I could be pleasant without being overbearing in my enthusiasm.

He looked at me for a moment, scrutinizing me, as though he recognized the difference already. He said nothing, though, as he finished filling his plate, then moved to the table.

I took two pieces of toast for my own plate, chose a seat across from him, and poured myself a cup of chocolate. Feeling the need for it, I took not one but two lumps of sugar, then poured my customary cream and sprinkled the cinnamon.

I felt myself being watched, and I glanced up at Mr. Donovan. He was regarding me with a frown.

"Am I being punished?" he asked. "Have I forfeited the right to smiling chocolate because of my reprehensible behavior last night?"

"What?" I asked in surprise. "No! No. I . . . I only realized that"—I stirred the cream I had just poured, making a muddle of the smile—"perhaps you are not as fond of my concoction as I am and that I had given you to think I expected you to have some each morning."

"Miss Russell," he said. "Do I seem as though I would drink something I truly disliked?"

I searched his face for a moment. By appearances, he might

not seem the type to do so, but I had a suspicion that either Valentine Donovan thought himself a worse person than he truly was, or he made a concerted effort for others to assume that of him. "With enough reason, yes."

His frown deepened. "If you believe I possess that sort of unselfishness, I am afraid you are bound to be disappointed in me again and again."

"I doubt that," I said. "Would you like some chocolate, then?"

"I would," he replied. "I find I am becoming a bit superstitious. I have begun to worry that my day shan't be a good one if it does not start with a warm cup of happy chocolate. But if you have tired of pouring it for me, I can do it myself—or attempt it, at least."

I smiled at him and rose. "I am quite willing to serve it to you."

"I thank you." He watched as I performed the ritual pouring, sugaring, creaming, and spicing. "By the by, I was wondering if you would wish to accompany me to the theater tomorrow evening."

My gaze flicked to his, and my hand stilled on the cream pot.

His glance shifted to the pot, and he used a single finger to tip the spout upward.

I looked back down, finding that the happy face had transformed into something . . . else.

Mr. Donovan tipped his head to one side, then the other. "Today's face has one unusually large eye."

"Perhaps it is winking." I twisted my mouth to the side. "No, I think you are right."

"Should I prepare myself for a peculiar day?" He smiled at me more than was usual for him, and I found my heart began to beat faster at the sight of it.

I set down the cream pot in order to sprinkle a bit of

cinnamon on top, glancing at him as he watched my movements. "Did you mean what you said about the theater?"

He chuckled softly. "Of course I did. I may be a cur, Miss Russell, but I am not so without remorse that I would extend such an invitation as a cruel pleasantry."

Anticipation took flight in my stomach like a flock of doves, and I clasped my hands together to keep from clapping them in excitement. I had never been to the theater, but I had always wished for the opportunity to go—to watch the drama unfold onstage, to see everyone in their finery, to laugh at the farce. It was unlike anything I had ever experienced, and Mr. Donovan was offering me the opportunity.

Remembering my determination to be more measured, I took in a deep breath and assumed a more dignified posture. "I would be delighted to accompany you to the theater tomorrow, Mr. Donovan."

His brow furrowed, his gaze going to my still-clasped hands hanging down in a more relaxed position. Only the whiteness of my knuckles would betray how difficult it was for me to contain myself.

"Do not mask your enthusiasm for life, Miss Russell," he said. "It is one of your finest qualities. Shall we say dinner at half-past six tomorrow, then?"

***

Diana had insisted I have one of her dresses altered to fit me, and it was ready just in time for the excursion to the Theatre Royal. The final embellishments at the neck and hem were finished with only an hour to spare.

I had pleaded with Dorothea to take special care with my hair for the evening, for I wanted to look my very best. It wasn't just for me, although my own pride was certainly a consideration; what I did and how I presented myself reflected upon Mr. Donovan and Diana as well.

As I slipped on my dress and waited for Dorothea to do up the clasps at the back, I regarded myself in the mirror. The silk underdress was a pale pink, but the sheer white overdress made it appear almost white, except at the neck and hem where Diana's seamstress had added braiding perfectly dyed to match the pink silk. My hair was done up with long curls framing my face in a way that made me look older. Old enough, perhaps, to suit Mr. Donovan.

I went still at the thought, wondering at it. Surely it was not Mr. Donovan I meant to impress by the way I looked this evening. I wanted to be admired by those attending the theater, stranger and acquaintance alike.

Looking at myself fixedly, I met my own gaze under the thick brows I had never thought much of until now. It was so much easier to notice all of my failings and flaws when I was surrounded with scores of young women my own age.

I chewed the inside of my lip. I had to admit to myself that it *was* Mr. Donovan's approval I wanted, just as much as I wanted it from anyone I might see this evening.

"There, miss." Dorothea took a step back and looked at me in the mirror, as well. "My, but you look fancy now. A real lady. If you don't have a handful of new suitors by the end of the night, 'twill be because they're blind, every last one."

I laughed nervously and turned away from the mirror. Dorothea took my hands in hers. "I hope you enjoy yourself tonight, Miss Russell. You deserve it."

I smiled, nodding and forcing myself to breathe. I *would* enjoy myself tonight. I wouldn't let the question of what everyone thought of me—not even Mr. Donovan—taint what could be a perfect evening.

It was impossible not to feel a bit of relief and victory when I entered the dining room, though. Diana and Mr. Donovan were standing at the table, and the latter looked up as I passed through the doorway, slowing in the act of lowering himself into his seat, an arrested look in his eyes. He was looking particularly handsome himself. His dark hair, which was normally left to its own devices, was styled with a bit of pomade, I assumed. The effect was enough to make my heart skitter a bit.

"You look a vision, Rebecca," Diana said as Mr. Donovan hurried up to pull out my chair for me. The result was another fluttering of my heart.

Oh dear. These reactions I was having wouldn't do at all.

Diana raised her brows enigmatically. "I imagine you will capture as much attention as the performers this evening."

I laughed, a bit of heat surging to my cheeks.

"As no one pays any attention at all to the play," Mr. Donovan said, "that is hardly a compliment."

A bit of my pride deflated, my smile wavering.

"How someone as inept at flattery as you has had as much success with women as you have, I shall never understand," Diana said, shooting him an annoyed glance.

Her brother scowled at her. "I was merely pointing out the weakness of your compliment, not disagreeing with the sentiment. You do, indeed, look a vision this evening, Miss Russell."

I wasn't at all certain how to take the compliment, for not only was it merely a repetition of what Diana had said, but it had been as good as forced out of him.

"Why do people not pay attention to the play?" I asked, hoping to change the subject away from myself.

"They are too busy conversing and ogling the other beautiful attendees," he replied. "You should prepare yourself for an inordinate amount of unapologetic staring."

Diana had invited one of her friends, Mrs. Henry, to accompany us to the theater, and by the time the four of us had arrived, my anticipation and determination to enjoy myself had both recovered.

The warm glow of the lights outside the columned theater beckoned me, catching the sheen of the dresses and waistcoats of those trickling in. The performance had started half an hour ago, but both Diana and her brother had assured me that no one arrived at the beginning, as it was unfashionable. I had a desire to see the entirety of the performance, but I had no wish to be unfashionable, so I made no complaint.

Mr. Donovan offered me his hand as I stepped down from the carriage, adjusting it to settle on his arm as he escorted me inside. He pulled his arm in nearer to him, just as I had taught him to do. I only wished it was because he wanted to do so and not because I had instructed him to.

My body buzzed with anticipation as we passed into the entrance hall, enveloped by perfumes, conversation, and the muffled sound of the play. With Diana and Mrs. Henry behind us, Mr. Donovan led the way up two sets of stairs to the box where we would be sitting. When we reached it, he opened the door and moved for me to pass through, which I did, only to stop almost immediately. The box was occupied.

I looked back to Mr. Donovan, unsure what to do. The gazes of those in the box turned to us, their conversation stopping. Mr. Donovan looked in to see why I had stopped, and his brows drew together at the sight of everyone within returning his gaze.

"Oh," one of the women said.

Diana slipped past her brother and me to address herself to those within. "Have we mistaken things? I thought we had decided that we would have the box on Mondays, Wednesdays, and Fridays, and that you would have it Tuesdays, Thursdays, and Saturdays."

The woman showed an apologetic gaze and a mouth full of clenched teeth. "I am afraid you *are* mistaken, Mrs. Russell. We most certainly said the reverse. I remember it quite well, for my sister comes to dine each Wednesday, and I thought how propitious it was that she should be able to accompany us here afterward. As she is now." She put a hand out to display the woman two seats away from her, wearing a hideous green turban and a gown a shade of yellow that made me feel as though I could taste the mustard from dinner again.

"Ah, yes, quite," Diana said with a smile. "Forgive us for inconveniencing you." She turned to me. "Duke and I decided to share the cost of a box with the Standerwicks. We do not come often enough to merit a box of our own."

"Oh," I said, trying not to betray my disappointment that we would be obliged to leave. I could see just the slightest bit of the stage from where I was, and I itched to see more.

"Is there a problem?" A head peeped around the partition that separated the box we were congregated in and the one beside it. It was a gentleman—a very fine-looking one, with golden hair, blue eyes, and a charming smile.

"No," Mr. Donovan said flatly, just as Diana said, "Yes."

They looked at one another, Diana with confusion, her brother with what I could only describe as a warning.

Diana ignored it. "It seems we mistook which evening was ours to use the box. My sister-in-law is here for the first time, and we are quite crushed she shan't be able to see the performance."

"No need to despair," the man said. "You may join us in our box. Eh, Donovan?" His eyes were on Mr. Donovan, a smile spread across his lips.

It was a very kind offer, and I looked to Mr. Donovan pleadingly.

"No," he said baldly.

Diana's eyes went wide. "Valentine," she chastised softly.

"We needn't put you out, Sutcliffe," Mr. Donovan continued. "We can find a place down in the pit. Or up in the gallery."

Diana drew back in revulsion.

"There is no idea of putting anyone out, Donovan," Mr. Sutcliffe said. "There are plenty of empty seats here. I am sure Miss Russell would prefer sitting in the comfort of this box to craning her neck in the pit or sitting so far away she cannot see a thing. What do you say, Miss Russell?" He looked to me, his handsome smile trained upon me.

I hesitated, conflicted between my desire to experience the theater at its best and my reluctance to go against Mr. Donovan. I let my gaze move to the part of the pit I could see and then to the gallery. It did indeed seem a more uncomfortable—and crowded—way to watch the play, which continued as we debated the man's offer. My gaze shifted to Mr. Donovan as I tried to gauge his mood, to determine why he was so reluctant to accept the kind invitation from an agreeable man.

"I would be happy to watch from anywhere," I said, hoping to strike a balance.

"I believe," said one of the Standerwicks with a bit of hesitation, "that there aren't any seats to be had in the pit or gallery tonight. I overheard as we were coming in that the tickets sold out this morning on account of Miss Blanchard coming in specially from London to perform."

"Then we shall return tomorrow night," said Mr. Donovan.

"Do not be ridiculous, Valentine," said Diana, her annoyance barely veiled. "We have already accepted an invitation to dine at the Woods' tomorrow night. We came to see the play, and see it we shall. It is very kind of you, Mr."—she paused, looking to the man offering us a place in his box—"Sutcliffe, was it?"

He nodded. "It is my pleasure, Mrs. Russell. Do come and make yourselves comfortable here."

Mr. Donovan's jaw was clenched tight, and I wished I could take him aside and ask him what had him so irritated. Was he simply put out about the misunderstanding? Or perhaps he regretted suggesting the theater at all. I tried to force him to meet my gaze, but his eyes were trained on his sister, who motioned to me to follow her.

"Come, Rebecca. We should take our seats."

Feeling powerless and more than usually confused, I obeyed the summons.

Chapter Fifteen
VALENTINE

"You mustn't mind Valentine," Diana said to Miss Russell. "He delights in being difficult."

Despite all my efforts to warn Diana off, she had ignored me. That was the problem with being so disagreeable all the time: no one ever believed you had any other reason for disliking something than your natural tendency to look askance on the world.

I had good reason, though. The last thing I wanted was to spend the next several hours in a confined space with Sutcliffe. His smiles didn't fool me. He was always up to something. No doubt he was curious about Miss Russell after hearing of my connection with her. I wouldn't put it past him to try to ingratiate himself with her, just as he had done with Nellie.

A flash of protectiveness over Miss Russell coursed through me. There were plenty of young women with more experience than she who had been captured by Sutcliffe's charms. Any thought I'd had of leaving her and Diana to fend for themselves evaporated. Diana wasn't familiar with Sutcliffe or his reputation.

With a gritting of the teeth, I left the Standerwicks' box and made my way into Sutcliffe's. I stopped short in the doorway.

"Mrs. Russell, Miss Russell," Sutcliffe was saying, "allow me to present you to Miss White."

Nellie was dressed in a fine gown of silver silk, trimmed with glinting spangles, her gold hair gleaming just as impressively in its careful coiffure. By appearance, she could have passed as a fine lady.

The three women exchanged curtsies, and I looked on, speechless, as Sutcliffe smiled at me knowingly. The dog. He had orchestrated this—or at least jumped at the opportunity presented to him.

Diana finally seemed to take notice of me. "We were obliged to introduce ourselves, since we did not have you to perform the task for us." She was displeased with me—that much was obvious—but I was every bit as displeased with her. Without her interference, I might have avoided this devilish situation. And it was not I who had mixed up which nights the box was available. If I had known, we could have come last night.

"You must meet Miss White, Mr. Donovan," Miss Russell said cheerfully. "Is it not very kind of her to share her box with us?"

I met Nellie's gaze, noting the impish light in her eyes. "Mr. Donovan and I need no introduction," she said, coming toward me and curtsying. She was doing her best to cover the accent that betrayed she was not genteel, and the effort was enough that Miss Russell might not notice it. But I did, and I would be surprised if Diana didn't notice it, too. Perhaps she would merely assume that Nellie had come from more humble origins, though.

"Yes," said Sutcliffe. "Miss White and Mr. Donovan are particular friends, you know."

"Oh," said Miss Russell, looking between me and Nellie with delight. "How wonderful! Then we may all be quite comfortable together. Here"—she scooted over toward Sutcliffe—"you may sit by one another, for I am sure you have a great deal to discuss."

Nellie kept her eyes on me, smiling as she replied, "How thoughtful of you, Miss Russell." She took the empty seat beside Miss Russell, leaving only the one between her and Diana for me.

This night was not going at all how I had envisioned it.

I took in a breath, ignored Nellie's gaze, and sat down in the only seat available to me. Miss Russell was engaged in conversation with Sutcliffe, a fact which made me grind my teeth. But, while she responded very civilly, it was clear that she was more interested in the play itself, and *that*, well, it couldn't help but make me smile. Who would have thought that someone as obscure and unaffected as Miss Russell would be the one to put Sutcliffe's very large opinion of himself in its proper place: firmly below *Two Gentlemen of Verona*.

Nellie leaned in toward me, keeping her voice low so that neither Miss Russell nor Diana would hear. "So," she said, "*this* is the infamous Miss Russell. I admit I am surprised. I did not think your tastes ran toward such . . . inexperienced young ladies."

"And I did not think yours ran toward such tiresome men."

She laughed, and the sound brought back memories of many evenings such as this we had spent together in the past. "Is that jealousy I hear?"

"Disappointment," I corrected. Nellie knew full well that Sutcliffe and I were something of adversaries.

"Sutcliffe is a generous man," she said.

"I can see that." I looked at the dress and the diamond drop necklace she wore. The knowledge that the money Sutcliffe had used to buy such things for Nellie was quite possibly money he had won from me at cards didn't particularly delight me.

"And," she said, "he has the added appeal of not having abandoned me."

"*Yet*, at least," I said. "Come, Nellie. If you expected sentimentality and tear-filled goodbyes from me, it was through no fault of mine. You knew what I was when we began."

"I did," she agreed. "And it is what drew me to you. What draws me to you still." She glanced down at our legs, which rested against each other.

Grimacing, I pulled away gently, for there was a candle-filled chandelier just above our box, illuminating us for anyone who cared to observe. She held my gaze for a moment, then turned and addressed herself to Miss Russell.

I tried to focus my attention on the play and not to pay the conversation any heed, but I was tense and annoyed. Nellie seemed to be taking stock of Miss Russell, going so far as to ask her questions about me and, when Miss Russell responded, taking the opportunity to demonstrate her own superior knowledge. There were enough veiled references to the type of association we had shared that I nearly intervened more than once. Based on the provoking glances she shot at me every now and then, Nellie was taking joy in my anxieties and frustrations. Months ago, I had enjoyed her contrariness; now, it merely aggravated me.

But Miss Russell was too pure and naïve to understand the references, and she listened with interest to the things Nellie said about me and was quick to compliment me based on her own experience. She was all kindness and curiosity, and she hadn't any idea she was speaking to a woman who was her opposite in most ways. Nellie had not come from happy beginnings, and her background had made her into the enterprising and determined woman she now was.

By the time the first half of the performance was over, I was feeling out of humor and restless. The moment the opportunity presented itself, I stood. "Miss Russell, would you care to accompany me for some refreshment?" I asked, my tone less warm than it would have been in other circumstances.

"Gladly." She accepted the hand I offered to help her from her seat. "Would you like to join us, Miss White?"

My hand instinctively tightened on Miss Russell's, and she glanced at me, her eyes widening as though she feared she had done something wrong. She had, but I could hardly tell her why.

Nellie looked at me, mischief in her eyes. I put as much warning as I could in my own gaze. There were limits to what I would tolerate from her.

"It is kind of you, Miss Russell," she said, "but I shall wait for Mr. Sutcliffe, I think."

Miss Russell nodded with a smile, and I opened the door for us to pass through, eager to leave the suffocating box.

"How very kind and agreeable your friends are," Miss Russell said.

Hearing her refer to Sutcliffe and Nellie as my *friends* had me unsure how to respond. She looked up at me and seemed to note my lackluster reaction to her comment.

"Do you not agree?" she asked.

I took a moment before responding. "Not everyone's kindness is as genuine as yours. Would that it were."

Her brow puckered as we arrived at the refreshment tables at the end of the corridor. They were spread with coffee and a few types of biscuits.

"They both *seemed* quite genuine," she said as she took a small plate. "And I am no one to them, so I think it a great kindness that they should invite us into their box when they could have easily left us to our own devices and kept the space to themselves."

Again, I found myself having to choose between two unpalatable alternatives: dashing Miss Russell's idealistic view of her fellow humans to bits or leaving her vulnerable to people with motives less pure than hers.

"You seemed put out by the invitation," she said. "I am very sorry if you would have rather returned home. I have so been looking forward to this since you asked me to go, and it is everything I had dreamed it would be. But I do not at all wish for the evening to be miserable for you." Empty plate in hand, she looked at me with concern. "We can go home now if you like. I have at least been able to experience the theater."

I felt a pang of guilt. I had been thinking primarily of myself—of the discomfort of being in a box with Sutcliffe and Nellie—of how the evening was not going the way I had envisioned it. But for Miss Russell, it was just as she wished it to be, and yet, she was offering to cut it short on my behalf because she sensed my displeasure.

I could manage another hour of discomfort if it would be an hour of happiness for her.

"I am afraid I often look miserable and put out." I tried for a smile. "But we shall not return home until you have seen the farce."

I tried to imprint the smile she offered me on my memory to prevent me from regretting my words.

As we took from the refreshments and ate them together, Miss Russell seized the opportunity to tell me what she had thought of the play. It was amazing how much she had watched given the amount of time she had been engaged in conversation. It almost made me wish *I* had paid better attention. But I was coming to find that Miss Russell looked on the world with different eyes than I did. Sometimes, I wished for a glimpse of things as she viewed them.

We passed Nellie and Sutcliffe in the corridor on our way back to the box, but Diana and Mrs. Henry were still there. Mrs. Henry addressed herself to Miss Russell, and together they walked to the balcony of the box. Diana, on the other hand, walked over to me.

"Not still moping, are you?" she said.

"You're a fool, Di." My annoyance returned rapidly at the memory of her meddling.

"For forcing you to stay at a place where it was your idea to attend?"

I glanced over at Miss Russell and, content her attention was occupied, leaned closer to Diana. "For forcing us to share a box with the last two people in this theater I wished to be near."

"Yes, you made it quite clear with your incivility that you preferred to go home. How could you do such a thing when you knew how much Miss Russell has looked forward to this? Besides, what have you against Mr. Sutcliffe or Miss White?"

I clenched my jaw and stared at her intently. I was fairly certain she wasn't wholly ignorant of the society I had been keeping for the past two years. The Admiral took delight in bemoaning and enumerating my excesses at family dinner, after all. "You mean Miss *Nellie* White?"

Comprehension dawned in her eyes. "Nellie?"

I said nothing, content that she now understood what she had done.

"Good gracious," she hissed with a quick glance at Miss Russell. "Why did you not tell me?"

"I thought the fact that she was an unmarried woman alone in a box with Sutcliffe would be enough to give you pause. Is it not part of your work as a chaperone to ensure you know the characters of those to whom you introduce your sister-in-law?"

"Forgive me for not being more attuned to the many places I might encounter your *Incognitas*."

I clenched my jaw more tightly. Diana was one of the only people in the world not to think the worst of me, but it was clear that in this moment she didn't care to extend me any grace. But I had learned long ago not to set people right when they said something unflattering and untrue about me. People would think what they would think.

"Perhaps in the future," I said through my teeth, "you will

not foolishly disregard my attempts to warn you. Or perhaps that is asking too much."

She narrowed her eyes and folded her arms across her chest as the performance started again in the background. "What has you angry, Valentine? The idea that Rebecca's innocence has been blemished, or the thought that her opinion of you might become tainted?"

She held my gaze intently, and I returned it with just as much force. Her question was more difficult to answer than I had anticipated, however. So far, I was fairly certain Miss Russell had no idea what sort of connection had existed between Nellie and me. What would she think of me if she discovered it? And why did the answer to that question matter to me? She knew I was a rake, after all. What difference did it make if she knew the identity of one of the women I had associated with?

A cry of pain sounded, and I whipped my head around.

Chapter Sixteen

REBECCA

I put my hand to the suddenly burning skin of my cheek as another burn scalded my forehead. I cried out again in surprise and pain, just as Mrs. Henry did.

Across the way and down in the pit, heads turned in my direction. I looked up at the chandelier above me, its candles glowing and reflecting off of the crystals around them. Some of the candles were beginning to gutter, the melted wax pooling at their bases and dripping down onto us below.

Mr. Donovan and Diana hurried over, and the former took my hand, pulling me out from under the chandelier as Diana shepherded Mrs. Henry away.

"Are you hurt?" Mr. Donovan's eyes searched my face, lingering on my cheek and forehead where the wax adhered to my skin.

The chatter of conversation in the theater had shifted, turning from the previous hum of constant conversation to hushed whispers. I didn't need to look to feel the eyes of the entire auditorium on our box.

"Stop the performance!" Someone cried out in the pit. "There has been an accident."

"Miss Russell," Mr. Donovan said again, commanding my attention. "Are you hurt?"

I shook my head quickly, though the places I had been burned stung. The heat filling my cheeks from embarrassment was as likely to scald me as the candle wax. How many times must one humiliate oneself before one became calloused to it? "No. I am well. They needn't stop the performance on my account."

"Devil take the performance." Brow furrowed, Mr. Donovan put a gentle hand to the wax on my cheek, using the edge of his thumb to pull it up, watching me for any sign of pain as he did so.

The touch of his hands on my face and the intensity of his expression sent my heart off like the shot of a gun at the races. I had never seen Mr. Donovan so close, never seen just how uniform the brown of his eyes was or how the stubble growing in on his jaw was sprinkled with red. The harsh slope of his brows contrasted with the softness of his skin on my cheek, making my heart beat all the more quickly.

He didn't seem to notice my reaction, so intent was he on his task.

"Did that hurt?" he asked.

I shook my head slightly. He continued to apply himself to the wax on my forehead. It was a larger piece, and he set his other hand on my arm to stabilize me. Once he had removed it, he flicked it to the ground. His eyes ran over my face, in search of any other affected areas and, finding nothing, his gaze moved to my hairline.

He touched his finger to a spot atop my head. "There is more here," he said with a grimace, "but I doubt I shall be able to remove it—at least not without pulling your hair and hurting you, which I do not wish to do."

His eyes dropped to mine, and our gazes met. We stared at

one another, his grip on my arm tightening imperceptibly as our eyes locked.

The door opened, and both of us glanced over. Miss White and Mr. Sutcliffe came through the door, looking around as though trying to understand what scene they had come upon. A few feet behind us, Diana and her friend were watching us. So, it seemed, was anyone in the theater who had a view of us—even if it had to be obtained on tiptoe.

Mr. Donovan's hand dropped from my hair and arm, and he took a small step back, his jaw hardening.

The interruption acted like smelling salts, reviving me from my stillness, for I hadn't moved since he had begun removing the wax. "It is of no account," I said. "Dorothea shall help me remove it at home."

"What happened?" Miss White asked. Her gaze jumped between Mr. Donovan and me. In my confusion, I found it easy to interpret her question to refer to the close contact Mr. Donovan and I had just shared rather than what had precipitated it.

"The candles were left too long without being trimmed," Diana explained, her eyes lingering on us for another moment.

"I shall speak with the theater to avoid any other victims." Mr. Donovan's voice was clipped, his tender demeanor replaced with brusqueness. As he passed Miss White, their gazes seemed to meet momentarily before he moved through the door and disappeared.

They are particular friends, Mr. Sutcliffe had said of Mr. Donovan and Miss White. I hadn't paid heed to that word *particular* at the time, but now it seemed terribly important. And that shared glance . . .

The hum of chatter in the theater had grown louder, and I began to feel a bit sick at the number of eyes on us. Mercifully, the performance began again, and I could only hope that people would forget about the interruption.

"Are you well, Miss Russell?" Miss White said as she and Mr. Sutcliffe came over to me.

I smiled, hoping it was a convincing one. "Yes, thank you. So silly. I should not have cried out so loudly when the wax dropped. Only it was such a surprise."

"Anyone would have," Mr. Sutcliffe said. "They should be tending the candles more closely. From the way some of them are drooping, it looks as though they have been economizing by using tallow amidst the beeswax."

"Yes, and when they have sold every ticket for an entire evening, they shouldn't *need* to make such economies," Miss White agreed.

There was a small knock on the door, and Diana went to open it. After a moment, she pulled it wide, revealing the Bradley sisters. Their eyes searched the box until they found me. They rushed over, all concern, and Miss White and Mr. Sutcliffe moved to make way for them.

"I am well," I said quickly, feeling sheepish from the to-do over such an insignificant occurrence. "It was just unexpected."

"Oh, but look at the red spots on your cheek and forehead," said Miss Maria, her forehead wrinkled in concern.

"It does not hurt," I said. It was mostly true. The stinging had generally receded, and I was eager to minimize talk of what had happened. Mr. Donovan was still gone, and I wondered when he would return. My eagerness to watch the performance had dissipated significantly, and I would gladly leave if given the chance.

"We were so worried for you," Miss Bradley said, her eyes shifting to Miss White and Mr. Sutcliffe. "We thought we should come see for ourselves that you were not too badly hurt."

"I am not," I reassured them. "But I would very much like a drink."

The Bradley sisters assented to this, and Diana and Mrs. Henry agreed to accompany us down the corridor. I didn't truly need a drink, for I had had one not twenty minutes ago, but I hoped leaving the box again would provide an opportunity to shift the conversation elsewhere. It was entirely possible, however, that I would find something near the refreshments to use to my further mortification. Coming to Brighton had acquainted me with that skill, at least.

The five of us left the box and made our way to the refreshment table, Diana and Mrs. Henry leading the way. The Bradley sisters took my arms, and we walked three abreast—a very tight and uncomfortable configuration—in the corridor, both of them leaning in toward me.

"How do you come to be sharing a box with Mr. Sutcliffe and . . . that woman?" Miss Maria asked in a low voice.

My brow furrowed at the strange way she referred to Miss White. Her accent was not quite so refined, but I hardly regarded that. I didn't share the prejudice some people had against those who had made their fortunes by industry. As long as people were kind, I was glad to know them. "My sister-in-law's box is shared with the Standerwicks, and there was a misunderstanding about which days the families would use it. Mr. Sutcliffe and Miss White kindly offered to share their box with us."

The sisters shared significant glances. "How terribly awkward it must be."

Feeling baffled, I was slow to respond. "They have both been quite attentive."

"Have they?" Miss Bradley asked. "Frankly, I am surprised Mrs. Russell"—she looked toward Diana to ensure she was not listening—"would countenance it."

"Diana was the one who insisted upon accepting the invitation," I clarified, bristling a bit on her behalf. "She wanted to ensure I was able to see the play."

Miss Maria blinked in astonishment. "But to subject you to

the company of one of her brother's . . . Paphians. It seems quite irresponsible. And strange."

I gave a little laugh, not wishing to seem ignorant entirely of what a Paphian was—or that I had apparently been subjected to one. Was it a political word? I had often heard Grandfather complain of Whigs and Tories, though I didn't truly understand what the words meant. Was Paphian yet another designation in that mysterious world? Did Mr. Donovan and Mr. Sutcliffe share radical opinions that the Bradleys thought I should not be exposed to? It seemed silly, if so. "I am sure I didn't regard it. It is none of my business, after all."

Their eyes widened a bit, and I wasn't sure whether the surprise was in my favor or not. How very difficult it was to pretend to be more knowledgeable than one actually was! If only Mr. Donovan had been here, he surely would have known just what to say.

"Well, that is very tolerant of you," Miss Maria said. "I thought perhaps Mr. Donovan and Mr. Sutcliffe would have a falling out, for Mr. Donovan has looked to be put out all evening. Though, to be fair, he often *does* look that way. But the way he attended to you after the wax incident . . ." She gave me a look full of meaning. "I thought he might kiss you right there in full view of the theater!"

"Kiss?" I said weakly. My mind reverted to when Mr. Donovan's hand had been on my arm and our eyes fixed on each other. It had lasted such a short time, and yet so much had passed in those moments. Not that I could say what exactly it was that had passed—or even if he had felt the same thing. All I knew was a . . . stirring within me.

"Even Valentine Donovan is not such a rake that he would kiss a woman at the theater," Miss Bradley said.

"No," her sister agreed. "But he seemed to have no thought of *her*"—she gestured with her head down the corridor toward our box—"in that moment, at least."

The only person she could reasonably be referring to was Miss White. The realization that I might have made a very incorrect assumption about the meaning of the word Paphian pressed itself upon me.

"No, he was *very* devoted to you, Miss Russell," Miss Bradley said. "And if that woman had not entered at that moment, who is to say what might have happened? I know *I* was on the edge of my seat—much more interesting than the performance, to be sure."

"Which reminds me, Miss Russell," said Miss Maria, "that you must tell us immediately if he *does* kiss you, and you must make it a point to remember *every* detail."

I nodded absently, my mind dithering between the idea of Mr. Donovan ever kissing me and my transforming understanding of Miss White—and what a Paphian was.

Chapter Seventeen

REBECCA

Diana, Mrs. Henry, and I accompanied the Bradley sisters back to their own box, leaving them there to the sound of their mother chastising their unchaperoned disappearance.

"I think perhaps we should return home," Diana said as we made our way back to Mr. Sutcliffe's box. "Removing that wax from your hair will take time, I imagine."

I nodded. "Yes, I think we should leave too." I wasn't feeling in the proper mood for a farce at the moment. Neither was I particularly keen on the prospect of being watched for the duration of the evening by those curious about the company in our box or the candlewax incident. Or by those who knew the precise nature of the relationship between Mr. Donovan and Miss White.

Diana patted my arm. "We will just give our thanks to Mr. Sutcliffe and . . . Miss White, and be on our way, then."

I didn't miss the hesitation before Miss White's name, but as we arrived at the door to the box, there was no opportunity to ask about it—not that I would have. I didn't wish to put Diana in an uncomfortable position, given how the Bradley sisters had responded to her decision to allow me in Mr. Sutcliffe and Miss White's box. She had been introduced to Miss White at the same time as I, so it was likely she hadn't known of the connection with her brother.

There was a liveried theater servant in the box, tending to the chandelier with the use of a stool and a snuffer. Mr. Donovan was in conversation with Miss White, and I felt a sting of jealousy as she directed her beautiful smile at him. There was something in the way she looked at him that I could easily see would be irresistible. Were all Paphians so beautiful? Was she a *confirmed* Paphian? Whatever the case, it made no sense for my stomach to twist and turn at the sight of them together.

I remained at the back of the box, away from the prying eyes of those in the pit and the boxes adjacent to ours, as Diana approached and spoke to her brother. He glanced at me as she spoke with him, then nodded.

Miss White came over to me, putting out her hands to welcome mine. I knew the slightest wish to deny them to her, but my conscience quickly overruled it. Whatever her connection to Mr. Donovan, I had no reason to dislike her. She had been nothing but kind to me, after all.

"We are sorry to see you go before the evening is over, Miss Russell," she said, "but we understand. I hope you are not too injured. It was a pleasure to make your acquaintance."

I smiled genuinely and pressed her hands. "You will be able to enjoy the evening in peace now that we are leaving. Thank you for welcoming us into your box."

Mr. Sutcliffe came over and, after I had thanked him sufficiently, he bestowed a little kiss on the back of my glove. His gaze moved to Mr. Donovan. "I hope Mr. Donovan will take the best care of a treasure like you, Miss Russell."

I swallowed and tried for a laugh as he took his place by Miss White's side again, offering her his arm and a warm look. I was unused to being spoken to in such a way. I had heard young women receive similar compliments with a nonchalant laugh, but I found myself rubbing the back of my glove where his lips had touched it. How was one to react to a man who flirted with one woman one moment and another the next?

Mr. Donovan was quiet on the journey home, and as my mind was full of the evening's events, the chore of maintaining conversation was left to Mrs. Henry and Diana.

It was strange, sitting beside Mr. Donovan in the relative darkness of the carriage. We had sat the same way en route to the theater, but it felt different now. I was aware of our legs bumping against each other with the swaying motions of the carriage, and it unsettled me. What was this I was feeling? And what was I to do with it?

But more than that, I worried for Mr. Donovan himself. He had planned this evening, but he hadn't seemed to enjoy it in the least. Was he jealous of Miss White and Mr. Sutcliffe? Was that why he had not wished to accept the invitation to join them in their box?

When we entered the townhouse some time later, Diana instructed water be prepared for a hot bath to be taken to my bedchamber. "I think that is the best way to remove the wax from your hair." She covered a yawn with a hand. "Shall I come see to it myself? I have been dripped on in the past, you know."

I shook my head. "It is kind of you, but there is no need. I am sure you are quite tired."

She smiled ruefully. "My yawning betrays me. I am afraid I have lost a bit of my stamina for social engagements. Before you know it, I shall be falling asleep in front of the fire. But I trust Dorothea to see to things." She smiled at me. "Goodnight, Rebecca. Goodnight, Valentine." With a swishing of her skirts, she took the stairs, leaving her brother and me alone in the entry way.

Mr. Donovan had loosened his cravat the moment we had

stepped inside, and his tailcoat hung over his left arm. He met my gaze for a moment.

"Good night, Miss Russell."

"Wait," I said, and he stopped.

When I didn't immediately say more, he turned toward me, a bit reluctantly.

I swallowed. "Are you angry with me?"

His brow furrowed. "What? Of course not. Why would I be angry with you?"

I lifted a shoulder. There was relief in hearing him react in such a way, but it meant that his low mood was caused by something else . . . or someone else. "For embarrassing you. Again."

The crease in his brow deepened, even as the edge of his mouth curled up. "Embarrassed me?" He took a few steps toward me. "The wax, you mean?"

I nodded. "They stopped the performance. Everyone was looking. And everyone saw—" I stopped.

"Saw what?" he asked.

I turned my head, unsure if I could manage to look him in the eye while I responded. I hesitated a moment. "Saw you . . . helping me."

"And what of it?"

I shifted my weight. How awkward it was to say this all aloud. "Just that we were quite close, and . . ."

His eyes searched my face, and his lip turned up at the edge. "Is that not what you wanted? I seem to recall the list you wrote made some mention of touching your hair."

I couldn't help a laugh. "I suppose it did. Is that why you did it?"

His smile wavered slightly. "No. No, it is not."

I nodded, wondering what to make of that. Or why I needed to make something of *anything*. "I suppose I am just embarrassed at my insistence on mortifying myself and those around me no matter where I go."

"Rebecca . . ." he said.

My lips parted at the sound of my Christian name in his voice. I had never loved my name as much as just now.

"Miss Russell, I should say," he corrected himself.

I shook my head quickly. "I do not mind it. It does seem strange to be so formal when we share such a close connection —and are living in the same house." I laughed, hoping to make my words light.

"It does," he agreed. There was a pause. "What I was saying, though, is that you need not concern yourself over what happened this evening—or any other evening. You have not mortified yourself or anyone. The wax was entirely the fault of the theater, and I took them to task for their negligence."

"You did?" I asked, somehow heartened at the thought of it.

"I did. But the point is, anyone who had scalding wax fall on them multiple times would have done just as you did. You need not feel embarrassment."

I sighed. "But what do you know of embarrassment? You are Valentine Donovan. I doubt you are even capable of feeling such a thing."

"Then you are mistaken."

I narrowed my eyes. "You are only saying that to make me feel better."

He shook his head.

I pursed my lips, still unwilling to believe him. What possible cause for embarrassment could someone like him have? Was it so mortifying being the most handsome man in Brighton and the object of so many women's interest? For I hadn't failed to notice how many women *did* regard him with anything-but-subtle fascination when we went anywhere.

"You must have heard plenty of rumors about me," he said. "You are friends with the Bradley sisters, after all, and they seem to take pride in knowing the gossip."

My heart stilled for a moment, wondering if he was referencing Miss White. "What rumors?" My voice was uneven, and I cleared my throat.

"About my parentage."

My brows knit. The thought of his feeling embarrassment made me feel . . . ill, almost. And a wish to comfort him. "And those rumors embarrass you?"

His mouth turned down at the edges. "Not anymore. But they did when I was young."

He had been hearing himself discussed in rumors since he was a child? I hated that thought. "And how do the rumors make you feel now?"

He frowned more deeply.

"Forgive me," I hurried to say. I was always doing something or other that proper young women shouldn't do. "I did not mean to pry. I am too quick to ask precisely what comes to my mind—"

"Which I like," he said.

I met his gaze, and he held it, as if to reaffirm what he had said. "I haven't considered your question in some time. I am not entirely sure what to feel about the matter of my parentage. I have more questions than answers, and many of those answers died with my mother."

"You never asked her any of them?"

His jaw shifted, and the muscles there grew more defined. "By the time I was old enough to understand what questions to ask, I did not have the opportunity."

"I do not understand."

His nostrils flared slightly, something that happened whenever he spoke of his father. "The Admiral had agreed to let me resign from the Navy after I passed my lieutenant's exam. But when that time came, he ensured the process was prolonged. As a result, I was not present at my mother's death."

I was silent at first, unsure how to respond. "I am terribly sorry. Surely, it was not done on purpose." There was a pause. "Was it?"

"If ever you have the doubtful pleasure of meeting the Admiral, you will see for yourself that everything he does is quite intentional. This was no different, I assure you."

It was difficult for me to believe that a person would do something so cruel—and to his own son. Well, perhaps not his own son, but someone he had raised as such. It seemed to me that many of Valentine's darker tendencies sprang from his relationship with his father. But he was also kind and good, little though he might admit it or even see it.

"What was your mother like?" I asked.

"An angel," he said softly. "An angel married to a devil."

I was quiet for a moment, trying to imagine both Admiral Donovan and his late wife. "I wish I could have met her." I looked at Valentine, trying to imagine what parts of his features he shared with her. "Do you resemble her?"

He shook his head. "We had the same eyes, but little else."

I smiled. "Your eyes are my favorite feature of yours."

He met my gaze for a moment, then turned away, and I wondered if I had spoken too freely—or given away too much of how I admired him. But I had been raised in a home where praise and compliments had been given sparingly, and I had promised myself never to withhold that from others.

"Your brows often look severe," I explained, "but your eyes . . . they are kind and deep."

His mouth turned up at the edge, a wry expression. "You see the reflection of your own kindness wherever you look, Rebecca."

His words brought to mind our discussion at the theater. *Not everyone's kindness is as genuine as yours.* He had been referring to Miss White and Mr. Sutcliffe.

"May I ask you a question, Valentine?"

He smiled slightly, and I wondered whether he liked hearing his name as I did mine. "A dangerous question all on its own, I think, if history is any indication. But, yes, you may."

I took in a breath, trying to brace myself for the answer. "What is a Paphian?"

Chapter Eighteen

VALENTINE

I stilled, staring at Rebecca. Her eyes were filled with a mixture of things: curiosity, wariness, anxiety.

"Who did you hear that from?" I asked. But I was fairly certain I already knew. "The Bradleys?"

She rubbed her lips together and nodded. "I thought perhaps they were referring to Mr. Sutcliffe, that it was a political term or some such thing, but I think it was rather Miss White to whom they were applying the term. What does it mean?"

I closed my eyes, feeling a bit sick at the discussion I found myself in. "Rebecca . . ." I shook my head, not meeting her gaze.

"You said you would answer my question," she said, seeming to sense my hesitation.

"I said you could *ask* me a question," I corrected.

The look of betrayal in her eyes burned my conscience, for my agreement to the question had been an implicit willingness to answer. And yet, I was hesitant.

Earlier this evening, Diana had accused me of being concerned with Rebecca's opinion of me being tainted, and I knew now that she was right. I *did* fear that. No one else in this world viewed me the way Rebecca did. She was determined to think the best of me, to describe my eyes as *kind and deep*. Was it so wrong to wish to preserve that?

It would be unforgivably selfish, particularly in the face of the young woman before me. She was asking for my help, asking me to help her navigate a Society she did not understand.

I let out a large sigh. "A Paphian is . . ." Dash it all! Why was it so hard to say the words? "It is a woman who offers herself as a . . . companion to men who wish for one."

"A companion," she repeated, as though she was trying to understand what that word encompassed.

"Not the sort of company your brother would wish for you to keep," I said. "I regret that you were made to share a box with Nellie—*or* Mr. Sutcliffe, for that matter."

"Nellie," she said. "That is Miss White?"

I nodded, regretting the informality. I had never referred to her as anything but her given name.

"And that is why she said she was your *particular* friend."

My lips pressed together. "Yes."

"And now Miss White is Mr. Sutcliffe's Paphian?"

The way she used the word might have been humorous to some, but I had no desire to laugh. "Yes."

She swallowed, and I wished I could see into her mind and know what she was thinking.

"If I had known," she said, "I would have found some excuse not to share their box. I am sorry for putting you in a . . . difficult position."

I blinked. "What?"

She lifted a shoulder. "I knew you were not in a good humor throughout the evening, but I hadn't realized that you were experiencing the pain of jealousy."

I struggled to respond. She thought I had been out of humor because I was jealous?

"It cannot be easy to see Miss White and Mr. Sutcliffe together. Though, I must say, it seems clear to me that she would rather be your Paphian than his." She smiled weakly.

I shut my eyes, shaking my head, for I could hardly understand the turn the conversation had taken. "Rebecca, I was not jealous. I was out of humor because you should not have been subjected to all that happened this evening. You should be angry with me and with Diana; you should certainly not be apologizing." I ran a hand through my hair and turned around. What sort of celestial creature was she that she would react in this way?

She didn't understand. That was the problem. Still, after a week of being together as we had been, she didn't know who I was, *what* I was.

"I think we should stop." I turned back toward her.

"Stop?" Her eyes filled with apprehension. "Stop what?"

"Stop *this*." I gestured to the air between us. "It is not helping you, and we cannot pretend that it is."

She took me by the hand, a pleading gesture. "It is, though. I promise you it is."

I shook my head and gently pulled my hand away from hers. "You would be better off not ever being seen with me again, Rebecca. That is the truth." I clenched my jaw, overcome with frustration. "I warned you. I tried to make you understand."

"I *do* understand," she responded.

"You do not." I whipped my head around, and the surprise in her eyes doused the flames of my anger—anger with myself. "You do not," I said softly. "You hadn't any idea with whom you were sharing a box this evening."

"But what does that matter?"

"It matters," I said as evenly as I could, "because my very presence in your life is corruptive." I didn't wish to be that influence on Rebecca. She deserved better than that. And as for myself . . . I could feel the connection strengthening between us, and there was nothing more frightening to me than that—and how much I wanted it.

And it wasn't just connection. I had felt something at the theater, that moment when our eyes had met.

I clenched my jaw. I couldn't even give that a thought.

She shook her head. "You are my only true friend, Valentine." The way she swallowed after made my heart twinge. "If it is not helping you, I shan't ask you to continue, of course." She paused. "Is that what this is about?"

I frowned. "No."

She looked unconvinced. "Perhaps being seen with me so often is keeping you from other . . . companions." The way she looked at me made it clear she was referring to Nellie. That she might have been worrying over such a thing made me feel a bit sick.

"Far from it," I responded. "It has been a success so far. Diana heard from the Admiral only yesterday, and she said he sounded encouraged." All of it was true. And while my association with Rebecca had produced some teasing comments, by and large, being seen with her regularly was doing what we had wanted it to do. The way people were looking at me was shifting, if only slightly. I had noticed it this evening. There was more interest, more curiosity, as though perhaps people were questioning their previous ideas of me.

"Then please do not put an end to things," she said. "Not on my account. I should hate to lose you." Her gaze flitted to mine. "As a friend. Though not a *particular* friend." There was that weak smile again.

I held her gaze, a strange thickness filling my throat. Never had anyone ever fought for me or expressed such a firm desire for my friendship. The way Rebecca saw me was not accurate—I knew that—but what did that matter? She believed she needed me, not just for what I could provide to her, but for my friendship, and I would not abandon her.

I took her by the hand, holding her gaze. "I shall *always* be your friend. As long as you wish for my friendship."

She pressed my hand, and I dreaded the inevitable moment when she realized my presence in her life would be of no value.

Chapter Nineteen

VALENTINE

Rebecca and I had agreed to be friends, and after our discussion the night of the theater, we seemed to settle into that friendship with a fair amount of ease. I found my time with Rebecca just that—easy. If anyone had told me I would be eager to spend time with a naive, optimistic young woman who, for all her experience of the world, might as well have been sixteen as her true twenty years, I would have laughed in their face—or perhaps ignored them like the madman they were.

But the truth was I found my wish for strong drink and high stakes at the gambling table least powerful when I was with her. Her *joie de vivre* made the things that had long held no interest for me a bit more entertaining and exciting once again. Whether it was a promenade along the beach full of enthusiasm for the feel of damp sand on her feet and the discovery of stray shells, or yet another dinner party with new foods to taste and people to meet, Rebecca found enjoyment in it. And while I would never match her energy, I found amusement and secret satisfaction in her pleasure.

But I was not the only one taking notice of or appreciating

Rebecca. More and more, I was obliged to forgo her company as other gentlemen asked for the pleasure of it themselves. And while I could celebrate such success for Rebecca's sake, I found the invitations did not have a positive effect on my own mood. There was a sense of protectiveness burgeoning inside me, a wish to deny the gentlemen what they wanted, not to mention a suspicion of *what* they wanted. I had known too many men who took satisfaction in opening the eyes of an innocent to trust anyone fully.

It was not my place, though, even if I doubted they would appreciate Rebecca properly, even if I worried what they might say that she might not understand. Her ignorance was likely to endear them to her as it had done to me. She had long since lost her hesitation in asking me questions, and though I had not lost my hesitation in answering some of them, I never could seem to deny her those answers. And the way she accepted it all was so practical that I could never find it in me to regret it.

Every smile from Rebecca bound me to her more, as though I had been starved all my life of the brightness she exuded. I could no more stop from soaking it up than could a dry sponge in the middle of the ocean.

Our friendship was not without encouragement, either. Indeed, Diana seemed to have an engagement for us to attend or a task she wished us to fulfill each day, all in preparation for the party she had decided to host marking Rebecca's entrance into Society.

"Strange, isn't it?" I said to my sister one morning when she asked for my and Rebecca's help dusting the library.

"What is strange?" She frowned at the menu for the week sitting before her and scribbled something on it.

"How incompetent your servants have recently become."

She dipped her quill again. "On the contrary. They are so occupied with other tasks that I cannot in good conscience ask them to do this on top of everything else. Besides, you assured me you would earn your keep here, you know, and it has now been more than two weeks since you arrived when you assured me it wouldn't be more than one."

"Then I shall just leave," I said, turning away.

"No," she cried out, turning from her task. "I need you here."

I smiled, but I was secretly relieved at her reaction. It was what I had expected, but if she had agreed with my departure, I would have been in a difficult position. I was no more flush in the pocket than I had been two weeks ago, and I didn't wish to leave. Since coming to stay with her, I had begun to feel that the world held less and less for me outside of the house's walls.

I faced her again. "You need me here?"

She nodded but did not expound.

"Come, Di. What is your game? And don't think I haven't noticed you throwing Rebecca and me together at every opportunity."

"I am not *throwing* anyone together," she said. "You made an agreement to help one another, and I am ensuring you both uphold your end of that bargain."

I shot her a look that said *I do not believe you.* She studiously ignored me, turning back toward the menu.

"If you could have the dusting done by tomorrow, that will be for the best," she said. "Phineas will be arriving on Thursday, and I wish for him to be able to look through the books without all the wretched dust there now."

"Phineas?" I said in surprise.

"Yes. I invited him to come stay."

I quirked a brow. "You mean, you lured him with the promise of books so that he would be here for the party." She hadn't ever said so, but I suspected Diana had an ambition to marry off both Phineas and me.

She shrugged.

"I wish you had not," I complained. "The Admiral will undoubtedly accompany him."

"Rest easy, dear brother. I told Father he needn't put himself out to attend."

I didn't mind having Phineas here. My guilt over leaving my younger brother to navigate the Admiral's moods on his own had persisted since my departure from Blackwick Hall. Phineas deserved a respite, and there was nothing that interested him more than a room full of unperused books.

"And what will Russell have to say when he returns here to find you have filled his home with Donovans?" I asked.

"He shan't." The clipped tone she used told me she felt more strongly about this than she was letting on. "Business at Birchleigh has become more complicated than he anticipated, which will keep him away another fortnight."

I watched her for a moment. She gave no indication that the words made her feel anything, but I wasn't fooled. It couldn't be easy to be so long away from her new husband, and against my will, I felt a bit of compassion for Diana.

She glanced up at me. "Rebecca is already in the library, so unless you mean to make her do the lion's share of the work, I suggest you join her sooner rather than later."

I sighed and walked toward the door. "Somehow I doubt Russell intended for you to make his sister into a servant when he made you her chaperone."

"Thank you, my dearest brother," Diana said, entirely ignoring what I had said. "Oh, and if you could inform Rebecca that I recommend she choose a Boulangère and the waltz for the first set, I would appreciate it."

I paused in the doorway. "The waltz? A bit dashing for a coming out party, don't you think?"

She smiled, full of her usual confidence and mischief. "Precisely."

I didn't particularly like the idea of Rebecca waltzing with someone, but I could hardly say as much to Diana. Or anyone. Besides, it was just like Diana to do something like this. She was not the sort of woman to do the safe or respectable thing. No. Rebecca's party would be talked of, just as Diana intended. "I will relay your message."

When I reached the library, Rebecca was on the third highest rung of the ladder, a feather duster in hand. Little breaths of dust, illuminated by the light pouring through the window, erupted in front of her with each swipe of the duster. She was humming something cheerful, as though there was nothing in the world she wished to do more than dust her brother's library.

I delayed notifying her of my arrival as I tried to catch the tune. It was *O Mistress mine, where are you roaming?*, which brought a smile to my lips.

As though she could hear the sound of my smile, she turned. "Oh, there you are. Perhaps *you* can reach the highest shelf. Or perhaps if I stand on the top"—she set a foot on the next rung.

"No," I cried out, hurrying over to her with my hands up in the event that she might fall. She stopped, looking at me with raised brows.

"I will do the top shelves," I said, my heart racing a bit.

"Very well," she said with resignation. "But if you are to have all the fun, perhaps you can at least push me a few feet that way."

I glanced over to the place she had indicated, my brow furrowing. Finding nothing, I returned my gaze to her.

She smiled. "I have always wished to glide along the library shelves on a ladder. Grandfather had only a stationary one in his library. It was terribly troublesome to move and not at all the adventure I wished for."

I gave a little chuckle, shaking my head at her strange ambitions. "I will oblige *if* you descend three more steps."

Her smile grew, and the little hint of playfulness in her eyes was entirely charming. "Are you worried for me, Valentine?"

Gripping the side of the ladder with one hand, she straightened her arm so that her body hung away from the ladder and the wall of shelves. It was a playful yet taunting gesture, and I almost hoped she would fall just so I might catch her in my arms.

"Worried to distraction," I said drily. "If you fall, I shall have to dust the entire library myself."

She laughed and, pulling herself more squarely onto the ladder, she took two steps down.

"And the third," I said, unyielding.

She obliged, then looked down at me expectantly.

"You are holding on firmly?" I asked.

"I am holding on for dear life."

With a little chuckle, I gave the ladder a push.

She laughed in delight as she slid a matter of eight feet to the side, and I watched with a smile of my own as she let her duster run along a shelf until the ladder came to a stop. She made dusting the library look less like a chore and more like amusement.

"Your turn," she said, giving a last dusting to the nearest books as she climbed down.

"*Not* my turn."

"*Yes*, your turn." She picked up a second duster that was sitting on the window sill and set it firmly in my hand. "You shan't regret it. I promise you." She gave me a push toward the ladder. "You said you would get the highest shelves, did you not?"

"I did." I yielded to the pressure she was putting on my back and put a foot on the bottom rung. "But there is no gliding necessary. In fact, gliding is outright forbidden."

"I disagree," she said. "Gliding is always necessary when it is possible. Go on, then. Just once."

I sighed and made my way up the ladder. My inability to say no to Rebecca Russell would be the death of me. I reached the rung fourth from the top and looked down at her. She was already poised to push the ladder and, when I gave a reluctant nod, she gave it a shove.

It was much harder than I had pushed her, and the ladder sailed across the rail as I gripped the side more tightly with one hand and attempted to dust with the other. It was a perilous affair, sending clouds of dust in front of me so that I had equally strong inclinations to laugh and sneeze. The way Rebecca's laughter followed behind me told me that she was running after me.

The ladder hit the end of the rail with a smack, testing my shaky balance with a jolt even as Rebecca stabilized the ladder with a hand.

"*That* was a proper push," she said.

"Was it?" I replied as I descended. "Allow me to rectify my prior attempt, then."

I moved, making space for her to take my place, but she did not. Her eyes were on me, playfully wary, as though she didn't know whether to trust me. After a moment of consideration, though, she stepped up.

"Brave woman," I said, hoping to make her rethink her decision.

She merely smiled and climbed up to the rung fourth from the top. "No. I trust you. You would never hurt me."

Her simple words caught me off guard. They were said so matter-of-factly, as though she hadn't a reason in the world to doubt them. And she was right. I couldn't imagine hurting Rebecca Russell—at least not on purpose.

"Well?" She looked down at me, waiting with her feather duster poised and ready.

I gripped the side of the ladder with my hand and pushed it hard, running along with it and hopping up onto the first rung to join Rebecca as we flew across the shelves, the skirt of her dress blowing against my smiling face.

Amidst sneezes, sliding, and a fair amount of laughter—more on her part than mine, of course—we dusted the library for the next hour. At the end of it, Rebecca wiped her hands together, surveying the library. "We did a fine job. If anyone happens to wander in here the evening of the party, they will be justifiably amazed by the admirable condition of it."

I was not fool enough to think anyone would truly enter the library the night of the party. This had all been an excuse for Diana to demand we spend time together. And I had enjoyed it, curse her.

"Speaking of the party"—I set down my duster beside hers—"Diana asked me to tell you she recommends selecting a Boulangère and a waltz for the first set."

"A waltz?" Her wide eyes told me that this was not particularly welcome information.

"Yes, and a Boulangère."

"But I do not know how to waltz."

"Oh." It wasn't surprising, really, that a young woman who had experienced her first real ball here in Brighton wouldn't know how to waltz. Many people didn't. It was such a recent addition to the ballroom scene in England—and not happily accepted by all. "We can tell Diana no, then. Nothing is set. The party is in your honor, and it is your prerogative to choose the first set." I knew a bit of relief, for it would mean I would not be obliged to watch, or even *picture*, the stupid dance.

"But she recommended it?"

"She did," I confirmed. "But that should not weigh with you." As soon as I said it, I realized I could have saved myself the trouble. Rebecca looked to Diana as an example of how to conduct herself in Society. She would not ignore her advice.

She chewed her lip. "Do *you* know how to waltz?"

"Regrettably," I said wryly. "Part of a bet I was unfortunate enough to lose."

Her anxiety gave way to curiosity. "You had to learn the waltz because you lost a bet?"

"Learn it and dance it—alone—at an assembly in some obscure village I have since forgotten the name of."

Rebecca laughed. "How delightful. Men have all the fun, don't they?"

"I assure you, there was nothing *fun* about the Master of Ceremonies dragging me from the ballroom floor—or how the orchestra ceased to play because all the other dancers stopped waltzing to watch me."

"I should like to have seen it," she said, clearly attempting to envision it. "My life has been so very dull compared to yours."

"Duller, perhaps, but certainly better spent. You were caring for your grandfather while I was making a fool of myself." She always spoke of him warmly, but I had read between the lines enough to realize he must have a difficult, stubborn personality. It was a wonder she had such a sunny disposition after spending so much time with only him for a companion. "Do you miss Millbury?"

She took in a deep, thoughtful breath and let it out slowly. "Sometimes. I miss Grandfather. I even miss Mr. Philpotts every now and then. I miss knowing my place. Everything was familiar." She looked at me. "I would be terribly lost in Brighton without you."

How did such a sincere, unflirtatious remark manage to set my heart racing?

"You would do just fine," I said. "Better, even."

"We shan't argue this again." She tilted her head to the side, looking at me with hesitation in the gentle slope of her brows. "If Diana wishes for a waltz, I wish for one, too. Would you dislike teaching me?"

"No," I said truthfully. I wouldn't dislike it one bit. In fact, I would like it far too much. But I hadn't time to truly contemplate that, for Rebecca was so enthusiastic in her gratitude, it required all my attention to receive it and dampen it to more manageable levels.

Only a few minutes later did it occur to me that this had likely been Diana's plan all along—to force me into teaching Rebecca how to waltz. As was true of all Diana's ideas, this one was an unwise one, and I would not let her make a mess of the friendly terms Rebecca and I had settled into. And by settled into, I of course meant that I was teetering dangerously on the edge of those terms, only maintaining any sort of equilibrium by sheer strength of will and the affection I had for Rebecca.

She deserved better than me, and she would realize that soon enough.

Chapter Twenty

REBECCA

The thought of performing a dance I hadn't had much time to practice before the party was admittedly daunting. It was difficult enough to remember the steps of the reels, minuets, and country dances I had learned from Mr. Abbot. I had given up my pursuit of perfection with those and was determined to simply enjoy myself, even though it meant treading on the shoes of my partner. I found I was not particularly adept at following the lead of whoever I danced with. My body was too impatient for it—another example of why I would never be the belle of Brighton, even if I had not been plagued with the broken vase or the theater candle wax incidents.

Good heavens! What other unfortunate mistakes awaited me? It was a daunting thought.

And while keeping company with Valentine was certainly having its intended effect in that I no longer sat out for dances or lacked for conversation partners wherever we went, I couldn't help but notice the variation in such partners. Few seemed to return for a second set, and that reflection was lowering. Surely, it would be better to have one or two determined suitors than a bevy of men who decided I was not to their liking after one conversation.

I had thought long and hard about what might be responsible for the lack of any consistent suitor, and I could not put my finger on any particular thing except that perhaps I was not like the other young women surrounding me. I did not know how to flirt or be coy. These were not skills I had been taught at Grandfather's, and my attempts to imitate what I had seen were unsatisfactory in the extreme. Indeed, when I had tried to use a fan to flirt with one gentleman, the episode had ended with my pinching my fingers between the sticks, something more than one person told me they had not thought possible.

The waltz, however, was something that could help in my wish to be taken seriously. Grace and Maria Bradley had spoken of it more than once in my presence, always with the utmost assurance that a waltz brought a man and woman into the sort of contact that couldn't but lead them to think of matrimony.

So, I would learn to waltz.

Dorothea did up the last buttons of my white dimity dress as I arranged the chemisette at my neck. I quite liked how Dorothea had taken to styling my hair. When I had first arrived in town, I had been asked by three different matrons if I had yet turned eighteen—a lowering occurrence, indeed. But that had since ceased, and I attributed it almost entirely to the new coiffures Dorothea had been trying.

"Will there be anything else, miss?" she asked.

"No, thank you."

Valentine and I had agreed to take a late breakfast and then begin our waltz lessons in the drawing room, and I felt a buzz of anticipation at the prospect. It was how I always felt before breakfast these days. Sometimes Diana joined us near the end, but often enough, it was just Valentine and myself, with our smiling chocolate and whatever conversation I forced upon him.

I couldn't help myself. My curiosity knew no bounds—about Society, certainly, but about him too. Valentine had known a great deal of sorrow, I had come to understand, not that he had said so in anything approaching such language, for he was not the sort to admit to it. But the more I knew of him, the more I found myself wishing to bring him happiness in whatever ways I could.

The bigger truth, though, was that I was doing precisely what I had assured him I wouldn't do. For I *had* promised not to fall in love with him. But that was the trouble with falling; it was not done intentionally, so how could it be stopped?

He was later than usual for breakfast and seemed to be in an unusually somber mood, less talkative than usual—and he was never particularly loquacious. But when we had both finished our food and drink and I proposed we move to the drawing room, he nodded readily enough and followed me there. Only the hard set of his jaw let me know that anything might be amiss despite his assurances to the contrary.

The drawing room was a handsome room, papered sage green with emerald curtains and gold trim. There were a few chairs and other small pieces of furniture littering the carpet, so we were obliged to do a bit of rearranging to make enough space for our lesson. Valentine rejected my suggestion that we call for the servants to perform the task, so I tried not to admire him too much as he moved piece after piece of furniture with such seeming ease.

By the time we had cleared room on the rug, there were a few beads of sweat on Valentine's brow. He shrugged out of his coat, and I diligently ignored the way his shirtsleeves adhered to his skin at the shoulders before he shook them out. While I had thought Valentine a devilishly handsome man upon our first meeting, further acquaintance had only improved him, for with it had come a familiarity with the subtleties in expression that told me how he felt—the various types of frowns he wore, the different angles of his reluctant smiles, the set of his jaw in frustration or determination.

He turned to face me, letting out a breath and setting his hands on the thighs of his pantaloons. "Waltzing, then."

I nodded and took in a breath, readying myself to learn.

"What you need to know first and foremost is that dizziness is your greatest enemy when you engage in a waltz."

"Dizziness?" I repeated.

"Dizziness," he confirmed. "The only way to combat it is to keep your eyes on your partner as you revolve. I can tell you this from my own experience *not* having a partner."

"Oh dear," I said, trying not to smile. "Whatever possessed you to agree to such a bet?"

He raised a brow, as though I should not have to ask such a question.

"You were bosky," I said.

A little snort came from him. "Where in heaven's name did you learn that word?"

I smiled enigmatically. "Diana said it once. I have been keeping track in a notebook of the expressions I have learned—mostly from you and a few from others. Those latter definitions I have had to assume from context, of course, so it is possible they are wrong. I was hoping you might agree to look over them and see whether I have properly understood them."

He whispered something under his breath. I could have guessed the word aloud, but I rather thought he might not like that in this particular moment. I had become familiar with Valentine's chosen oaths, for he did not whisper them as well as he thought he did. "Your brother is likely to call me out if he discovers this notebook of yours."

I raised my brows. "Really? That is very promising, for then we might check off the duel from my list." I wrinkled my nose. "Though perhaps it would not be ideal to have my own brother as one of the participants. Less romantic, I think."

"It is that rather than the thought of me lying dead of a gunshot wound which deters you?"

The comment took me from my imaginings, and I met Valentine's sardonic gaze. "Duke would never *kill* you, of course. Naturally, he would delope. Or perhaps a little grazing of your arm would serve better. Just here, for example." I touched my hand to the top of his arm, near the shoulder. What a stir it would cause if people knew that Valentine Donovan, confirmed rake, had been injured in a duel on my behalf. The firmness of his arm under my hand distracted me for a moment, and I pulled it away. "You could wear a bandage around your coat at the next dinner party we attend."

One of his brows cocked. "A bandage on the outside of my clothing?"

"Well, you could wear one underneath, as well, if you are worried about your shirtsleeves becoming soiled by the blood."

"How very generous of you. Perhaps we should focus on the waltz and leave the discussion of a duel until your brother can give his own creative suggestions. Or have you decided against learning the waltz? No doubt there is something more shocking you would prefer—a public duel?"

I laughed. "You are teasing me now! But you are right. We should concentrate on the waltz." I took in a deep breath and straightened my shoulders. "I am ready to learn."

"Very good," he said. "We haven't any music, unfortunately, so we will simply have to count."

"I could hum," I offered.

"If you prefer it, certainly. Now, for the positions." He took in a breath and stepped closer to me. "We both set our hands about one another's waist. Like so."

I sucked in a breath as his hand wrapped around mine, every thought flying out of my head besides the sensation of his fingertips and palm cradling my side. I had been escorted by

Valentine, danced with him, even, but this . . . this was something different, and my heart knew it.

"We both do it," he said.

I glanced up at him, blinking. "What?"

"You are to set your hand at my waist, as well." The words were tight, his jaw set, as though he didn't relish repeating himself.

I forced a laugh. "Oh, of course. Silly of me." I set my hand in its place, noticing an almost imperceptible tightening of his muscles beneath my hand, and those muscles were already very firm indeed.

He nodded. "Our other hands are joined above our heads."

I obliged, forcing myself to focus on the mechanics of the movements as he described the figures and steps the dance required, and to hum as we performed them. It was a difficult thing with our faces so near to one another and nowhere to look but into his eyes or at his lips. We found ourselves colliding a few times with my mistakes.

The third time I stumbled into him resulted in an instinctive tightening of his hand about my waist. I stepped back, breaking away.

"What is it?" he asked. "Are you tired? Should we take a respite?"

"No, no," I said. "It is only that . . . well, I am not a very good dancer, as you well know, and I wonder if perhaps the waltz is not such a good idea, after all."

"Nonsense. You are a perfectly good dancer. I have danced with you myself and watched you many other times. You never look happier than when you are dancing. It is only that you do not yet know these steps well enough to enjoy yourself."

I nodded, keenly aware that that was *not* the reason I was struggling. How was I to keep steps and figures in my mind when I was losing myself in Valentine's eyes? Or imagining how it would feel to kiss him?

There was nothing in his demeanor to imply *he* was struggling, though. Valentine was simply fulfilling a duty. And that was to be expected, for what was it to waltz with Rebecca Russell when he had experienced so much more with other women?

But it was not Nellie White's nor any other Paphian's physical intimacy with Valentine which I most envied, though I certainly *did* envy that. It was the thought that they might know him better than I did, that in their association with Valentine, they might have become privy to parts of his character that I hadn't yet or might never still come to know.

"I am being silly, of course," I said. "Let us try again."

He nodded and, with that set jaw that told me he was determined to help me learn, he put his hand at my waist and joined the other to mine above our heads. An uncontrollable shiver coursed through my body at his touch, and his gaze leapt to mine. Something told me that, if Valentine knew what I was feeling for him, he wouldn't hesitate to end things immediately. There would be no more cups of smiling chocolate in the mornings, no more asking him to explain the complex rules and expectations of Brighton Society, no more trying to make him smile and laugh. And that was a prospect I couldn't bring myself to accept.

"Forgive me," I said. "Mr. Abbot always had the coldest hands, and I think it is ingrained in me to shiver when I am learning to dance."

Valentine frowned. "Mr. Abbot."

I nodded. "He was my dancing master. He had retired from formal teaching, but as a friend of Grandfather's, he agreed to help me."

"And how old was he?"

"Eight-and-seventy."

Valentine looked less than pleased. "Of course he was. And he did not wear gloves when he instructed you?"

"He did," I stuttered, "but they were terribly thin and worn so that I could still feel his cold, wrinkly skin beneath the tattered fabric." Why was I lying? And not even a good lie. No one would believe it.

Guilt gnawed at me. Mr. Abbot had *always* worn gloves, and I had never felt whether his skin was cold or warm. But I had felt Grandfather's skin plenty of times, and *his* was always terribly cold. I had felt Mr. Philpotts's one time as well, and his had been frigid. "I think older people suffer from cold hands quite frequently," I offered in support of my fabrication. Even to my own ears, I sounded desperate. And I *was*. Desperate to keep Valentine from knowing how his touch made me feel things I had never felt before, things he did not want me to feel.

He frowned deeply. How could a man look so very handsome with such a foreboding expression? "You continue to flatter me by these comparisons to men about to stick their spoon in the wall."

I tilted my head to the side, momentarily distracted.

"Yes," he said resignedly, recognizing the cause for my curiosity. "*To stick one's spoon in the wall*. It means to die. You can add it to your collection of cant phrases, which I hope will be of great comfort to you when Duke has shot me dead in a duel."

I couldn't help but laugh. "I am not comparing you to old men because you are *like* them. It is quite a different thing, I assure you, to be held by a hunched, wrinkly man of eight-and-seventy than to be held by"—I bit my tongue to keep *the most handsome man I have ever seen* from slipping through my lips—"than to be held by you." Somehow my choice of expression still sounded infused with a great deal of implication.

His eyes searched mine for a moment. We were still in position to begin waltzing, and the arm held above our heads was beginning to tire. "Well, I doubt you will be waltzing with any old men at the party, so you had better accustom yourself to a less trembling grip and a sprier step."

"Of course," I replied, wondering if I would react in the same way to being held by another gentleman. I suspected not. "Let us continue."

Someone cleared their throat, and both of us turned our heads to look to the doorway, where the sound had originated. Two men stood there, one with a somber expression and hair caught somewhere between gray and white, the other with sandy blond hair and large, wiry glasses perched atop his nose. Diana hurried up from behind them and she pushed her way through, her harried and apologetic gaze on us.

Valentine's hands dropped, and I followed suit with my own, wondering how soon all of us might choke on the thick air around us—and whether I was looking at the two people I believed myself to be looking at.

Chapter Twenty-One

VALENTINE

From the expression on Diana's face, it was clear she hadn't known the Admiral intended to come. Phineas, too, looked grim and apologetic.

But that didn't change the fact that the Admiral *was* here, and the sight of him, with his impeccably pressed clothing and stern expression, made my stomach churn and my chest tighten, just as they had the last time we had seen one another.

It would be too easy to start where we had left off. Ironically, he had demanded I leave Blackwick, and now here he was, pursuing me so that I couldn't escape him. I wanted to say as much, but experience told me that things would only escalate from there, and I wouldn't subject Rebecca to such ugliness.

I held the Admiral's gaze. "Isn't there some picnic we are meant to be attending, Diana?"

There was no immediate response, and I moved my gaze to my sister, whose mouth was open, as though she wasn't entirely sure how to respond. There *had* been an invitation to a picnic today, but after a week full of supposed gaiety, I had convinced her to decline it.

I was regretting that now. It would be better to attend some picnic than to be obliged to spend time in the Admiral's company—and safer than how I had just spent the better part of an hour: my hand about Rebecca's waist and our faces near enough that I had been able to memorize every shade in her eyes and wonder if, in some other version of life, I might have been worthy to hold her without the waltz as an excuse.

"Yes," Diana said slowly. "The picnic at the Wolcotts. We should change, certainly, or we will be late."

We wouldn't. If memory served, the picnic did not start for another two hours, but I didn't care. I needed a reason to be out of the Admiral's presence, even if it meant enduring more time making conversation with people I didn't care a fig about.

"Very good," said the Admiral. "We will join you."

I clenched my jaw.

"Without an invitation?" Diana asked.

"George Wolcott is a friend," the Admiral said. "He will be glad enough to see me, invitation or no."

"That makes one of us," I said under my breath. I had wanted to escape the Admiral, and now I would not only be attending a picnic I had never wished to attend, I would do so in his company. I turned to Rebecca beside me. She looked like a doe facing down a group of hunters. My anger fizzled a bit. "We can continue this later, though I think you have the way of it nearly." I tried for a reassuring smile, and her posture relaxed at the sight of it, her own ready smile appearing.

"Liar," she said softly.

I put a hand over my heart. "On my honor."

Her eyes twinkled. "*Have* you any?"

"Touché," I said with a chuckle.

Diana cleared her throat, and I found all eyes on us.

"Yes?" I said in annoyance, then waved a hand. "You are all dismissed to dress."

The last thing I wanted was to be squeezed into a carriage with the Admiral—the closer the quarters, the more explosive the result, I had found—so I insisted on taking a hackney.

"Join him, Phineas." The Admiral was watching me as though my idea was merely a veiled intention to abandon the picnic altogether and visit the club. Not a terrible idea, in truth.

Phineas looked at me to gauge what I thought of this, his gaze careful behind his glasses. He was a good sort of brother. Never interfering, generally quiet, but his willingness to oblige the Admiral's eternal demands irked me.

My real hesitation was leaving Rebecca with less company in the carriage to insulate her from the Admiral. I doubted she had ever met someone like him. He was a bit like the vase we had broken—unique and unpleasant. The only difference was that the Admiral was not part of a pair. Thank heaven for that.

But Diana was perfectly capable of ensuring he did nothing to make Rebecca uncomfortable, so I gave Phineas a little nod to show I was happy enough for him to join me.

Once the hackney had been secured, Phineas and I climbed inside.

"You cannot be looking forward to this any more than I am," I said, settling in. The greatest similarity Phineas and I shared was our reluctance to engage in an endless array of social activities. But where my reluctance was rooted in impatience for shallow and meaningless polite talk, his stemmed from his all-consuming preference for books and study.

"No," Phineas replied. "But Father insisted I come."

"Of course he did. And naturally, you obliged."

He looked at me for a moment, then turned his head to the side, silent.

"Say it," I said.

"Say what?"

"Whatever it is you were just thinking but decided against saying. You know I have a thick enough skin for it."

He studied me through those wiry glasses again. "Fine. Some battles are not worth fighting."

"By which you mean to say, that for you, *none* of them are worth fighting." That was not fair, really. While Phineas was not one to come out in open opposition to the Admiral, he had always found ways of quietly rebelling. His need for glasses from a young age was undoubtedly due to all the sneaking off to read in the dim light. He had been teased frequently for his bookishness and his lack of interest in the rougher parts of sailing. On one occasion, I had stepped in to stop the unkindness, resulting in a scuffle that had earned me a black eye and a bloody lip. Phineas hadn't thanked me for it, either. He had seemed frustrated more than anything, for he preferred to ignore rather than engage.

"I did fight him on his intention to come to Brighton, Valentine. But it was no use. He was set on it."

"Why? Why throw me out only to follow me?"

"Diana's letters had him curious—and doubting. He insisted on coming to see your supposed progress for himself."

I sighed. That was the problem with doing everything you could to convince someone you would never do as they wished: the moment you did, they refused to believe it. "Thank you for trying, Phin."

I sipped from a glass of lemonade at the refreshment tables covered by canvas tents. The plates and glasses had been picked over, and most of the guests had settled in the seats on the lawn, conversing and eating to the sounds of the small orchestra the Wolcotts had hired. It made this the perfect place to escape mind-numbing conversation, and Phineas seemed to agree, for he was nearby, taking his time eating the licorice on his plate.

There were perhaps sixty people in attendance, and Lord Newham was one of them. I had seen him far more frequently of late. Part of me wondered whether it was intentional on his part, this coinciding of our schedules. But it could just as easily be that he had always attended this sort of event, while I had eschewed such things. I felt the familiar prickle of curiosity at the sight of him. He had the same thick brows as me, the same hairline, and a similar nose shape. Certainly his propensity for glowering made us similar. Or perhaps I was so desperate for answers that I was imagining it all.

Either way, one didn't simply go up to a man and introduce oneself. If he had any wish to know me, he would undoubtedly have sought an introduction by now. And if he didn't wish to know me, why should I wish to know *him*?

Over the rim of my glass, my gaze settled on Rebecca. She was in conversation with a group of people comprising of the Bradley sisters and two young gentlemen, one of whom she had danced a set with at an assembly earlier in the week.

My mouth turned down at the edges. She held a glass in hand, but it was lemonade rather than the ratafia I knew she preferred. I blamed the Bradleys. They were harmless for the most part, but they were silly young women, and the effect they had upon Rebecca was to make her more conscious than ever of the image she presented to Society. I found this frustrating. To watch Rebecca in public was to see an altered version of her, restrained and less quick to smile. It was a shame, in my opinion. But clearly, I was not the one to apply to for advice on pleasing Society.

"She seems an unexceptionable young woman."

I didn't need to turn my head to know that the Admiral had joined Phineas and me at the refreshments. I pulled my gaze from Rebecca and set my empty glass down on the silver platter with the others. "Of course she is. She is Russell's sister."

"Which begs a few questions, doesn't it?"

I turned fully to him. "And what questions are those?"

He met my gaze with his own unflinching one. "How you, of all people, managed to pique her interest."

The top of my lip curled up. "This effusive flattery is unmerited, Admiral."

"What reason have you ever given me to flatter you? I am sure I am not the first one to ask the question. The claims Diana has made about your behavior paint the picture of a swift change indeed."

"Hence this lovely, unannounced visit." I poured myself another glass, this time of ratafia.

"I received a number of bills the other day, Valentine," the Admiral said sternly. "If you expect me to pay them, I expect firm evidence of real progress. Diana has always been prone to underestimate your faults—or overlook them entirely."

"Yet more flattery." I took a sip from the ratafia to keep from throwing it in his face.

"Understand me, Valentine," he said. "I shan't be hoodwinked into paying your bills."

I clenched my teeth, and my grip on the glass tightened dangerously. "Perhaps if you would provide me the inheritance my mother left me, you wouldn't be obliged to do so. What precisely do you accuse me of?"

"That remains to be seen. Suffice it to say that if you are attempting to pull the wool over my eyes, you will catch cold. And I shan't be there to save you from the sponging house when you inevitably end up there."

"Oh," I said, only just keeping my voice from shaking as I set the glass down a second time, "content yourself, Admiral. That is something I would only expect of a father." I turned, but he caught my wrist.

"I may not be your father," he said in a low tone that trembled with anger, "but I have raised you and paid your debts, and you would do well to remember that."

Phineas came up beside us, partially blocking us from the view of those sitting out on the lawn. "Perhaps this conversation is better suited for a different venue," he said as two footmen approached to clear away dishes.

Using as much controlled force as I could manage, I wrested my wrist from the Admiral's grasp, swallowing the bitterness in my mouth as I turned away. I paid no heed to the dozen or so heads that were turned in my direction, staring.

Blood boiling, I made my way away from the refreshments and lawn toward the way out. When I felt like this, the only thing I had found to make it go away was drink—a great deal of it. There had to be an inn or public house somewhere nearby.

"Valentine." Rebecca's breathless voice reached me before she did.

Shutting my eyes, I slowed until she came abreast of me.

"Where are you going?" She came around to stand in front of me. Her chest rose and fell under her fichu from the hurry to catch up with me, and her eyes held a worried look.

"To lift my hand to my head, as they say," I said, too frustrated to come up with a plausible lie.

"That means to drink to excess, doesn't it?"

"It does."

She looked at me, her gaze thoughtful, and I felt as though she was seeing a great deal of me—things I didn't particularly wish anyone to see. "You *could* do that, or"—she smiled at me as though her next words promised a treat—"you could take a walk about the gardens with me. Maria says they are some of the best in Brighton."

My heart was still beating quickly, but no longer was its thudding deafening in my ears. I wavered between the two options Rebecca was giving me. The oblivion brandy offered was an enticing alternative to what I was feeling just now, but Rebecca clearly hoped I would choose the gardens, and somehow that mattered to me.

"I believe the roses are in bloom," she added as an enticement.

I hadn't ever cared about a rose garden in my life, and I certainly didn't care about one just now. I glanced behind Rebecca, noting a few sets of eyes on us.

"Roses it is, then," I said. I couldn't—wouldn't—leave her, embarrassing her as I had at Peckley House two weeks ago. If she wanted my company in the rose garden, I would give it to her. And afterward, I would have my brandy. Or as much of it as the coins in my pocket would afford me.

Chapter Twenty-Two

REBECCA

I had been certain Valentine would say no to a walk in the gardens. There was little appeal in it for someone like him, but it had been the only thing I could think of—the only alternative to his losing himself in drink alone.

I didn't understand the relationship between Valentine and his father, but I had seen enough to tell me that behind all the anger, there was a great deal of pain—likely on both sides. I couldn't help Admiral Donovan, for I didn't know him, and I wouldn't have dared to try even if I had, but the realization that Valentine was hurting deep down affected me. I might not be able to take that pain away, but perhaps I could share in it or relieve it.

He offered me his arm, and though I was under no illusion that he was particularly happy about my proposed promenade, I was determined he would not regret it—not if I could help it. But the tightness of his arm told me he was still feeling the effects of the interaction with his father.

"I thought I saw you pour yourself a glass of ratafia," I said. "Have you changed your opinion of it?"

He smiled slightly, and his arm relaxed infinitesimally. "No,

Rebecca. It is still the vile stuff it ever was. But while we are on the subject, I noticed *you* chose the lemonade. Have *you* changed your opinion of ratafia? Seen the light?"

I shook my head, looking over at him with a teasing expression. "It is still the delicious stuff it ever was."

He made an expression of distaste, but it was tempered by the glint of amusement in his eyes. "Why do you deprive yourself of something you enjoy?"

I shrugged. "I suppose it is because I feel my credit is feeble enough to be overset by people's general dislike of the drink. It sounds silly when I say it, but there you have it."

His brow pursed. "You do yourself and others a disservice by concealing the most endearing parts of your character."

We stepped under an archway and into the gardens, and I smiled ruefully. "My affinity for ratafia is the most endearing part of my character?"

"Parts," he clarified. "I said *parts of your character*, of which your strange palate is just one."

I wanted to ask what the other endearing parts of my character were, but I wasn't certain I truly wanted to know. *Endearing* sounded like the sort of word one might use to describe a child, and I was tired of being seen like a child—particularly by Valentine.

"I am not the only one to hide parts of my character, am I?"

He glanced at me, his eyes narrowing slightly.

My heart galloped a bit, but I had promised myself not to withhold praise. After the bit I had observed of Admiral Donovan, I had the sense praise was not something Valentine had much experience with. "The face you show to the world is not the one I have come to know."

He looked away. "And what makes you think the face you know is the true one?"

I stopped, turning in front of him so that he, too, was

obliged to stop. "Can they not both be? We are all more than our reputations."

He held my gaze. "Try convincing the Admiral of that. He suspects our ruse, Rebecca. It is why he has come—to reveal it as a farce meant to persuade him to pay my debts. You should prepare yourself to be questioned by him."

I wanted to ask Valentine whether, for him, it *was* a farce. But I was a coward. I was too afraid of the answer—too afraid of his answering untruthfully to avoid hurting me. "Very well," I replied. "If he does, I shall tell him the truth."

His gaze jumped to mine, and I could see he had misunderstood me. But he nodded. "Of course. You shouldn't lie for me."

"I will not need to."

He shook his head. "He knows me too well to believe someone like you would allow yourself to be courted or even befriended by someone like me without receiving something in return."

"Then he is wrong." My voice grew softer. "Wrong on my account, at least, for I was drawn to you from the moment I met you. It was I who had to convince you to participate in this ruse, as you call it. But it is not a mere ruse for me, Valentine. You *are* my friend, and I would wish for you to be my friend even if it served neither of us."

The smallest of shifts under his cravat told me that my words meant *something* to him.

"And I yours," he said, holding my eyes until my skin erupted with shivers. How easy it was for me to see what I wanted to see, to hear more than what he was saying.

But I hadn't brought Valentine into the gardens for this.

I smiled gratefully, then turned. We began walking again, following the hedges toward the center where Maria had said the rose garden was.

"What is it that causes such grief between the two of you?" Timidity made my voice soft.

He didn't answer immediately, and our feet crunched on the gravel walk. "Everything."

I didn't respond, waiting to see if he would elaborate.

"He has always resented me, treated me with . . . contempt, I suppose. I could never live up to his expectations, could never compare with my brother Theo, no matter how hard I tried. When people began to tease me about being illegitimate, I didn't believe it, didn't *want* to believe it. But, the more I thought on things and the more I noticed how differently the Admiral treated me from my other siblings, it became the only thing that made sense."

"He knows, then?" I asked.

"He knows. He admitted as much today. Early in my parents' marriage, he was gone for long stretches of time. It was difficult for my mother, I think. She had Theo, and she had hoped to join the Admiral on his voyages. But he refused to have women aboard, insisting she stay at Blackwick. My mother felt abandoned, I imagine, and I gather the Admiral was not particularly pleasant even during those short periods when he *was* home. I can only assume she yearned for comfort and company and . . . I am a result of that."

"But I thought your family lived together aboard your father's—the Admiral's—ships?"

"One of his ships—the Dominance. But that was after all of this. He bent his own rules in an attempt to prevent a recurrence of what had happened during his time away. But he never forgave me—or my mother."

We emerged into the rose garden, a circular area surrounded by low hedges with winding paths between a colorful array of flowering bushes. I took a seat on a wooden bench surrounded by deep red blooms, but my gaze went to the lawn, searching for Admiral Donovan. He stood in conversation with Mr. Wolcott near the refreshment tent. "You are a reminder of his failings."

Valentine took the place beside me. "If you knew the Admiral, you would know he *has* no failings—not any that he would admit to, at least. I am a scourge to him."

"*You* are not a scourge," I said. "His own mistakes and his humiliation are the scourges. He has unfairly chosen to make you the target of his anger instead of accepting his own responsibility."

Valentine looked over at me, his dark eyes full of . . . something. Contemplation, perhaps. Or maybe it was hope. Either way, the intensity there held me riveted, as if he wouldn't believe me if I broke my gaze away.

Finally, he closed his eyes and, resting his elbows on his knees, he rubbed his lids with his palms. "I am tired of the anger. The struggle. The fighting."

I wanted to put my hand on his back, to comfort him, but I refrained. "Then do not engage," I whispered.

He dropped his hands and looked at me. "And let him win?"

"One should always let old people win."

He smiled a bit, shaking his head at my comment.

I sighed. "Perhaps not engaging would mean *you* would win, Valentine. For would it not be a victory of its own to leave such conflict behind?"

He shook his head. "I do not think I am strong enough. The anger . . . it consumes me when I see him. I can feel it in my veins. I can taste it on my tongue." Even saying the words, his jaw tightened and his hands balled into fists.

"Which is why you seek refuge in . . . Blue Ruin?" I looked a question at him, for I wasn't entirely sure what Blue Ruin was. I had heard it in passing at a ball last week and forgotten about it until now.

He chuckled softly. "My preference has always been brandy, if you must know."

"Brandy rather than . . ."

His smile grew. "Gin. Blue Ruin is gin."

"Ah," I replied. "And does the brandy help?"

His smile faded. "Very temporarily, yes."

I looked away to conceal my face from him, for I was not skilled at feigning seriousness. "Perhaps I shall try it next time *I* am angry."

"The devil you will," he said.

I turned my face toward him, letting him see my smile. Valentine seemed to have a real fear of his influence over me.

He relaxed, chucking me under the chin playfully. "You will be the death of me, you know."

"I certainly hope not," I said. "I would miss you terribly."

His expression sobered, and under his cravat, his throat bobbed.

My heart shot to action. Why could I not think before speaking, like a respectable person?

A little breeze blew through the garden, tossing a few rose petals in the air and to the ground. I reached down and picked one up. It was a coral pink, the color fainter near the center. I tilted my head to the side, regarding it. "Whenever *I* am angry, the garden is the first place I go."

Valentine's brow puckered, the hint of a smile on his lips. "You, angry?"

"Oh, yes," I said. "I have a dreadful temper."

"You terrify me," he said. "And what sort of things make Rebecca Russell angry?"

"Oh, any number," I replied. "Grandfather could be terribly stubborn and ill-humored, particularly whenever I expressed the desire for a more social existence than the one we lived." I smiled wryly. "Once, when he refused to travel to London for the Season, I became so angry, I tore up the stitching on three samplers." I frowned, rubbing the petal between my fingers.

"And did you go to the garden after your sampler rampage?"

"I did. Millbury House has a small but lovely one."

"And did it help?"

I nodded. "Perhaps you could try it."

He looked around. "Is that not what we are doing now?"

"Yes, but it is more than just *being* in the garden. Here." I picked one of the blooms beside me, taking care to avoid the thorns. I handed him the stem, and he took it from me with a quizzical look.

"Am I to become the garden?" he asked teasingly.

"In a way, yes. You are to use all of your senses to experience it. Go on, then. Close your eyes."

He did not oblige. "I thought I was to use all of my senses. How am I to use my sight if my eyes are closed?"

"You have seen the garden already, have you not? Now it is time to use your other faculties. Sight is such a powerful sense; it often drowns out all else." Perhaps I should have closed my eyes too. Every time I looked at Valentine, I felt his attraction. But his draw was far more than mere physical attraction. I loved everything about him.

His eyes narrowed suspiciously. "Do you intend to play a trick on me the moment I close my eyes?"

I pursed my lips and shot him a look. "If you are too proud, I shall do it myself." I took the bloom from him and, once I had it in hand, I closed my eyes. I took in a slow deep breath, taking note of everything my vision had overwhelmed. "First, I pay attention to the smells." I inhaled slowly, bringing the flower to my nose. "The subtle, sweet scent of roses, a whisper of wet soil. Then, I listen for the sounds—distant conversation, a bee buzzing nearby. I note the feel of the velvety petals between my fingers, the—" I stopped, for I had been on the verge of mentioning the feel of Valentine's arm against mine.

I opened my eyes, handing the flower to him. "The point is, when I allow myself to take in the garden in such a way, it reminds me that my anger, as powerful as it may be, is but a piece of life. There is beauty and peace despite it all if I will but pay it any heed."

Valentine took the flower, looking at me for a moment before his eyes dropped to the rose, which he twirled slowly between his fingers. It was mesmerizing, the way the spinning made the petals all run together into a whirl of pink.

After a moment, the twirling stopped, and I glanced up at him. His eyes were shut, and his chest rose with a steady intake of breath. He brought the flower up to his nose, inhaling slowly, and I watched him. He looked so peaceful, his body relaxed, his dark lashes lying in a crescent against his cheekbones. The contrast to how he had looked when I had first come upon him a quarter of an hour ago—eyes bright with anger, muscles taut, jaw flexing—was stark.

I felt a surge of affection for him, and with it, a fierce wish for the opportunity to show him that affection. I wanted to take his face between my hands and tell him what I thought of him, that the friendship I had with him was beginning to fall woefully short of what I wanted to share with him.

His eyes opened and his gaze met mine. My cheeks warmed, as though he might see into my mind by merely looking at me. "Well?" I said. "Better than Blue Ruin?"

He smiled and took to twirling the rose again. "Better than Blue Ruin. And less expensive."

"Better than brandy?"

His smile faded slightly, and the sides of his mouth turned down as he looked at the flower. "Better than brandy."

I felt a flood of relief, and it emerged as a shaky laugh. I hadn't truly thought he would appreciate my silly little trick.

Diana emerged into the rose garden. She quirked a brow and settled her gaze on us, hands on her hips. "Here you are. You are making me look like a very lax chaperone, you know."

I rose to my feet. "I am terribly sorry. I did not think there would be any objection, as there is no privacy here and there are other couples walking the gardens."

She smiled. "Do not be silly. I am not angry with you. I *am* a lax chaperone, after all. And you are right—I have had my eye on you from the lawn. But I cannot let Valentine dominate your attention for the entire picnic"—she shot him a significant look —"when there are a number of young men asking for you, Rebecca."

"There are?"

She nodded. "I promised to retrieve you myself."

I glanced at Valentine. I would have happily spent the entire picnic here with him in the garden, but it was hardly in my best interest to indulge my rapidly increasing need for his company. And yet, after the more somber nature of our conversation in the garden, I didn't wish to leave him.

With a crooked smile, he gave a nod, as if to say, *you can leave.* He rose to his feet, the rose still in his hand. "I think I shall see if Phin wishes to return to the house. Someone should certainly take advantage of the immaculately dusted library."

"Not just yet," Diana said, stopping him with a hand on his arm. "There are one or two young women hoping for a bit of conversation with *you,* as well."

My heart plummeted into the pit of my stomach. It was an unreasonable reaction. I should be happy for Valentine. I was already aware that attitudes toward him were shifting; it had become a more regular occurrence for other young ladies to inquire about him. The intrigue was always apparent in their eyes.

I found Valentine's gaze on me, and I forced a smile. "I have been very selfish, stealing you away, haven't I?"

How was it possible to simultaneously be happy for Valentine and to wish to keep him to myself?

Chapter Twenty-Three

VALENTINE

Normally, I would have consigned Diana and whoever she imagined wished to speak with me to the devil and gone on my way. But my time in the garden with Rebecca had produced a strange sequence of emotions in me.

When she had first come upon me, I had been consumed with anger. But it was impossible to stay angry in Rebecca's company. Instead, the anger had given way to something raw. Her words and presence had been balm to the wounds I had never wanted to admit to. And the ridiculous rose exercise—I had done it for her, for I hadn't wished to offend or hurt her, but it had done just as she had said. It had cooled the remaining embers of my anger, leaving me with nothing to distract me from the way I felt. Not just about things with Admiral, but the way I felt for her.

Only a fool could have thought me deserving of Rebecca Russell, and I was no fool—or at least, I was a fool, but not foolish enough for *that*. A man like me, who had wasted half of his adult life in dissolution and anger, had no right to do anything but dream of an alternate existence where a woman like her would deign to consider me in such a way. Rebecca was an angel, and though she might condescend to friendship with me, angels simply did not marry devils—at least they didn't do so and come out unscathed. My mother and the Admiral were a perfect example of that.

So, I reluctantly agreed to talk to the young women Diana mentioned, hoping that, somewhere in those conversations, I might realize that it was not just Rebecca who appealed to me. Perhaps my desires were changing and all those young women who had never held any appeal for me would do so now.

But I had no such luck, and after enough time that I would not be considered entirely lost to any sense of civility, I begged leave of them and found Phineas, who quickly agreed to return to the house together.

I dreaded dinner and seriously considered absenting myself from it altogether. But Diana had anticipated such a decision on my part, and she forbade me from leaving, so I prepared myself for a supremely unenjoyable evening biting my tongue.

When we sat down at the dinner table, my eyes were immediately drawn to the two vases full of white roses on either end.

"Aren't they beautiful?" Diana said as she took her seat. "Rebecca was the one who arranged them."

I glanced at Rebecca, and she met my gaze with a small smile that told me it had been done intentionally—done for me, knowing that my temper would be taxed by sitting down to dine with the Admiral present.

Over the course of the meal, I did have to bite my tongue on a number of occasions, but each time, I found Rebecca looking at me, as though in acknowledgment that my patience was being tried. And then, I would glance at the roses, and somehow, those silly flowers made it a bit easier, a bit less miserable.

And when the women rose to leave us for the drawing room, Diana spared me the prospect of sitting over port with the Admiral with some excuse about needing my help with tasks for the ball. I readily assented, not caring if the tasks entailed emptying chamber pots or writing invitations.

I t was eight o'clock, and I made my way downstairs warily. It was the time of morning Rebecca and I generally breakfasted, but the Admiral was also an early riser, and I wouldn't set foot inside until I was certain he was not there.

I kept my boots to the rug as I approached the door to the breakfast room, which was open. I could just see Rebecca, pouring cream into her cup. I smiled slightly as she pulled up the pot of cream, then let two drips fall.

". . . admittedly surprised to hear you and Valentine were, well, connected, I suppose."

I stopped, moving to the side of the door and listening to the Admiral's voice.

"And now that I have met you," he continued, "my surprise has only grown."

"Oh?" Rebecca asked. "Why is that?"

The Admiral gave a humorless chuckle. "Surely you know Valentine's reputation, Miss Russell."

I clenched my fists, preparing to walk in and put an end to the conversation. But Rebecca's voice stopped me.

"I do, sir, yes. But I do not set too much store by such things." The clinking of her spoon against the glass told me that she was stirring her chocolate. She never stirred it once the cream was in. "I find people are much more than their reputations, don't you?"

"Certainly a reputation cannot convey *everything* about a person," he replied, "but that is where their value lies, I think. They condense things into a form Society can manage, reducing a great deal of information to the most important bits."

"Or the most controversial ones, perhaps," she replied. I

could hear her smile in her voice, and I was amazed by how she could say something so contrary in such a palatable way. Those same words in my voice would have instigated a veritable explosion. "I can only imagine what *my* reputation must be—breaker of vases, interrupter of plays—and though those things are true, I assure you I am much more than those things incidents would imply. Just as Valentine is more than what people say of *him*."

"Breaker of vases," the Admiral repeated. "What vase is it you speak of?"

I put my hand on the wall, drawing nearer to hear the answer, as though I couldn't already hear everything well enough.

Rebecca's stirring ceased, and a pause ensued.

"Is it Mrs. Lawrenson's vase you are referring to?" the Admiral asked. "Wolcott said it was Valentine who broke it while in a drunken stupor when he mentioned it at the picnic yesterday."

"He was not in a drunken stupor," Rebecca said, the first hint of annoyance in her voice. There was a pause. "I should not have said anything. Valentine most particularly asked me not to, so if you will please disregard it, I would greatly appreciate it."

"Do you mean to say, Miss Russell, that it was *you* who broke the vase?"

My jaw tightened at his clear ignoring of her plea.

"It was," she said, "but Valentine insisted on taking the blame—and bearing the cost."

I shut my eyes. Rebecca didn't know that Diana was the one who had paid for the vase.

"Did he now?" the Admiral said. "That does not sound at all like him. Valentine will do anything to shirk his responsibilities."

My fingers tensed on the wall, though there was nothing there to grip. It was one thing to have the Admiral tear my character to shreds to my face; it was another to hear him doing it behind my back, and to Rebecca, of all people.

I inhaled deeply in an attempt to calm my budding anger. Rebecca's roses would have come in handy right now—or a cup of the chocolate she had poured.

"Oh, on the contrary, sir," Rebecca said, "he has been most helpful since my arrival. I cannot tell you how much I appreciate his kindness toward me, his patience with my lack of experience, his willingness to be a friend to me when I had none. I cannot imagine these last three weeks without him. I have asked a great deal of him, and he has obliged me, even when it did not serve him to do so. He is the best of men, and I imagine you must be very proud."

My throat thickened. It was like listening to someone describe a stranger. I had never thought of myself as kind or patient, and certainly not as *the best of men*. But somehow Rebecca thought of me that way, saint that she was.

I had always assumed that saints did not associate with sinners, that their very nature would be offended by the disparity in goodness. I had been wrong. True saints did not make sinners feel worthless or lesser; they recognized and emphasized the best in those sinners, choosing to see them for what they could be rather than limiting them to what they had been. In Rebecca's presence, I did not forget my flaws and failings; I was simply inspired to do and be better.

The Admiral cleared his throat. I could only imagine what his expression must be now to hear me characterized in such an unrecognizable way. "I find the person you are describing . . . unfamiliar, so forgive me for asking such forward questions, but my curiosity consumes me, for I can find no other way to explain what I am hearing. Are you, in fact, in love with Valentine, Miss Russell?"

Every muscle in my body tensed.

"I-i-in love?" Rebecca's soft voice answered. "Oh"—a shaky

laugh—"I do not know if I would say that. That is to say, I admire him greatly, of course, and I consider him my nearest friend and someone whom I would trust with my life, and naturally one cannot but notice how handsome he is, as I am sure you will agree . . ." The words had been tumbling off her tongue with rapidity, but she suddenly trailed off, as though she realized how her protestations sounded.

With her voice gone, the only thing I could hear was the beating of my own heart in my ears.

"I see." The Admiral's voice made it clear that he was entirely unconvinced.

I stood stock still, my mind spinning. Did Rebecca truly return my regard? It seemed impossible, but . . .

"Miss Russell, you seem a very good young woman, if a bit naive. May I be frank with you?"

"O-o-of course."

"I hope you will not take my warning amiss, for it is meant with your own well-being in mind. Valentine knows how to be charming when it serves his ends. It is his greatest asset in obtaining what he wants. I urge you to make certain there isn't something he wishes for from *you*. For I assure you, once he has what he wishes for, he will not hesitate to dispose of you as he has so many other women."

I hardly heard his words or Rebecca's response, for I was still trying to fathom what I had heard, what I had *felt* from Rebecca's words—the simultaneous hope and dismay I felt at the realization that she loved me. *Me*.

The door opened wider, and Rebecca emerged, pulling it closed behind her. She stopped short at the sight of me, her eyes wide. And for a moment, our gazes locked, my eyes searching hers and hers searching mine, as though we were seeing each other for the first time.

"Valentine." Her voice was weak, and she cleared her throat. "Were you coming for breakfast? I have just finished."

"I was. Until I heard the Admiral's voice."

Her eyes became more alert, and she swallowed visibly. "Were you . . . have you been standing here long?"

I hesitated. Her behavior told me she would be acutely embarrassed to know what I had heard. But I didn't wish to lie to her.

I tried for a smile. "Long enough to know I do not wish to breakfast with the Admiral." I hoped it struck the balance between reassuring her and avoiding a lie. Before she could ask any clarifying questions, I continued. "I am glad to have found you, though. The ball is but two days away, and I wondered if you felt confident enough in your waltz or if you wished to go over the steps again." The words spilled out of my mouth before I could truly consider them.

She gave a weak smile. "Confident? No. But after a quarter of an hour of practice, I think I would feel much better."

"Of course," I said, my stomach sinking. "Shall we? Unless you have other engagements at the moment?"

She shook her head. "The dressmaker is coming for a final fitting at half-past ten, but nothing until then. I wouldn't wish to monopolize your morning, though. I am certain you have more important things to do."

"More important than avoiding the Admiral? Unlikely. Come. I believe the furniture we moved remains where we left it. I would like for you to feel prepared for tomorrow—for you to dazzle the crowd with your waltzing."

I led the way toward the drawing room.

"I shall never dazzle," Rebecca said with a laugh. "It is simply not in my nature. But I would like to be proficient, at least."

I wanted to correct her, to let her know that she *did* dazzle, that the reason men were not more assiduous in their attentions toward her was a combination of my looming but ambiguous presence around her and the fact that they didn't know what to do with someone as good as she was. She was different, and people were simultaneously intrigued by and wary of different. I knew that well.

But I couldn't say those things to her. It might reassure her for a moment, but it would change things between us, setting us on a path I knew was wrong to tread. And I cared for her too much to open that possibility to her. It would be to take advantage of her naivete, for it was a path she would not choose once she better understood that there were far better options than me. The Admiral was right to warn her against me, and that fact troubled me as much as anything.

"Then we will make you dazzlingly proficient," I said.

But even despite my holding my tongue, things in the drawing room were fraught, every touch magnified ten times, every look full of something that made my blood run hot and my heart ache for more.

I couldn't give Rebecca more, though. I had nothing to offer her but a tattered reputation, financial woes, and brokenness. She deserved infinitely better. She deserved everything life had to offer her. She had cared for her grandfather for so long; it was her turn to be cared for, to be taken care of, and I could not provide that for her.

As I held her close to me, her lips near enough that I could memorize their every curve, could imagine how it would feel to press mine against them, anguishing reluctance consumed me. I had never truly thought someone like Rebecca would fall in love with someone like me. And now that she had, it was my undeniable responsibility to make her see the reality: any man would be better for her than me.

Chapter Twenty-Four

REBECCA

Never had a dress fit me so perfectly as the one I now wore. Diana had encouraged me to choose a celery green silk that matched the walls of the drawing room—she was adamant that it was the most flattering color on me. I had been hesitant at first, wondering if I would simply blend into the papered walls, but as I looked at myself in the mirror, I could admit she had been right. The fabric brought out the light green of my eyes, which I had generally thought a strange, undefinable color. The dressmaker had embellished the gown with a wide champagne ribbon at the waist and gold spangled netting at the hem.

Dorothea had spent the last hour curling my hair with tongs, and she was transforming it into a becoming coiffure, with small roses arranged in a sort of crown. As she worked, all I could wonder was what Valentine would think when he saw me.

Our waltzing lesson had been . . . peculiar. I had a suspicion Valentine had listened to enough of my interaction with the Admiral to hear my bumbling and entirely unconvincing arguments against being in love with him. Had I realized the Admiral would ask me such a direct question, I might have been better prepared to respond to it. As things stood, I was left to seek the balance between convincing him that it was not all a ruse and convincing *myself* that I was not fully and entirely in love with Valentine. I had failed miserably at the second. I hoped I had succeeded at the first.

Valentine had been so business-like and stiff as we practiced the waltz that my stomach had swum at the thought that he might be angry with me for doing what I had promised not to do. But twice, I had seen something in his eyes that had challenged that assumption—something like desire, and it had sent a cascade of chills down my spine.

Dorothea paused, looking at me in the mirror. "Are you well, miss?"

"Yes," I said, rubbing at the raised skin on my arms the memory of his gaze had caused. "Just caught a small chill."

"There's a bit of a draft from the window," she said, stepping over to close it. "I'm nearly done with your hair now. Master Valentine won't be able to resist you, miss. If anything can push him to ask for your hand, seeing you tonight will do it."

My cheeks flamed. "Dorothea."

"Oh, forgive me, miss," she said hurriedly as she stepped behind me again. "I shouldn't have said anything. Only, there's been so much talk of it belowstairs, I suppose I forgot my place for a moment. Please don't be angry with me."

Wishing I had a fan to cool my cheeks and that it wouldn't cause even *more* talk belowstairs for me to employ it just now, I let out a breath. "I am not angry with you." I hesitated. "What sort of talk is there belowstairs?"

She looked wary.

"I shan't be upset," I reassured her. "I am merely curious." I wasn't *merely* curious. I was ravenously so.

"Very well," she said, picking up another pin and losing her temporary timidity. "One of the maids and one of the footmen

were saying that Master Valentine was only toying with you—
that you aren't the sort of woman he's likely to court."

My heart began to race, but I kept my voice as steady and
nonchalant as I could manage. "And what sort of woman is that?
Did they say?"

She tipped her head from side to side, as though we were
enjoying a comfortable bit of gossip, when the truth was that
my heart was on tenterhooks. "He's always been one for women
with lighter coloring, if one judges by his mistre—" She
stopped, her eyes wide.

"His mistresses?" I finished for her, forcing myself to smile
calmly. If I showed even a hint of hurt, it would be the topic of
discussion in the servants' hall tonight.

"Well, yes, miss. But I told them, I said, Master Valentine has
changed his ways. Mark my words! I don't think they believed
me, but you and I know, don't we, miss?"

I smiled at her, feeling sick inside. I didn't *know* anything
except that I wanted Valentine Donovan, that I was entirely and
helplessly in love with him.

When I went downstairs for dinner, my gaze
searched for Valentine amongst the greenery and
the white and yellow rose arrangements Diana had
caused to be brought into the entry hall for decoration. But
Valentine wasn't there. We would dine earlier than usual in
order to be ready for the coming of the guests at eight, and
evidently, we would do so without him. I itched to ask his
whereabouts, but I lacked the courage to do so, particularly after
my encounter with the Admiral. He was a stern man, and he had
made it clear that he had no belief in my affection being

returned by Valentine. And from Dorothea's words, he wasn't the only one.

I t wasn't until a quarter to eight that Valentine finally appeared at the top of the staircase. The sight of him stopped my heart. He wore a black tailcoat, a champagne waistcoat, and a frown. His focus seemed to be on the ground as he made his way down the stairs, as though his thoughts were consumed, but it came up once he reached the bottom, settling on me. He slowed, the frown disappearing for a moment as his gaze took me in.

My relief at seeing him dispelled my unwelcome thoughts, taking me over to him. "I thought perhaps you had decided not to come."

His frown had resumed its place, but he shook his head. "I wouldn't miss it."

I smiled a bit. "No, you are too good a friend to me for that."

His frown seemed to deepen. "Yes."

"There you are!" Diana emerged from the drawing room. "The guests are beginning to arrive. I think we shall trust the refreshments and music to hold people's attention until, say, a quarter to nine, when we will begin the dancing. Come, both of you—you especially, Rebecca, for you are the reason people are here."

I nodded, and Diana flitted away as quickly as she had come. At the mention of dancing, a little tremble of nerves coursed through me.

"You needn't be nervous," Valentine said, guessing at the cause of my silence. "You know the figures perfectly."

I met his gaze and smiled weakly. "Dazzlingly proficient? I would be less nervous if *you* waltzed with me."

His mouth opened, then shut, his lips tightening together in a grimace. "I am afraid I have promised the first set to Miss Goulding."

My stomach churned, a sea of disappointment. Valentine didn't dance. Everyone knew that. But tonight, he would be waltzing with Miss Goulding. I tried not to show my hurt or jealousy. "Of course." I forced a laugh. "I am certain there will be a dozen women wishing to waltz with you."

"Rebecca," he said grimly, "this is for the best. Tonight is what we have been working toward. I have served my function, and now it is time to let other gentlemen have their chance with you."

I couldn't even manage to say anything, for my throat was suddenly thick. What if I didn't want any other gentlemen to have their chance with me?

His brow grew more dismal. "Focus your efforts on enjoying yourself. You deserve that."

"Rebecca!" Diana shouted in a whisper from the drawing room door. She motioned for me to come, and I turned and hurried toward her before the stinging in my eyes could betray me to Valentine.

Taking in a deep breath and blinking away the threatening tears, I lifted my chin. For years, I had wished for an opportunity like tonight's. No, that was untrue. Tonight was *more* than I had ever hoped for, and Diana had worked tirelessly to ensure it would surpass all my expectations.

I stepped into the drawing room and paused, marveling at the sight through eyes still slightly pricking with tears. The room had been transformed, the rug removed, and a grand chandelier, glowing with candles, hung from the ceiling. White and pale yellow roses punctuated the greens and golds, and a small orchestra inhabited the side of the room by the fireplace. The guests were beginning to filter in, and I hurried from my stupor of amazement to join Diana in greeting them.

From that moment, the night became a whirlwind, my time

and attention consumed with trying to remember names and to make conversation. I was much more practiced than I had been upon my arrival, but my mind was elsewhere, and my gaze constantly attempted to track Valentine's whereabouts.

When it came time to begin the dancing, Mr. Trussler asked me for the pleasure of the first set, and I tried to accept the invitation with as much graciousness as I could muster. I liked Mr. Trussler well enough, but he had one glaring fault: he was not Valentine Donovan.

Having his arm around my waist and our faces so near each other was not the electrifying experience it had been when I had practiced with Valentine. It simply felt strange and awkward. My gaze searched amongst the set and found its target easily: Valentine dancing with Miss Goulding.

She was a graceful vision, with her flowing pink skirts, the beautiful, rippling feather in her golden hair, and perfectly rosy lips and cheeks. Her gaze was locked on Valentine, intent and . . . inviting. *He's always been one for the women with lighter coloring.* With a clenching stomach and the beginnings of dizziness accosting me, I looked away, fixing my gaze on my partner and forcing myself to make conversation with him.

After an eon, the waltz ended and I curtsied to Mr. Trussler. I couldn't stop my gaze from searching out Valentine, though. He was bowing to Miss Goulding, but as he rose, his eyes flitted to me. Our gazes held for a moment, and for the briefest of seconds, I thought I saw a glimmer of regret in his.

Miss Goulding addressed a remark to him, taking his attention again, and soon the Boulangère began. By the time it was over, I was eager for a respite. I made my way to the refreshment tables with Diana and found both ratafia and lemonade on offer. I paused in front of the ratafia.

Diana glanced at me and, noticing the object of my gaze, she grimaced. "Yes, that was one of Valentine's requests. I tried to dissuade him, but he was adamant."

I glanced over at him, standing beside Phineas in the corner. Their heads were close as Phineas spoke. "Actually, I quite like it," I said, a rush of affection filling my chest.

"Oh." Diana blinked. "Then I am glad Valentine suggested it." Her gaze shifted behind me. "It looks as though you have some friends wishing to speak with you. I shall leave you to do so in peace." She gave me a little wink and stepped away.

I turned and found the Bradley sisters and Miss Goulding approaching. Liking people had always come easily to me, but I found it very difficult indeed to feel anything but stinging envy as I greeted Miss Goulding. I had always liked the color of my hair, but tonight, I found I wished for it to be as flaxen and glimmering as hers.

"What a splendid party," Miss Maria said. "Never did I think to have the opportunity to *waltz* this summer, but when Mama learned that Mrs. Russell was the one arranging for it, she relented. Oh, what an adventure it was!"

"Indeed," said Miss Goulding with a significant glance around our circle. "One quite sees what all the fuss is about, for it is so very intimate."

My stomach tossed and churned.

"And you dancing with Valentine Donovan," Miss Maria said with a bit of awe. "I thought certainly *you* would dance with him, Miss Russell. Has something gone amiss between the two of you?"

"Maria," said Miss Bradley with a hint of censure, "you will recall her telling us from the beginning that his kindness and attention to her is due to the connection they share and nothing else. Besides, Miss Russell is too pure, too cheerful for a man like him. A reformed rake undoubtedly wishes for a wife with a bit of . . . experience."

"Well," Miss Goulding said, "I, for one, am glad for it, for I have had my eye on him for some time. Only Mother would never even allow me to speak with him until she became convinced"—she turned to me—"thanks to you, Miss Russell— that he was finally reforming. When she agreed for me to stand up with him for the first set this evening, including a waltz, of all things, I could hardly believe my good fortune."

I tried to smile and could feel how woefully I failed, but Miss Goulding seemed not to mind.

"And you *do* have experience, don't you, Miss Goulding?" Miss Maria leaned forward and lowered her voice, her eyes alight with excitement. "Is it true that Mr. Sutcliffe tried to kiss you at Vauxhall?"

Miss Goulding's mouth drew up in a cryptic smile. "Oh, I couldn't say, I'm sure. But"—she looked around at all of us significantly—"suffice it to say, on the carriage ride home, I was frightened lest my mother smelled his cologne on me."

The Bradley sisters' eyes widened, and Miss Maria's hand came up to cover her mouth.

Miss Goulding looked satisfied with the reaction and let out a thoughtful sigh, her gaze searching amongst the crowds. "I do think I prefer Mr. Donovan to Mr. Sutcliffe, though, for he presents more of a challenge. A heart yet unbreached."

"Are you well, Miss Russell?" Miss Bradley asked.

"Oh yes," I said, the tone of my voice every bit as unconvincing as my smile. "I am just parched after all the dancing." I continued sipping my drink as an excuse for my silence, but the ratafia only made the turning of my stomach worse.

"Mr. Sutcliffe and Mr. Donovan are not on happy terms, though," Miss Maria said. "Do you not fear that, if Mr. Donovan begins courting you and word of your"—she leaned in again— "*tryst* with Mr. Sutcliffe were to reach him, he would be angry?"

Miss Bradley laughed, exchanging a condescending glance with Miss Goulding. "Oh, Maria. You have a great deal to learn of men, I think. They do not wish for naive, young wives. It is their mothers who insist on such a thing—or the appearance of it, at least."

"Precisely," Miss Goulding confirmed. "And *I* think Mr. Donovan would deem it a victory over Mr. Sutcliffe, for I understand they have something of a competition betwixt them to steal away the attention of each other's women."

Finding my glass was empty and my stomach near to turning itself inside out, I excused myself to refill it. I tried to swallow down the emotion in my throat. I wasn't even sure what it was. If people thought ratafia tasted loathsome, they should try jealousy, disappointment, and embarrassment. It was far worse.

The word *endearing* pressed itself upon me again and again. It had been how Valentine had described my personality. Now more than ever, the word troubled me. I was endearing, and men like Valentine did not want endearing women. Neither did they want naive ones, and I had betrayed the full extent of my naivete to Valentine, asking him all the questions I dared not ask others. I was not blonde or as beautiful as Miss Goulding, either, and I certainly was not as experienced. I could not flirt and entice with my eyes, I could boast no real suitors, I had never had the cologne of a man on me as Miss Goulding had.

"Take care, miss, or the glass will overflow."

I blinked, bringing the world back into focus. I had been using a ladle to fill my empty cup, and it was near to spilling over.

"Good heavens," I said, setting the ladle back in the bowl and glancing at the man who had warned me. He must have been somewhere near his sixtieth year. His hair had turned gray, for the most part, but a few sections revealed that it had once been dark. He had a brooding sort of face that might have intimidated some, but I knew better than many what could be hidden behind such a façade. "Thank you, sir. My mind was elsewhere."

His lip moved slightly as though he was trying to smile, an expression that did not come naturally to him, I gathered, for his forehead was creased in a frown, making the smile almost dissonant. "I gathered as much."

I laughed shakily. His response did not invite a continuation of our interaction, but I was eager for a distraction from my conversation with the Bradleys and Miss Goulding. "I do not think we have met, sir."

"We have not." His eyes surveyed me for a moment, and there was something that struck a chord there, a hint of the familiar. "I am Lord Newham."

"Pleased to make your acquaintance, Lord Newham. I am Miss Russell." I curtsied. I wasn't entirely certain how this man came to be at a ball held in my honor when I had never before met him or heard of him. He was far too old to be considered a potential suitor for me; Diana might be unconventional, but she cared for me far too much for *that*. "Do you know my brother, Duke? Or perhaps my sister-in-law?"

He raised the glass of punch to his lips, not responding immediately. "I knew Mrs. Russell's mother once upon a time." His hard eyes were a bit misty, fixed on some point ahead of him. I followed his gaze, which seemed to be centered on Valentine.

A thought came to me. I surveyed his face, the full brows, the shape of the nose, the clear propensity for frowning, even the timbre of his aging voice. Realizing that I was staring, I turned my gaze away, my heart beating quickly. "I envy you. I have heard enough about her to understand that she was an uncommon sort of woman."

"She was indeed."

"Did you know her well, then?"

There was a pause. "Quite well, yes."

Again, the response did not invite further questions. But I was too curious now whether my suspicions were correct, curious to know about the mother—and father—of the man I had fallen in love with. "What was she like, my lord?"

His mouth turned down at the edges, and his expression became more thoughtful. His eyes turned to me. "She was a bit of heaven on earth, Miss Russell. Soft, good, warm-hearted, and all that despite a difficult life—and one cut far too short." His gaze turned back to the ballroom.

I held a glass full of ratafia, but I hadn't any desire for more, for my stomach was full, and my attention was rapt. "She sounds every bit as lovely as I had imagined. Do you find her children to be like her?"

"I do not know them well enough to say for certain, but I think perhaps the second son least like her of them all."

I frowned and looked over at him. "Valentine, you mean?"

He was frowning as he watched Valentine. "I believe that is his name, yes." He took a drink.

I wasn't fooled. He knew Valentine's name, and the fact that his focus was still fixed upon him told me that my suspicions were correct: this was Valentine's true father.

That he should think Valentine unlike his mother made my heart ache and my temper rise. He had obviously believed Society's interpretation of Valentine's character. Why were those who had every reason to love Valentine so critical of him, so quick to assume the worst?

I tried to control the trembling in my voice as I responded. "Of course, I did not know Mrs. Donovan, sir, but I do know Valentine, and I can tell you that, if the words you have used to describe Mrs. Donovan are true, he is very much like her."

He met my gaze, his dark eyes searching. They were the same deep, uniform brown I had come to know and so admire.

I turned my focus to Valentine, watching as he threaded his way through the crowds. The mere sight of him made some of my frustration ebb. "When I arrived here, sir, I knew nothing of the world outside of the home in which I was raised. Valentine was the first one to befriend me. He has gone out of his way to make me comfortable, doing things that do not come naturally to someone of his temperament. He has been, more than anyone else, the one to help me navigate a Society I, quite frankly, find bewildering. I shudder to think what I would have done without his kindness." I looked to Lord Newham again, meeting his gaze with my chin raised slightly. "If Mrs. Donovan was soft, good, and warm-hearted, Valentine is certainly her son. And he, too, has lived a difficult life, as you may know better than most."

A flash of distress illuminated his eyes.

I set my glass, still full, on the silver platter beside me. "It was a pleasure to meet you, my lord."

Chapter Twenty-Five

VALENTINE

If the curtains by the windows hadn't been so dense and hot, I would have slipped behind them an hour ago. The only reason I hadn't left the ball already was that I didn't wish to leave Rebecca on the most important night since she had arrived in Brighton.

It seemed silly now, for we hadn't spoken since the ball had begun, and I couldn't bring myself to seek her out. To be fair, she had not sought me out, either, but from the way I found her gaze searching for me every few minutes—almost as often as my own gaze sought *her*—I knew that she would have if circumstances had been different.

It was my fault. What I had said to her about having served my function in her life had hurt her. I had nearly recanted it right then and told her I would waltz with her all evening if she would let me. But I had refrained. I was doing this for her. If she would only allow herself a moment to realize it, she would understand what everyone else knew: any man at this ball would be a better choice for her than me.

"How was your waltz with Miss Goulding?" Diana had come

up beside me. She had a way of doing that, I had found. "She looked quite . . . fixed upon you."

I sighed in annoyance. It was true. I had come to know the look in a woman's eyes when she wanted to welcome more from me, and Miss Goulding's eyes and smiles had not been at all subtle. She was precisely the reason I detested dancing. Whenever I surrendered to pleas to engage in the activity, the partners chosen for me were inevitably the sort of women who were fascinated by my reputation and the exhilaration of danger I apparently posed to them.

"It was long," I replied.

"Well, I do not pity you. You should have done the sensible thing and asked Rebecca." Diana sent me a sidelong glance, but I said nothing in reply. Sensible was not the word I would have used. Selfish, certainly, but not sensible.

"It was kind of you to suggest the ratafia on her behalf," she said. "You might have told me that was the reason for it. How in heaven's name has she developed a taste for the stuff?"

I couldn't help a smile. "I haven't any notion." Like a magnet, my gaze sought her out again, and when it found her, I stilled. She was in conversation with Lord Newham, of all people. I hadn't even known they were acquainted.

Diana followed the direction of my gaze. "When I saw the invitation to Lord Newham amongst the others, I nearly threw it out, you know, for I certainly hadn't written it. I haven't spoken to him above twice, and Father hates him. But then I realized *you* must have been responsible for inviting him."

She was right, of course, but I kept my silence. My curiosity over my parentage had been slowly growing, and when I had seen the stack of invitations, I had made the impulsive decision to send one to him, all for the slim possibility that there might be some interaction between us, some . . . answers, perhaps? But now that he was here, I found my pride too strong. Or perhaps it was that my courage lacked.

"You should speak with him, Val," Diana said, her voice more calm and less teasing now. "I have seen him looking at you a dozen times. Almost as much as I have seen you look at Rebecca."

I ignored the latter part of her comment. "If Newham wanted the connection, he would acknowledge me."

"Perhaps," she said. "Or perhaps he is waiting for you to show some sign *you* would welcome it."

I watched Lord Newham and Rebecca. He was looking at her, his expression somber and intent. She said something, then, with a small curtsy, turned and walked away, looking more haughty than usual. Rebecca and haughty. Those were two words I never would have thought to use together. What I wouldn't have given to know what they had spoken of.

"I miss Duke," Diana said suddenly.

I turned to look at her. She was staring out over the drawing room. It was unusual for her to admit anything that smacked of the more tender emotions, and I felt a niggling guilt over how focused on my own problems I had been. Diana had been without her husband for weeks now, and it occurred to me that she had thrown herself into the planning of this party to distract herself from her loneliness.

Wrapping an arm about her, I pulled her closer to me, setting a kiss on her temple. "And to think of all the time you spent fighting him off."

She chuckled lightly. "I was a fool."

"And I told you as much."

"You did. More than once. But now *you* are the fool."

My smile faded, and I released her gently, letting the distance between us widen.

She faced me. "Do not resist it as I did, Valentine. Life is too short." She put a hand around my arm and squeezed, then left my side.

Diana didn't understand. She was almost as guilty as

Rebecca of being blind to the truth. I wasn't resisting love. I was acting upon it by ensuring Rebecca received what she deserved.

Yates came up to me, smiling and breathless from the reel he had just finished. "When you danced the first set, I admit to hoping you would continue the trend."

"One would think you knew me better by now."

"Yes, well, I have been surprised by you more than once recently, you know. Do you not intend to dance with the Russell girl?"

"No." I wanted to dance with Rebecca as I had wanted few things in life. I wanted my hand about her waist, to look into those enchanting eyes, and the constant mention of it was not helping me in any way.

"Are the rumors true, then?" Yates asked, a hint of surprise in his voice.

"What rumors?"

He gave me a quizzical look. "Come, now. Coyness doesn't suit you, Donovan."

"You can either tell me or leave, Yates. I have no interest in playing games."

He shrugged. "They say that you are done with her. That you've had what you wanted and are pursuing . . . bigger and better things."

I whirled around, taking him by the throat. "Next time someone has something to say about Miss Russell, tell them they can say it to my face."

Eyes wide, Yates stared back at me. He tried to nod as much as my hand gripping his throat would allow. Aware that our interaction had not escaped the notice of those around us, I released him.

I pulled down on my coat, clenching my jaw with regret at my explosive reaction. "Forgive me."

"Nonsense," Yates said, straightening his cravat and looking far too composed for a man who had nearly been strangled.

"There is nothing to forgive. I merely thought you would wish to know what effect your actions are having upon Miss Russell's reputation."

"What actions?"

Yates didn't respond, and all the people who had been watching us began to lose interest in the strange interruption. No doubt they dismissed it as another of my vagaries.

"What actions, Yates?" I repeated impatiently. When he didn't respond, I sighed in annoyance. "I shan't strangle you again if that is your concern."

He chuckled, rubbing his throat. "You've the devil's own grip, Donovan. What I mean is that you have stayed away from her all evening. Anyone can see the girl is pining after you, and you haven't so much as stood beside her. Given your reputation, there are some who think you have . . . well, compromised her in some way, and now you have lost interest."

I let out a string of curses under my breath. No matter what I did, I was bound to hurt Rebecca. This was precisely what I had been concerned over from the beginning—that people would assume the worst of her because of *me*. And of anyone in this world, Rebecca Russell deserved that people should assume the best.

"Thank you for telling me," I said tightly. "Forgive me for . . ."

Yates gave a wry chuckle. "If you apologize again, Donovan, I will begin to worry over you. I haven't any use for apologies. A little choke from you is hardly the worst we have been through."

He was right, of course. We had both done worse to each other in our lowest moments. I turned to leave, but he stopped me.

"I've had word from Jones. He says the case should finish at the court within the week."

I didn't move. This was the most welcome news I had had in some time, and I hardly knew what to do with it, particularly on the heels of such *unwelcome* news. The courts had been holding the money for nearly two years now—two years of being obliged to apply to the Admiral for money. A significant portion of that time I had been obliged to spend at Blackwick Hall because I had no alternative.

Finally, though, it would be over. That deserved a celebration.

But I had no desire to celebrate at the moment. Eyes focused on Rebecca, I thanked Yates and left his side. I had to quash the rumors, but I had to find a way to do it without giving Rebecca to think there could be more between us than friendship. It was the devil of a balance to strike.

She had taken to conversing with Phineas on the edge of the ballroom floor. Her cheeks were becomingly flushed, and I wondered if it was a result of her conversation with Lord Newham. Regardless, I had never seen her look more beautiful than she did this evening.

"Valentine." Diana cut off my progress and grabbed my arm. "Father and Lord Newham are having . . . an encounter."

I grimaced, looking behind her to where Rebecca was, then to the Admiral and Lord Newham. They were standing near the refreshment table, just as Lord Newham had been when he had been speaking with Rebecca. They might have been attempting to stare one another into the ground.

"And you think adding me to it will help?"

"No," she said. "But I can distract Father if you will distract Lord Newham."

I pinched my lips together, squaring her with a churlish expression. This was another of Diana's opportunistic ideas—her way of getting me to speak with Lord Newham, as she thought I should do.

The Admiral took a step toward Lord Newham—one step *too* close, though Lord Newham responded by closing the distance even more, the effect somewhat lost due to his halting gait. If we didn't intervene, Rebecca's ball was likely to include a bout of elderly fisticuffs. At least Rebecca knew enough now not to accuse the men of having by-blows—though she wouldn't be wrong in Lord Newham's case.

Throwing aside my hesitation, I made my way toward them, trying to maintain a quick but inconspicuous pace, with Diana on my heels.

Neither of the men spared even a glance in our direction as we stopped beside them.

"You are not, nor ever have been, welcome near this family, my lord," the Admiral said. Even when he was being rude, he insisted on using proper titles.

"Father," Diana chastised.

"I will have you know, I was invited," Lord Newham responded.

"Ha!" the Admiral scoffed. "I am quite familiar with the sort of *invitations* you perceive people to be extending to you, Lord Newham."

"*I* invited him," I interrupted before the two of them could fling our family's less-than-pristine history in front of the guests.

The Admiral's head whipped around to me, his nostrils flared and his jaw clenching. "*You.*"

"Yes, I. If you would like to expel your anger at me, perhaps I can persuade you to do so somewhere upstairs. Rebecca does not deserve that a scene should be made here."

The Admiral stared at me and then Lord Newham. After a tense moment, he whirled around and walked away.

I was aware of Lord Newham's eyes on me, and after a moment of hesitation, I met his gaze. His expression was not a happy one, certainly not fatherly.

"I shall not stay where I am not wanted," he said in a gruff voice, turning for the cane that rested against the nearest wall.

I reached for it. "Allow me to escort you to the door, my lord."

"I need no assistance." Lord Newham snatched at the cane I held, but it was farther than he had thought, and though he managed to wrest it from my grasp, he lost his balance as a result. I scrambled, managing to catch him by the arm before he fell to the floor.

Discordant notes sounded as members of the orchestra were distracted from their task. Heads turned toward us, and a hush fell over the guests. I ignored it as I helped Lord Newham to his feet.

Before he was entirely stable, he pushed me away.

Clenching my jaw, I stepped to the side. Whatever thought I had had of speaking with him fled. This man wanted nothing to do with me. Why he had accepted the invitation to come in the first place was a mystery, as was why I had thought to extend it.

The sting of his behavior toward me, and in front of all the guests, no less, began to course through my veins like boiling water. "Forgive me," I said tightly, "for my attempt to be a decent son to yet another unwilling father."

I turned and walked away, willing my anger to cover my embarrassment and hurt until people inevitably lost their interest again.

Chapter Twenty-Six

REBECCA

My eyes were wide as I watched Valentine shoulder his way through the crowds and stalk from the room. Lord Newham, on the other hand, tottered in the opposite direction using his cane.

"Excuse me," I said to Phineas. Keeping my eyes on the door Valentine had disappeared through, I gathered my skirts and made my way across the room. I checked the library first, for Diana had ordered a few tables to be set up there for those who preferred card playing to dancing.

But Valentine was not there.

I checked every door lining the corridor, peering into the darkness until I was certain each one was vacant. A journey up the stairs and to Valentine's bedchamber was just as fruitless, and I closed the door with disappointment and a hint of worry.

As the latch clicked, I glanced toward the servant staircase, and an idea occurred to me. I dashed toward it and took the winding staircase down the three flights to the servant quarters. I emerged into a dimly lit corridor, but a rattling near the butler's pantry called my attention, and I hurried over, stopping short on the threshold.

Valentine held the iron handle of the door to the cellar and was shaking it violently. When it refused to give way to his efforts, he released it and kicked at the wooden door, releasing a string of curse words, of which I was secretly pleased to understand every one. But my pleasure was but a wisp, overshadowed by my concern. This was what Valentine did when he didn't know where to go, or what else to do: he went for the liquor.

Putting a hand on his hip, he scrubbed the other one harshly over his jaw, turning away from the cellar door. He caught sight of me and slowed. A sequence of emotions passed over his face.

"Marsh has the key if you wish to call for him," I said. I didn't truly want Valentine to drink away what he was feeling, but it needed to be his choice to refrain.

"You should be upstairs."

"Not if you are down here."

"I am not pleasant company—and I will be even less so once I open this door." He gave it another kick, and I couldn't help but admire his restraint, for he made no sound of pain despite how much it must have hurt his foot. It occurred to me that perhaps there was a different pain outweighing that one, though.

"I am not afraid of you, Valentine."

He pulled the knot at his throat until it loosened. "You should be."

I took a few steps toward him. "What happened upstairs?"

"What happened was what anyone might have anticipated." He tugged at the end of the cravat until it slid out from the collar of his coat. "You say I am fortunate to have two fathers, but which is preferable, Rebecca: one father who, though gone now, loved you dearly while he was alive? Or two living men who despise you? What positive can even *you* find in being so unwanted?"

"You are not unwanted," I said.

"Saying it does not make it so."

"*I* want you." The words escaped me before I could stop them. But I couldn't regret them, hanging as they did upon the air.

He had been threading the cravat through his fingers, but he stopped, though his gaze did not come up to meet mine. "You shouldn't." His voice was soft, and he resumed his distracted threading.

"I shouldn't do a great many things, but I do not care—not anymore." I took another step toward him and grabbed him by the hand, stilling it. "Valentine, I do not know what Lord Newham thinks, but I do not believe he would have come tonight if he hadn't some desire to know you. When we spoke of you, he couldn't hide his interest, much as he tried. But, whatever his thoughts or feelings about you, whatever the Admiral's thoughts and feelings about you, you mustn't let them hold greater sway in your life than the thoughts and feelings of those who know and love you best."

Jaw tight, he stared down at our hands. His thumb brushed against my gloved finger for the briefest moment, making my heart thump in my chest.

The words to tell him how I felt came to my tongue, the urge to share my deepest feelings surging like a bubble to the surface. But I bit my tongue. It was not the right moment. He was consumed with other concerns—concerns he had been harboring and battling for far longer than I had known him.

I reached up to my hair, locating one of the small roses there and giving it a little tug until it yielded. I reached for his hand, opening it and placing the rose in his palm. I looked up at him with a small, hesitant smile as I closed his fingers over it.

His frown softened slightly, and he stared down at our hands.

"You can deaden your senses with drink for a night, Valentine," I said softly, keeping my hold on his hand, "or you can use those senses to recognize the good that still exists."

I rose up on my tiptoes. Closing my eyes and leaning in, I kissed him softly on the cheek. My own senses filled with the scent of the soap he had used to shave and the feel of the beginnings of stubble. The kiss had been an impulsive gesture to convey my affection for him, but suddenly it didn't feel like enough. I was wading in the waters, but I wanted to immerse myself in them. I wanted to wrap my arms about him, to move enough for our lips to touch. I wanted to leave with his cologne lingering on my skin.

A clattering sounded in the kitchen, and I jumped back, blinking.

Valentine's eyes were on me, dark and alert. His hand hovered in the air with the rose, as though he hadn't moved since I had given it to him. He had been standing rigid, and I . . .

Heat flooded my cheeks. "I shall tell Marsh to come down," I said, my voice rough and uneven.

I turned and left.

Valentine was not at breakfast the next morning. The Admiral was, but as he was in a foul mood, I declined to drink my cup of chocolate. Somehow, it felt wrong to drink it without Valentine there. I settled for a few bites of toast before I made a retreat from the room with the excuse of needing to see to correspondence.

The end of last night's ball had been long, and I had been distracted, wondering what Valentine was doing downstairs. As promised, I had sent Marsh down, but I had been too afraid to ask the butler what had happened when he reappeared upstairs a few minutes later.

Had Valentine thought about the moment in the pantry with me? Had it merely been an unpleasant surprise to him?

The way he had grazed his thumb over my fingers . . . a chill swept over my skin at the thought, leaving bumps in its wake. Was I wrong for hoping such gestures meant something more to him than mere friendship? To wonder if it was his insistence on thinking the worst of himself which kept him from acting on such feelings?

Despite the intensity of planning and executing a ball in such a short period of time, Diana insisted that we leave the house once she had finished her breakfast. It was to be a shopping expedition, though what we needed the day *after* a ball, I hadn't any idea. However, I was so preoccupied wondering about Valentine that a diversion was welcome.

We stepped down from the carriage at the edge of Duke Street just before noon, both of us with our reticules in hand.

"What precisely are we looking for?" I asked as I took in the bustling activity filling the narrow street.

"I haven't any idea," she replied. "Something is bound to take our fancies, though, don't you think?" She looked over at me and smiled. "You look befuddled."

"Do I? I admit I am quite unfamiliar with the activity of shopping. Grandfather thinks it a great waste of money, and I suppose I can see why he would think such a thing if we haven't any specific purchase to make but are simply determined to spend money."

Diana laughed and hooked her arm through mine. "Your grandfather sounds prodigiously entertaining. But though we do not have a particular purchase in mind, we *do* have a *purpose*." She began walking, and I followed suit.

"Which is . . .?"

"Distraction," she replied.

I glanced over at her, wondering how she knew I needed any such thing, but she was busy looking at the nearest window—a cobbler's shop with a pretty display of boots, slippers, and the like.

"While I had the ball to plan, I could keep reasonably distracted from Duke's absence," she continued. "But now that it is over, I feel his absence more keenly than ever. Hence our shopping expedition." She pulled us to the cobbler's window, and we stopped in front of it. Diana narrowed her eyes, tilting her head to the side as she inspected a pair of leather half-boots. "You must know that about us Donovans, Rebecca. We will do anything to avoid feeling unpleasant emotions." She made a disappointed face and pulled us away from the window. "I think those are too narrow for my feet."

I hardly heard her last words. My mind was too fixed on the previous ones. *We will do anything to avoid feeling unpleasant emotions.* She was right—about Valentine, at least. Rather than hurt, he would drown himself—in alcohol, in cards, in women. The realization pained me. It pained me because it spoke of a man so full of hurt, he would do anything to escape it.

"Ah, let us step in here for a moment," Diana said, oblivious to my thoughts. "It is not the best draper in Brighton, but it is by far the most extensive, and I have a mind to have a dress made up in time for Duke's arrival."

The bell on the door jingled as we stepped through, and my eyes widened. Fabrics of all colors, textures, and sheens were draped, rolled, and folded in row upon row. Young ladies in bonnets inspected, touched, debated. I had never seen anything like it.

Under the windowed shop wall were rolls of muslins— white, dyed, printed, embroidered. I reached a finger and touched the nearest one, a beautiful jaconet.

"You should look for a sturdier one, I think," Diana said. "A gray, perhaps. We will be retiring to Kent soon, and your current ones will dirty in a trice there, for I imagine you will like to walk a great deal. It is quite pretty at Birchleigh. I shall be just over there, looking at the silks."

I nodded, but her mention of Kent had my stomach in coils.

Once my brother returned to Brighton, we wouldn't remain much longer. And then what would happen? I hadn't secured any real suitors, and if Birchleigh Hall was anything like Millbury, there would be no gentlemen to speak of in the vicinity. All the expense and trouble Diana, Duke, and Valentine had gone to on my behalf had been for naught.

But beneath those thoughts lay another concern. I doubted Valentine would join us at Birchleigh Hall. But what, then, would he do? Return to Blackwick with the Admiral and Phineas? The thought alone was distressing.

I reached for a gray muslin nearby, and my hand bumped someone else's.

"Miss Russell! What a pleasure to see you."

I didn't even need to look up to know who was speaking to me, for I recognized the accent quickly. Miss White—Nellie, as Valentine called her—was standing beside me. She was wearing a vibrant violet dress with half-sleeves and the neck cut low. Her hair, a glowing golden blonde, peeped out from her bonnet in the form of loose ringlets. She was as beautiful as I had remembered her.

"Good day, Miss White." I hated the surge of jealousy I felt being near her. I hadn't any idea whether Valentine still kept company with her, but the thought that he might turn to her in his time of emotional distress made me sick to my stomach.

"It looks as though we want the same thing." Though her hand was on the muslin, the smile she wore and the tone she used as she said the words dripped with implication. "I understand you had a ball last night."

"I did." I moved to the next muslin in the line of fabrics. It was far too dark for me to wear, but I had no desire to fight over the gray one with Miss White. As I pretended to inspect it, I tried not to betray the thought in my mind: was it Valentine who had told her about the ball? What if he had sought her out after our encounter in the butler's pantry? That thought made me hurt in ways I had never before felt.

"And how was it?" she asked. "Agreeable?"

I managed a smile. "Yes, thank you. Very agreeable." It was strange speaking of it, not only because a great portion of it had *not* been agreeable, but because I wasn't certain whether she felt she ought to have been invited. I had a kind heart, but not kind enough to invite the mistress of the man I loved to a party held in my honor.

"Valentine did not wish to join you today?" She looked around as if she might see him somewhere inside the shop. Her use of his Christian name made me clench my fingers. "I suppose it *is* a bit early for him—he was always one for staying abed late." The glint in her eye as she smiled at me dripped with implication.

I swallowed. I hadn't known Valentine as a late riser. He had taken breakfast with me early, as I was accustomed to doing. But Miss White's knowledge of him was different in a way that I didn't know what to do with it. Except to feel even more sick to my stomach.

"I am not certain where he is," I said truthfully. "I am here with my sister-in-law."

"Ah, well," she passed behind me, close enough to brush against me. The way she was behaving now was entirely different from her demeanor at the theater. There, she had been kind; here, she was almost . . . threatening. "It is no matter. I shall be hearing from him soon, undoubtedly." She looked me over. "Playing at reform cannot hold a rake's attention for long, as we all know. Good day, Miss Russell."

She drifted away, greeting Diana as they encountered each other at the end of the long path between the fabrics. Diana looked at Miss White down her nose and gave the merest hint of a smile—or was it a sneer? —then passed her by without a word.

"Was that woman talking to you?" Diana asked when she reached me.

"Yes," I said, busying myself with the fabrics. "For a moment."

"If I had noticed her in the shop, I would never have left your side. I can see from the look on your face that she was being unpleasant. What did she say?"

I shook my head, trying to shake Miss White's words and presence along with it. "Nothing important."

Diana looked at me dubiously, her lips pinched. "I do not believe you for a second. She was making mischief, wasn't she? Speaking of Valentine, I assume."

I didn't respond, for my eyes were becoming blurry, the printed pattern on the muslin I had bent down to look at running together in an unidentifiable muddle. If I spoke, Diana would immediately know how overset I was.

"Rebecca," Diana said, taking my hand and pulling me up to stand. I blinked quickly, for the last thing I needed was to make a scene in the draper's shop. Seeing the gathering tears in my eyes, she hesitated a moment. One or two heads were turned toward us.

"Ah, this one is quite lovely," Diana said a bit louder than necessary as she crouched down. "Come take a closer look."

I obliged, grateful for what Diana was doing—she was giving me time to compose myself.

"Rebecca," she said in a near-whisper. "I imagine you are aware by now who and what Nellie White is." Her voice grew louder. "I do not think I have ever seen such a pretty pattern before." She lowered her volume again. "Please believe me when I say I would never have agreed to sit in Mr. Sutcliffe's box at the theater if I had known then what I know now."

I took in a deep breath, willing my emotions to settle. "It is not your fault."

"It is, though. That is my duty as your chaperone—to keep

from exposing you to people like her." She squeezed my hand, looking me intently in the eye. "Nellie White is a jealous woman who is trying to hurt you. I have it on good authority that Mr. Sutcliffe is done with her. She is desperate, and she chose you as the target of her ire. Do you know why?"

I shook my head.

"Because she is threatened by you—threatened by what she saw at the theater between you and Valentine."

My cheeks warmed and I looked away. "There is nothing between us."

"My dear, your assertion is positively overwhelmed by the evidence. Recall that I was there, too, to see the incident with the wax. And plenty of things since. I know my brother enough to recognize how he looks at you. But I shan't speak of it if you do not wish me to." She rose, pulling me up alongside her. "No, you are quite right. On closer inspection, the pattern looks to have been applied on a terrible slant. It will not do at all. I shall have to order in from London."

I allowed Diana to lead the way out of the shop, dithering between despair at the conversation with Miss White and painful hope at the one with Diana.

Chapter Twenty-Seven

VALENTINE

The night of the ball, I had left the butler's pantry before Marsh had even come, assuming Rebecca had indeed told him. I hadn't truly wished to enter the cellar, not after having a moment to reflect upon things. In fact, there had been alcohol enough upstairs if that had been my true wish.

But I was tired of the same routine I had kept for the past two years—trying to douse my feelings in flames until there was nothing left but embers. The flames scorched those around me; they licked at my happiness until it was harder to feel *anything*. And nothing had reminded me of that fact more keenly than Rebecca's presence in the pantry.

Any thought of drinking myself into oblivion had disappeared the instant she had kissed me on the cheek. The tenderness of the gesture, particularly on the heels of her words, had made my throat thick. And when she had lingered there, her warm breath on my cheek and the whisper of her lips near, I had gone still, terrified of the things I was feeling, of the way my arms begged to be free to wrap around her, the way my lips pled to have their way.

I had resisted as long as I felt I could—a pathetic matter of seconds—when the crashing in the kitchen had sounded. A merciful diversion, though I had wondered a hundred times since what might have happened without it.

It had taken a few minutes for me to calm my racing heart once Rebecca had left. With the rose in hand, I had left the butler's pantry and hurried up the servant staircase to my bedchamber. There, I had lain upon my bed, fully clothed, and shut my eyes, holding the flower and trying to do what Rebecca had taught me to do. At some point, I had fallen asleep.

When I woke early the next morning, I didn't move, paying attention to the novelty of the experience. The memory of the previous night came over me quickly, but there was no pounding headache, no sluggishness, no parched throat, and, most significantly, no regret.

I *had* regrets, of course, but they were all for my treatment of Rebecca. I should never have agreed to her hare-brained idea, no matter how much it had done to help me. I hadn't ever deserved such help, for I had been responsible for the ruination of my own reputation, while Rebecca . . .

Yates's revelation made me sick to my stomach—that people would think such a thing of someone as pure and principled as Rebecca Russell, and for no other reason than that she had chosen to befriend me, to be seen with me.

But how to fix it was not immediately apparent. To continue being seen with her when I knew her feelings for me, when I knew my feelings for *her*, was damaging in its own way. I didn't know how to protect her, or if I *could* protect her. The damage had already been done, and I seemed the last person in the world to be able to rectify it.

Saddled with such a burden, I stayed away from her and away from the Admiral, whose presence would only confuse me more by adding to the muddle of emotions I was trying to untangle. I sought refuge with Yates, who asked no questions when I arrived at an uncivilized hour of the morning and informed him I would be sleeping at his residence for the foreseeable future. And when he desired entertainment at the club, he made no protest at my refusal to join him. I had no appetite for such things.

Apparently, I did have an appetite for one of the apple tarts his cook had made. I had it brought to me, where I ate it in the comfort and privacy of my bed. Contrary to what my stomach had insisted on upon seeing the tart, eating the entirety of it did not assuage my frustration or my growing sense of despair at arranging the future in a satisfying manner. Indeed, my only reward for such indulgence was protracted, uncomfortable regret and a fiery determination never to eat apple tarts again.

My resolve held strong until far into the morning, at which point I awoke from my pie-induced slumber. Feeling hungry and dissatisfied, I tugged the bell pull, calling for two more pieces of tart to be brought to me with all haste.

I was near to finishing the second piece—for a gentleman finishes what he starts, no matter the personal cost—when Yates barged into the room unceremoniously.

Upon seeing the state of me, shirtless and with crumbs scattered on both my person and the plates around me, Yates swore, his expression half amusement, half concern.

I forced down the last bite of the second piece of tart and pushed away the tray holding the plate as my body attempted to reject what I had forced it to consume. "Your cook *must* be persuaded to stop making apple tarts, Yates."

He reached for the bell pull and yanked it. "*You* must be persuaded to stop acting like a pig. What the devil, Donovan?"

"Leave me be. Don't you have something better to do than pester me at this unholy hour of morning?"

"It is noon."

I made a sound of irritation. "That is impossible. Where did the morning go?"

"Perhaps you ate it."

A scowl was the only response I gave him, sliding down so that the blankets covered me more fully. I intended to go back to sleep—if the crumbs in the sheets would allow such a thing.

Yates strode over to the curtains and pulled them open. "Newham has been taken ill."

I paused in the act of brushing crumbs toward the edge of the sheets.

Yates folded his arms and looked at me. "It was all the talk at the club last night. They don't think he shall recover. Evidently, he has been ill for some time."

I frowned, unsure what to feel at such news. "How long does he have?"

Yates shrugged. "A few days perhaps. There is no saying, really. I simply thought you should know."

I gave a nod, and Yates soon left me in my bed of crumbs and contemplation.

I t took a great deal more charm and charisma than I was wont to display, but the butler at Lord Newham's residence did, in the end, agree to inform his lordship that I had come to call upon him. I stood on the stoop, tapping my finger impatiently on the wrought-iron railing to my side. I was confident my presumption in coming here, particularly after the events of Rebecca's ball, would be met with a resounding rebuff, but life had equipped me well for such a thing.

This was perhaps my last chance to . . . to what? I wasn't even certain what I had come for. A desire to take Lord Newham to task and tell him what I thought of him battled with the need to ask him, once and for all, whether he was, indeed, my true father. All I knew was that I had become too familiar with regret to wish to spend the rest of my life wondering and wishing I had acted while Newham was still alive, even if my efforts to speak with him met with failure.

The butler returned momentarily, his face haughty and stoic as he appeared in the doorway again. "His lordship will receive you in his bedchamber."

I blinked in surprise, but the butler allowed no time for gathering my wits. He turned on his heel and led the way, leaving a footman to close the door behind us.

Lord Newham's residence stood in contrast to his dour demeanor. I would have assumed Lord Newham preferred mahogany and deep blue carpets, but his residence was full of creamy marble and light stone floors that must have cost a fortune. The butler led me up a staircase carpeted in pale green, then turned directly left, opening the door and announcing me.

I stepped inside the room which, though decorated in similarly light colors, was dim due to the curtains being drawn together. The door shut behind me, and my stomach, still full of that delicious but regrettable apple tart, churned with nerves.

Newham sat against a plethora of pillows, his head adorned with a cap that made him look older than usual. "What do you want, Donovan?" His voice was markedly weaker than when I had seen him at the ball.

He might think to intimidate me with such direct talk, but I was a match for him there. "I heard you were about to receive your last rites."

He scoffed, which turned into a hacking fit. I strode over to the bedside table and poured from the pitcher there, handing him the glass. He took it from me and drank deeply, successfully quelling the cough.

"I am not dying," he said.

I made no response, for I wasn't sure whether I wished him to be right or not.

"Why have you come?"

I met his gaze, trying to decide what I most wanted from this man. Was it to rail at him for bringing me into an existence such that I grew up the subject of rejection and ridicule? Such that I was incapable of providing the life deserved by the woman I loved?

No. He bore only partial blame for that. Besides, what was done was done. I wanted just one thing from him.

"I want to know if you are my father."

He stared at me, and I knew the answer already, looking at him there in his bed. But I wanted to hear him say it—if he would. The silence grew protracted, and while it was answer enough, it was not the way I had wanted my answer. This man had done nothing for me, his own son, my entire life, and even here on his deathbed, he could not be convinced to tell me the truth, to say a few words.

My nostrils flared. "Answer me, dam—"

"I am."

I went still, and Newham held my gaze. He *was* my father. I was the bastard son of Lord Newham. Years of suspicion and uncertainty, a childhood of rejection and teasing slid from my shoulders. I breathed out slowly.

"I swore to Admiral Donovan I would never tell you as much," he added.

"Why?" Was the Admiral so intent on making my life miserable that he refused me the truth?

"Pride, of course. You know what he is. When he returned from his assignment and discovered the connection your mother and I had shared, he challenged me to a duel. Your mother did what she could to pacify him, and he thought better of it—of the scandal that would ensue. Instead, he insisted he would claim you as his own, that no one should know of the circumstances of your birth. He made me swear to stay away from your mother, from you, and to never speak the truth or he would have me ruined—and then run me through."

My teeth clenched. In short, the Admiral had reacted in

anger, then reversed course to salvage his own reputation. I wasn't naïve enough to think he had done any of it for me or my mother.

"Much good that promise did," I said. "My parentage has been a matter for Society gossip for as long as I can remember."

"Well," he said, "you have hardly made it an aim to quell gossip about yourself, have you?"

"I suppose not."

"You are as headstrong and foolish as I was," he said, regarding me through critical eyes.

It was not a compliment by any means, but the fact that in me he saw himself . . . well, I had never had a father claim any part of me—especially not the less savory parts.

"But there may be hope for you yet." He leaned his head back and closed his eyes. "You have a young woman who loves you. Miss Russell, isn't it? It is not every young lady who will take a man like me to task."

I looked at him intently, remembering when she had walked away from him haughtily. "Did she?"

"She most certainly did. Chastised me like I was a young schoolboy."

I couldn't help a smile. "She is out of the ordinary."

"She is." Newham opened his eyes, leveling a stern gaze at me. "So stop acting like a fool and do whatever is required to deserve her."

I gripped the handle of the chair beside me. "I'm afraid we are past that possibility."

"Don't be stupid, Valentine." The words were harsh, but my name softened them. "My life would be very different—as would yours—if I hadn't given up on deserving what I wanted. I was in love with your mother before she ever knew Admiral Donovan, but I convinced myself she was above me. The result of that laziness and idiocy is that you and I sit here as we do today." He leaned back again, as though the fervor of his words had drained his last bit of energy. "Now, get out of my sight and set your mind to things like a man."

I swallowed and gave a curt nod before turning to make my way to the door.

"Valentine," Newham said as I set my hand on the doorknob.

I turned and looked back at him.

He didn't speak for a moment. "When I've recovered, I will best you in a game of piquet."

My lip drew up at the corner. "I don't gamble anymore, sir, but I will gladly best you in a game of chess whenever you see fit to try your luck against me."

Chapter Twenty-Eight

VALENTINE

I hardly knew what to make of my conversation with Lord Newham. It was a beginning, I supposed. It bore the mark of potential. He would never claim me publicly, but he had done so privately, and that was more than I had expected when I had set out for his residence.

He had also given me advice regarding Rebecca, and though I would have been forgiven for ignoring such counsel from a man who had never really spoken to me until today, I couldn't ignore it. I hadn't known he and my mother shared a connection before her marriage to the Admiral, and it haunted me to think what might have been, what regrets he must live with. I did not want to go through life with such a burden, to watch Rebecca marry another man because I had decided against doing everything in my power to have her.

But Rebecca should know what people were saying about us, what damage had been done to her reputation by her association with me. I owed her that, at least.

Marsh welcomed me through the front door of the town house with a smile, and I tried to return it, though I found it difficult to focus on anything but how to approach the conversation ahead of me.

"Do you know where Miss Russell is?" I asked as Marsh took my hat.

"I believe she is in the library, sir."

I gave a nod, wondering if she was there with Phineas. A spasm of jealousy shot through me. Phineas was precisely the type of man Rebecca deserved—an even temperament, thoughtful disposition, and saddled with no sordid history or crushing debts.

I stepped from the entry way into the corridor just as the Admiral emerged from the breakfast parlor. "A word, Valentine."

I clenched my jaw. Nothing grated me more than the Admiral speaking to me as though I was still a disobedient midshipman on the Dominance.

"*A word*, Valentine," he repeated when my obedience was not immediate.

I gave a stiff nod and, looking toward the door that led to the library, I followed the Admiral into the breakfast parlor. He shut the door behind us and clasped his hands behind his back. He might have been concealing a switch there based on his demeanor. "Where have you been?"

I didn't answer immediately, considering whether to submit to this unmerited questioning. What I did was no business of his, much as he might try to make it so.

"With Yates," I finally replied.

"Captain Yates," he corrected me.

"Forgive me, Admiral," I said, holding his gaze. "*Captain* Yates."

"And why have you returned?"

"I thought you would have left by now." I had hoped it, at least. The only reason the Admiral would remain here after the ball was to keep his eye on me.

His expression grew more stern. "You should return to Captain Yates's residence."

I said nothing, my eyes on him.

"You must be aware," he continued, "of the unfortunate rumors circling Brighton over your connection with Miss Russell."

My nostrils flared. "I am." It gave me no pleasure to admit such a thing to the Admiral. He already thought little enough of me as it was.

"When Diana sent me word of the *progress* you were making," he said in a hard voice, "I did not anticipate it would be duping an inexperienced young woman—and the sister of your own brother-in-law, of all people! The last thing this family needs is yet another scandal attached to your name."

"I have duped no one," I gritted out.

"Do not be a fool, Valentine. The ball the other night put on public display how fully you have charmed that girl into loving you—and then dispensed with her company now that you have tired of her."

His words seared me, but only because it pained me to hear Yates's words confirmed.

"Nothing untoward has happened between Rebecca and myself," I said with a desperate attempt at calm.

"Neither Society nor I believe you," he replied. "You have made sure of that with your despicable reputation." He strode closer to me and jabbed a finger into my chest. I refused to let the violence of the gesture move me from my place, to allow him to push me even an inch.

"You will marry that girl, Valentine," he said through clenched teeth.

My lips drew up in a sneer. "If I ever marry," I said, my voice dangerously quiet, "you can be certain it will not be to please *you.*"

He held my gaze, his eyes blazing blue. "Then you shan't

have a penny from me. You may drown in your debts for all I care. I am done with you." Turning, he reached behind him and picked up something from the table—a small stack of correspondence. He shoved the papers into my chest. "Those are the most urgent ones. Now get out."

Grasping the letters in my hand, I strode out of the room, slamming the door behind me. I didn't know where to go—all I knew was that I needed to put as much distance between the Admiral and myself as physically possible.

A vase of roses, leftover from the ball, caught my eye as I walked through the entry hall, and I slowed. What about Rebecca? I had come to speak with her, and I couldn't leave her wondering where I was or why I had not spoken to her since the ball. The letters in my hand trembled with my anger, and I shut my eyes, wishing things hadn't become so complicated, wishing I hadn't been so foolish in the past. By telling me to marry Rebecca, the Admiral was giving me an order I would have given anything to obey. But I couldn't marry Rebecca, couldn't ask her to marry me when she deserved infinitely more than what I could give her.

I gripped the letters more tightly. They were just one evidence of the mess I had made of my life. If I wished to be free of my debts, a great deal of the prize money I had coming to me would be used up paying them. And then where would I be left? I had nothing to offer Rebecca—nothing at all—except for the supposed protection of my name. What good was that when I had spent the last two years ruining that name?

"Valentine," Diana said from the top of the stairs. "You returned."

"No," I said. "I am leaving. On the Admiral's orders."

Diana hurried down the stairs with her skirts in hand. "This is not his house to give orders in."

"No," I said. "But when did that ever stop him? Besides, he is right to send me away."

"Nonsense," she said. "Why would you say such a thing? I have never in my life heard you agree with him." She put a hand to my forehead as though to check for a fever.

I swatted it away, in no mood for humor. "There are rumors."

She took my unpleasantness in stride, squaring me with her clear gaze. "You mean Sutcliffe's rumors? Or Nellie's?"

I frowned, and Diana's lips pressed together. "Father went to the Brighton Club yesterday. It seems Sutcliffe spoke with him directly. He came home in a rage. But after my own conversations with a few people, the rumors do not seem to have spread. I think Sutcliffe meant them to reach you more than he meant for them to be transmitted amongst Society."

I breathed a small sigh of relief. "And Nellie?"

The mere mention of her name was enough to put a flash of anger in Diana's eyes. "Let us just say that she has been hard at work as well. Rebecca and I encountered her at the draper's the other day. I didn't note her presence there until it was too late." She looked at me significantly, and malaise filled my stomach.

"Too late? What did she do?"

Diana glanced down the corridor as though afraid we might be overheard. "It was what she said. Rebecca wouldn't tell me precisely, but the look on her face was enough to make it clear that it was mischief—relating to you, I am certain. I tried to mitigate the damage as well as I could . . ." She looked at me intently. "You *do* love Rebecca, don't you, Valentine?"

I clenched my jaw and looked away. To be asked such a question outright when I had been trying to persuade myself out of such love . . . "It doesn't matter what I feel. I cannot marry her."

"Hogwash," Diana spat.

"Don't be a fool, Di. You know what I am, and you know that Rebecca deserves better." If Diana was right and the rumors had only been meant to make my life more miserable, perhaps Rebecca's situation was not so dire as the Admiral or Yates had made it sound. She could still find someone worthy of her affections, someone who could properly take care of her.

"I know nothing of the sort," Diana said. "I know that both of you deserve to love and be loved. I know that I have never seen you as happy or at peace as you have been recently. And only a sapskull would be ignorant of the fact that she is madly in love with you too."

A door down the corridor opened, and I watched Rebecca emerge, a vase of roses in her arms.

Diana looked at me significantly. "Don't be a fool, Valentine." And then she walked back up the stairs. How many more people would call me a fool before the end of the day?

Chapter Twenty-Nine

VALENTINE

Rebecca stopped at the sight of me, blinking, as though she thought she was seeing things. The sight of her filled me with aching wishes of what could never be—what *should* never be. But she deserved to know what had been happening, why I had left, and why I was leaving again.

I walked toward her, and she offered me an unconvincing smile. It was full of uncertainty, and I wished I could replace it with one of her usual, joyful ones. In time, she would regain that. She couldn't be brought down for long; it was not in her nature.

She set her burden on the table next to the door, wiping her hands down her skirts. "With all the decorations from the other night still sitting in the drawing room, I thought we could put the vases of flowers around the house for a bit of cheer." She paused, looking at me hesitantly. "Would you like one in your bedchamber?"

The veiled hope in her voice, the implication that she wished for my return made it difficult to swallow. "It would be put to better use elsewhere. I am returning to Yates's."

"Oh."

We stayed in the silence for a moment, looking at one another. I didn't want to leave. I wasn't ready to say goodbye, but I had no reason to delay. Rebecca was a bright spot in my overwhelmingly dark life, and I didn't know how to return to the abyss after knowing that light.

"Would you like help?" I asked.

Her expression brightened a bit. "I would appreciate it very much." She offered another courageous smile that tugged at my heart. How could she be such an angel to someone like me? I knew for a fact that *I* didn't deserve Rebecca Russell, but I was beginning to wonder if *anyone* truly deserved her.

I moved to open the door wider, and she passed through with a soft "thank you" and a glance up at me that twisted my heart.

The room was a beautiful ruin of the ball, with vases of flowers covering every bare surface area and the chandelier hanging low, already cleaned but not yet raised again after the removal of the candles. I set down the letters from my creditors on the side table, wishing the contents could be set aside just as easily.

Rebecca went to the nearest vase and took to tidying the roses inside, pulling off the petals that were drooping and browning. There was a nervous energy about her, a quickness to her motions I didn't quite understand. But neither did I know how to say what I had come to say.

She turned toward me suddenly. "You have been avoiding me." She pulled her lips in, as though the words had come out without her intending them to.

I opened my mouth, planning to refute it, but I couldn't. I *had* been avoiding her. "I am sorry. I have only been thinking of your well-being."

Her brows drew together. "You think it serves my well-being to be deprived of you?"

"I have always thought so," I pointed out softly.

"And I have always disagreed." She said it with more passion than I was accustomed to hearing from her. A hint of anger, even.

"Rebecca . . ." My voice was plaintive, and I stepped toward her, needing her to understand. "I was earnest when I told you before the ball that my usefulness in your life had been spent. I doubt whether I ever *was* anything but a harm to you. You have looked to me for guidance before—I must ask you to trust me now."

"Trusting you to tell me the meaning of words is not the same thing as allowing you to decide my future, Valentine."

I sighed. She had a point. "My withdrawal is necessary to allow other gentlemen the opportunity to come to know you." The very words made me sick with jealousy. I swallowed down the acrid taste, and it burned like brandy.

"To what end?" she said. "None of them wish for that, and neither do I."

"The more they come to know you, the more they will love you. It is inevitable." How many words that went against a man's true desires could he say before his tongue rebelled against him? I was nearing that limit; I could feel it.

"It is not inevitable." There was a small pause as she swallowed. "You know me better than any of them, and you do not want me."

I stared at her, momentarily bereft of speech. Her eyes were filling with tears, as though saying the words aloud had taken something from her she could never get back.

"Are you mad?" I said, my words soft but harsh. "I have *never* wanted someone the way I want you, Rebecca. I am being driven to the brink of reason with it. I can hardly—" I stopped myself. There was no use belaboring the point.

The way Rebecca was looking at me, though, her eyes wide with surprise, told me she hadn't been aware.

I looked away, for to look at her was to want her. "The

important thing," I said in a level voice, "is that I cannot give you what you deserve."

"Is this about the money? The debts? I have a generous dowry, Valentine—five thousand pounds—and Grandfather has assured me he means to leave a significant—"

"Stop." I gripped the edge of the table beside me. "On no account would I agree to that." I took in a breath, trying to calm myself. That Rebecca should offer her own inheritance to pay for my irresponsibility was more than I could bear. It was the greatest reproach I could imagine. "The money is only part of it."

There was a pause. "Is it Miss White?"

My brows drew together. "Miss Wh—" I cut myself off, rearing back slightly. "You mean Nellie?"

She said nothing.

My resistance creaked and groaned under the weight of her hurt, and I stepped toward her. "Is this what you have been thinking since the night at the theater? That I have been pining after her?" Gently, I nudged her chin up so that she would meet my gaze.

Her eyes, pink and shining with threatening tears, stared back at me. "I cannot compare our friendship with what you and"—she swallowed—"Nellie had. Or *have*. But I can tell you that every touch between us has connected me to you in ways that . . ." She shook her head, not meeting my eye. "I cannot describe it. But the point is that I can only imagine what you must feel for one another after the sort of connection you have shared."

"Rebecca." I thought I might split in two from the way my insides writhed. Putting my hands on either side of her face, I lowered my head to seek her gaze. "You are right. What you and I have cannot compare to what Nellie and I had. *Had*, Rebecca, for that is all in the past."

She swallowed.

"And the reason it cannot compare is because my connection with her was borne of convenience and selfishness. I regret it for a hundred reasons—on my account, on Nellie's account, and on your account, to name but a few." I clenched my teeth and dropped my hands from her face. "But my regret does not change the past. And it does not change the fact that she is not the only woman with whom I have shared such a connection. My behavior in the past has been inexcusable. But it would be just as inexcusable and selfish of me to ask you now to be with me."

She shook her head, taking my hands in hers. "I think you have been hurting for a very long while, Valentine, and hurt can lead us to do strange things. That does not mean you do not deserve happiness now and in the future. Perhaps you deserve it all the more."

I looked down at our joined hands, wondering how I could keep my resolve intact much longer when she held my hands in such a way and offered me such unmerited mercy. "You make allowances for me I do not deserve." Allowances even the man who had raised me did not make for me. I raised my eyes to her face. "Why?"

She met my gaze squarely. "Everyone deserves mercy. And who am I to say that, in your place and with your pain, I should have acted any differently than you?"

I searched her eyes. "Does your charity never exhaust itself?"

She gave a soft, rueful chuckle. "I have struggled mightily to have any charity at all for Nellie. More, in fact, as time goes on. When I first learned she was your soft-skirt—" She paused. "That is what it is called, isn't it?"

It was the strangest thing to laugh in such a situation, but I couldn't help myself. Rebecca had the power to make me smile in the most unlikely of circumstances. It was what I so loved about her. "Light-skirt. But close enough."

"Light-skirt," she repeated, as though committing it to

memory. "When I first learned *that*, it was not your physical intimacy that troubled me, but the thought that she might know you better than I do—better than I ever would. "

I shook my head, but she continued.

"But once Grace Bradley asked if you had kissed me yet . . ." Her gaze dropped to my lips, and she rubbed hers together as though tasting an imaginary kiss between us. It sent a pulse of desire racing through me, and I unintentionally tightened my grip on her hands.

She looked up at me again. "I began to be jealous of Nellie—and all the others—for a whole new reason. And I began to wonder if you *had* ever thought of kissing me."

A million times. It was all I could do to keep from doing so now, to keep my gaze from straying back to the curves of her pink lips.

Her brow furrowed as she looked up at me. She took a small step toward me, setting my every muscle on edge. "He has kissed so many other women, I thought to myself. Why not me?"

"Because I do not deserve to kiss you, Rebecca." The words tore from me. "I do not deserve any part of you. Everyone but you realizes that. Any man would be better than me."

"I do not care what everyone else realizes. And neither should you. You pride yourself on not caring what people think, yet you let them determine how you see yourself. I cannot bear to see it anymore, Valentine. If there are people who refuse to accept you as anything but a rake, who refuse to allow you to change, it is a fault in *them*, not in you, that makes it so."

My throat grew thick, my eyes burning in a way I hadn't experienced since discovering my mother's death—one of three times in my life I had cried. My mother was the only one who had ever said anything to me like Rebecca was saying, who had believed better of me than I believed of myself. And to have Rebecca echo her felt like a message from beyond the grave, all the more powerful for the fact that Rebecca was not *expected* to believe the best of me as a mother was.

"I do not know how to deserve a happiness like you," I said, my voice thick.

She dropped my hands and reached hers up to my face, just as I had done with her minutes ago. "You deserve every bit of happiness you are willing to receive, Valentine. Can that happiness not be with me?"

I rested my forehead against hers, clenching my eyes shut. Part of me said to give in to what I wanted, to what *she* wanted, while the other part of me demanded I resist, insisting that I would never be worthy of her.

Her gaze was on my mouth, and her thumb brushed from my cheek to my lips, sending shivers rippling across my skin, igniting the embers of desire glowing inside me. I had experienced Rebecca in enough ways to know I loved her—I had seen her beauty, listened to her joy, felt her hands and waist in my hands, smelled her sweet scent. But I wanted to taste her lips, to experience everything of her there was to experience. I wanted her in all my senses.

"Do not test me, Rebecca," I pleaded, feeling the weight of my weakness, for I knew somewhere inside me that, if I kissed her, I would never be the same, would never be content with a life without her.

But that was already true. The moment I met her, everything had begun to change for me. I was not the man I had been when I had come upon her eating brioche buns in the kitchen at midnight, warning me against gout. "I am not strong enough to resist."

Her voice came in a whispered plea. "Then do not resist." She tipped her head so that I felt the ghost of her lips near mine, melting the last bit of my resistance away.

I lifted my chin slowly, tentatively, until my mouth met the delicate velvet of hers. A shudder ran through me, a potent mixture of pleasure and unparalleled bliss. Her lips were softer, more inviting than I had imagined them—as soft and inviting as Rebecca herself, welcoming me to explore them, to forget everything beyond us.

And like that, I was lost. Entirely. Completely. Irrevocably.

She put a hand on my chest, and I covered it with mine, lacing my fingers through hers and feeling the knocking of my heart through it all. Wrapping my hand around her waist, I pulled her gently into me as our mouths met again and again, tilting and turning in a soft, slow exploration of one another.

I thought I had kissed women before, for I had kissed to distract, kissed to forget, kissed to fill a void. But I knew now that I was wrong. I *hadn't* ever kissed. Not until now. Everything before had been a sham, a shabby imitation of something ineffably sublime. Every second with Rebecca in my arms was a concert of emotion, a duet in the expression of love, a coupling of desire and tenderness that I had never before experienced.

A handle turned, and the sound of the door opening broke our lips and bodies apart.

Breathless and disoriented, I turned my head and stilled.

Duke Russell stood in the doorway, staring at Rebecca and me. His stunned gaze traveled back and forth between us, as though he wasn't certain he could trust what he was seeing.

Surprise gave way to anger, his nostrils flaring and his jaw tightening. "Leave, Rebecca." The words were hard, flinty, but his eyes were not on her. They were fixed on me.

"Duke," she said, her voice pleading for understanding. "I can exp—"

"Enough," he said, his voice louder than I had ever before heard it. When he spoke again, it had regained its calm. "I will speak with you later. Leave. Now."

Still, Rebecca hesitated beside me. I turned my eyes to her ' ~ave her a reassuring nod. She held my gaze for a moment, her cheeks pink and her chest still rising and falling rapidly, then she walked toward the doorway.

Russell's eyes never left mine, even as his sister passed by him, and I braced myself for what was to come the moment the door closed.

Chapter Thirty

REBECCA

I was not normally one for nervous habits, but I both paced and chewed at my thumbnail as I waited outside of the drawing room. The suddenness of my brother's return had put an abrupt stop to the most inconceivably glorious minutes of my entire life, replacing it all with a tangle of dismay and anxiety.

Impulse told me to charge through the door and defend Valentine from whatever attacks he was now facing. But I trusted he knew his relationship with Duke. I would have time to speak with my brother later.

The door opened, and I whirled around as Valentine emerged. My heart plummeted into the pit of my stomach at the sight of his expression. I had never seen it so dark.

He took a few steps before noticing my presence. His expression relaxed a bit, and I hurried over to him. He took a step back, putting out a hand that held a few letters, and I stopped, my dismay returning. What had Duke done? What had he and the Admiral said?

Anger shot through my veins, and I hurried past Valentine, only for him to grab my hand, preventing me. I turned toward him, ready to fight him off. I was prepared to do anything—shout the curse words I had learned from Valentine at Admiral Donovan, challenge both him and Duke to a duel—if it meant undoing whatever damage they had done to the understanding we had reached.

"Let things lie, Rebecca," he said softly, keeping my hand in his. "It is no use."

Desperation began to rise in my stomach, clawing up into my throat. "They cannot keep me from you."

"But they can." The quiet in his voice made me feel more desperate than anything. "You aren't of age."

"I shall be in November," I said, my voice coming out almost frantic.

Valentine nodded. He swallowed and looked down at our hands, his thumb rubbing mine distractedly. "I am not surrendering, Rebecca. But it will take time to prove myself to your brother. If it can be done. And if your affection for me remains."

I squeezed his hand, my eyes brimming with tears. "Never doubt it." That he hadn't given up hope, hadn't abandoned the idea of us eased the despair enough for me to breathe. "I shall love you far beyond the day I stick my spoon in the wall."

His mouth turned up in a half-smile, and I gave a watery chuckle. The amusement faded quickly, though, and our gazes met. The gravity of the situation, so quick on the heels of such joy, made the moment heavy, and our hands gripped each other's tightly.

"You will hear from me," he said. "Somehow."

I nodded, wishing I could keep the tight hold I had on his hand and prevent him from leaving. To have had him so near so recently and to think of the possibility that I might never again . . .

With a final press of the hand, he let go, turning and walking through the arched doorway that led to the entry hall, then disappearing. I watched him go, a knot in my throat. It wasn't until the door shut behind him that I took my eyes from the place he had disappeared.

Duke stood in the doorway of the drawing room. How long had he been there? Next to him stood the Admiral, a stern expression on his face. He, too, seemed to have witnessed what had just transpired.

All the frustration that had pent up inside me during my pacing of the corridor bubbled up anew, and I stalked over to my brother. Despite the fact that our relationship over the years had been conducted largely by post, I had always quite liked Duke. But just now, I wanted to slap him. And the Admiral too.

I hadn't lost my senses, though. Not completely. Not yet. There would be plenty of time for slapping later.

"May I speak with you alone, Duke?" I asked tersely, glancing at the Admiral.

"I shall give you your privacy," the Admiral said stiffly, and he turned away from us. My fingers gripped at the sides of my skirts impatiently as he walked down the corridor and disappeared into the library.

Once he was well out of earshot, I shifted my gaze to Duke. "How could you, Duke? You haven't any idea of the situation—"

He put a hand up. "I haven't the energy right now, Rebecca. We will speak of this tomorrow when I have had time to settle my emotions. And when I have seen my wife, who is the reason I am here in the first place. There is no need to rush into things."

I clenched my hands into fists, wanting to ignore his request, for my feelings were like the boiling water in a teapot. Left much longer, they would force themselves out—very likely in the same loud and unpleasant shrieking.

But there was wisdom in what Duke said. If Valentine and I were to have any chance of making him believe the truth about what we felt for one another, a night's rest and reflection would help. Screaming like a teapot would serve no one. Perhaps I could consult with Diana in the meantime, too. She would help Duke see reason. I knew she would.

"Very well," I said.

Duke's expression was inscrutable as he walked over to me, dropped a quick kiss on my forehead, and went on his way up the stairs.

―――――

There was no opportunity for speaking with Diana that day or that evening. Whether Duke was purposely trying to keep me from her or whether they were simply eager for time alone together, they did not descend from upstairs at all.

When the Admiral, Phineas, and I gathered in the dining room and discovered that neither Duke nor Diana meant to come down but had ordered their own dinners to be sent up to their bedchamber, there was an awkward pause.

"I shall follow suit," the Admiral said, turning to the footman. "Bring my dinner to me in my bedchamber."

The footman nodded, and the Admiral left without another word. I couldn't regret it. It was a relief not to be obliged to make conversation with him all evening when I had nothing civil to say.

"What of you?" I asked Phineas. "Shall you take your meal upstairs as well?"

He gave me a measuring look through his glasses. "Do you wish for company?"

I thought for a moment. The afternoon had been interminably long, and the evening would be the same, filled with worry over Valentine. Would he buckle under the stress and take to drinking the troubles away? I assumed he had returned to Captain Yates's as had been his intention before our interlude in the drawing room, but there was no way for me to know. I could only wait to hear from him.

"I will eat here," Phineas said.

My expression must have betrayed how much I disliked the prospect of spending the evening alone, and I sent him a grateful smile.

My experience with Phineas had been limited since his arrival in Brighton, for he spent a great deal of his time poring over books in the library. But I found in him an easier conversational partner than I had imagined. Indeed, he seemed able to converse on a host of topics with ease, successfully distracting me as we ate. But behind it all, the same preoccupations simmered under the surface.

Near the end of the meal, I set down my utensils and looked at him.

He met my gaze and grimaced slightly. "It is not the same without Valentine, is it?"

I shook my head, trying to ward off the lump in my throat. "We must help him."

He nodded. "You have my support, if that means anything."

"It does. A great deal. My brother might not be inclined to believe *me*, but he shan't be able to help taking you seriously."

"I would not offer my help if I did not believe it in the best interest of both you and Valentine." He looked at me for a moment. "I have watched Valentine struggle and fight—himself, my father"—he shrugged—"everyone. But now . . . well, he is quite altered. Your brother will see that, I trust."

I sat at the breakfast table at eight o'clock, staring at the pots of chocolate and cream in the middle of the table, unable to persuade myself to pour either into my cup. I had drunk chocolate in the morning for at least a year, but somehow it had come to feel like a tradition to be enjoyed only in Valentine's company.

The door creaked open, and my brother stepped inside. His eyes settled on me for a moment before he continued to the sideboard.

"Did you sleep well?" he asked in his calm way as he filled his plate.

"Not particularly," I replied. "You?"

"No."

I sighed. I had had plenty of time to think about things during those wakeful hours, and I couldn't deny that making an enemy of Duke was the worst possible route to my goal. "You are worried about me. And angry with me, perhaps."

Lips compressed, he brought his plate to the table and sat down. "I am trying to make sense of it all, Rebecca."

I nodded.

He picked up his knife and reached for the butter. "It is an understatement to say that Valentine Donovan is not the man I would have chosen for you."

"Why?"

His knife slowed, and his gaze fixed on me. "I doubt any man wishes his sister to marry a rake."

"And what if he is not the rake you think him?"

"Rebecca . . . you must realize that I have known Valentine longer than you."

"But not as recently and not as well," I countered.

"How much change can there possibly be in a matter of weeks?"

"A great deal. But if you refuse to accept him as anything but a rake, that hardly matters, does it?"

He frowned deeply as he buttered his toast. "I, as much as anyone, want the best for Valentine."

"Is that true? The best? The very best?" I held his gaze, but he was silent. "Or do you wish for him to continue paying for his mistakes all his life, as so many others seem to wish?"

"No," he said softly. "That is not what I wish at all."

"And what does Diana say?"

He blew out a soft laugh through his nose, shaking his head. "She is entirely set upon the match."

Bless Diana. She might just be the means of salvation for Valentine and me.

The door opened suddenly, and Captain Yates walked in unannounced. His gaze took in the room, and he doffed his hat, dipping into a hurried bow. "Forgive me for bursting in on you in such a manner."

"What is it?" I asked, my stomach filling with lead.

"It is Donovan." He spun the brim of the hat in his hands. "He has been arrested. Taken to the sponging house."

The silence following this announcement was deafening.

"The bailiff came upon us as we were walking to the bank," Captain Yates said. "Donovan meant to apply there for a loan to pay his debts, not that he had much hope of them granting it. But now . . ." He grimaced. "If I hadn't my own financial troubles to contend with, I would pay the bail myself."

"How much is it?" Duke asked.

"Fifteen pounds. It is his tailor who laid the complaint."

"Thank you, Captain," Duke said somberly.

Captain Yates gave a nod and set his hat back on his head. "I shan't interrupt you any longer. Only send word if I can be of any assistance."

It was not until the captain had left and the door was closed that I found the ability to speak. "Will you pay the bail?"

Duke's lips turned down at the sides as he set the butter knife back in its place. "I do not know."

"You do not know?" I cried incredulously.

Duke set his hands on the edge of the table and looked at me. "Valentine's debts have been paid for him for years. Where has that brought him? It has only enabled him to continue accruing them, Rebecca, for there are never any consequences. And if you think that I shall give you my permission to marry someone drowning in debt, who, once those debts are paid, shall merely dive into the waters once again, you are being unforgivably foolish. And that is only if he *does* mean to marry you, a fact which Admiral Donovan contests."

"Admiral Donovan does not know Valentine at all."

"I rather think he would disagree, being Valentine's father."

"He is not his father. Not in name *or* deed. He seems to have thought the worst of him from before he was even born and then spent his efforts since then making Valentine believe the worst of himself." I held Duke's gaze, willing him to understand what seemed beyond his grasp. "How is Valentine to pay his debts from the sponging house? Or, if you will not pay the bail, from debtor's prison?"

Duke's grimace deepened. "A night or two in the sponging house shan't do him any harm. Indeed, it may well help him. And in the meantime, I will try to make sense of his financial situation with Admiral Donovan."

I took in a breath, trying to calm my temper. Never had I been so out of humor with anyone. I had no hope that Duke speaking with the Admiral would do Valentine any good at all.

No, if he was to be extricated from debtor's prison, it would have to be by other means.

Chapter Thirty-One

VALENTINE

"And here we thought we'd be lettin' ye go, Mr. Donovan, sir." One of the bailiff's workers stood in the doorway, smiling at me with crooked, yellow teeth and the smell of tobacco heavy about him. *Bailiff's dogs*, they called such men. I thought the term an insult to dogs everywhere.

The Admiral's footsteps could still be heard retreating down the creaky corridor of the sponging house, but even if they had not, the thumping of my heart was evidence of the sort of visit his had been.

It was late morning, and the Admiral had arrived but a quarter of an hour ago. A short visit that might have ended differently, as the man said.

"We're glad not to lose ye so soon, though," he said.

"No doubt," I said, taking a seat on the thin, tattered mattress. Since I had arrived, the bailiff and his dogs had drunk four bottles of various spirits and eaten half a dozen fowl. Aside from the general disgust with which I regarded their behavior under the influence of such spirits, my greater annoyance was that all of this was to be added to the account they were keeping of *my* expenses at the sponging house. Three shillings for the doubtful pleasure of sleeping on the premises, two shillings for a bit of bread and cheese, and the same exorbitant rates for drink and a candle once dark fell.

Knowing as I did the debts already on my shoulders, I couldn't but cringe each time they chose to enter my room—if the space could be called any such word—for they generally came with a bottle in hand, ready to flaunt their consumption in my face, offering me the dregs of the bottle and whatever flesh was left on the bones of their food. It had taken every bit of my willpower to deny myself the drink offered, knowing it would at least make the misery of the place a bit more bearable. All I could do was close my eyes and try to imagine myself back in the rose garden or, preferably, in the library with Rebecca, her arms wrapped around me and mine around her.

"I have told you already," I said. "I cannot pay the debt brought against me. I wish to be transferred to the prison."

"Ah," he said with faux disappointment, "ye make me sad, ye do, sayin' fiddle faddle like that, Mr. Donovan."

I was nearly made to smile, thinking of what Rebecca would say if she could hear such talk. No doubt she would bemoan the absence of her notebook.

The bailiff's dog waved a hand. "We'll give it another day or two here, eh? A fine cove like yerself is bound to 'ave friends ready to sport the blunt." And without another word, he shut the door, leaving me to myself.

I suppose I should have been grateful that I *was* by myself. When I had first arrived, there had been another man—a chandler—staying in the same room. He had been fortunate to have a small enough debt for a relative to pay it.

The last eighteen hours had felt like an eternity. I had heard reports of the conditions at sponging houses, but the experience was worse still. The dampness, the dimness, the general squalor . . . it was atrocious.

My window faced the street, but thick iron bars had been put in place to prevent any *ideas* from being executed. If I wished for the benefit of fresh air, I was allowed five minutes in a sort of caged garden at the back of the house—supervised, of course, by one or both of the bailiff's dogs.

Part of me hoped no one would pay these men a penny on my behalf, while the other part of me would have given anything for my freedom. My request to send a letter had been granted—for a price—until the bailiff's dog had opened the letter, seen that it was addressed to a woman, and thrown it in the fire. They were only interested in allowing me to communicate with people who could pay them the money they wanted.

I let myself drop back onto the bed, cringing when my spine hit one of the boards protruding from under the mattress. Shutting my eyes, I grasped at the memory of Rebecca's touch, of those sweet kisses she had offered me. That all felt like a different lifetime. By now, she would know of my presence here —Yates would have seen to that.

Perhaps it was the influence of the miserable sponging house, but I had been trying mightily to fend off the fear that those moments with Rebecca had all been a dream, that if I ever *did* manage to leave this place or debtor's prison after it, her sentiments would have changed.

With such unhappy thoughts and feelings for company, I dozed off.

T he jangling of keys jerked me awake. I sat up on my bed, blinking the sleep from my eyes, remembering the hellhole I was in.

The door opened, letting in a stream of light, and I blinked at the woman who entered.

"Nellie?" My voice croaked, scratchy from sleep.

She was dressed in a long-sleeved, pink gown, with short kid gloves covering her hands. Smiling, she pulled on the strings of her straw bonnet and removed it. The bailiff's dog who had opened the door shut it behind her.

I frowned. The Admiral's visit had been carried out entirely under the surveillance of one of the dogs. From all I knew, that was a procedure they followed quite strictly. They didn't wish for secret communications between their wards and visitors.

"What are you doing here?" I asked, standing up.

"I heard you were here, and I had to come," she said. "I haven't had even a moment alone with you since you returned to Brighton."

"We have both been otherwise engaged."

She walked toward me. "But now we aren't."

I took a step back, and she checked in her progress toward me. "Don't tell me you're still playin' at the reform game, Valentine."

"It is not a game, Nellie. Things are different. *I* am different."

She looked me over, as though trying to decide whether to believe me. "I was certain you'd have tired of your schoolroom miss by now."

My brow furrowed as I remembered what Diana had told me of their encounter with Nellie the other day. "Is that what you said to her?"

She held my gaze. "I only reminded her that before she came along, I was the woman in your life. It seems you could use remindin' of it as well." She took another step toward me.

"I need no reminder," I said, matching her step with one of my own in the opposite direction. "That is all in the past."

"It doesn't have to be. I could free you from this place, you know." She put a finger to the necklace she wore. "This piece alone would be enough. We could—"

"I mean to marry Rebecca, Nellie," I interrupted. "If she will take me."

I saw the sting of pain in Nellie's eyes, but she veiled it

quickly. Guilt pricked at me. I had always thought Nellie as indifferent as I was. I had been wrong. She was a skilled actress, that was all.

"Well," she said, "marryin' her doesn't have to spell the end for us, now, does it?"

I grimaced, well aware that I was primarily to blame for the fact that Nellie would make such an assumption about how I would conduct myself after marriage. "It does, though."

She gave a brittle laugh. "Never thought I'd see the day when Valentine Donovan would let himself be ruled over by a simperin' miss."

"You may call it whatever you like, but if you mean to speak of her in such a way, you can leave."

Her eyes flashed and her nostrils flared. More evidence that this was not the business transaction I had assumed it to be for her. I had been a blind, selfish fool.

"I never meant to hurt you, Nellie. I swear. And I am truly sorry if I have. You deserve better than this, though—than what you had with me or Sutcliffe." I nodded at the necklace she wore. "You should sell that and use the money to make a life for yourself. You are a smart, enterprising woman. I have no doubt you will find success."

Despite the sincerity of my words, her expression only grew harder.

"I wish you well with your little doll," she said. "*If* she'll take you, which she'd be a fool to do." Turning on her heel, she left the room without another glance backward.

The door shut with a thud, and the jingling of keys thereafter told me the bailiff's dog had been nearby. Listening in, more than likely.

I slumped back down on the bed, rubbing my eyes with my hands. I couldn't fault Nellie for the manner of her departure. I recognized what had prompted it: pain and embarrassment. I had a whole past of decisions made in such a state.

I could only hope that, with time, Nellie's resentment and anger would ebb enough for her to forgive me—and to choose a different life for herself.

I laid down again, cursing as the same board lodged into my back. How long would I be here? When would the bailiff be satisfied that he would have no money out of me or anyone I knew?

Chapter Thirty-Two

VALENTINE

I felt the ire of the bailiff's dogs keenly. In their eyes, I had deprived them of money now not once but twice, and they had their revenge in the amount of food and drink they consumed that evening. I didn't even want to know what astronomical amount had been added to the initial fifteen pounds leading to my arrest.

I stood at the window, my hand on the cool iron bars, letting the light that slipped between them fall on me as I imagined myself outside. The bailiff's home, which acted as a sponging house, was on a narrow, cobbled street with little light even on the sunniest of days, and today was not sunny.

There is beauty and peace despite it all. Those had been Rebecca's words in the rose garden. I breathed in, wishing I could inhale those flowers again, but the stench of the sponging house was all that met my efforts, leading me to cover a cough.

A carriage clattered nearby, and I strained for a glimpse of it —evidence of life beyond these bars. Fortune smiled upon me, for it drew nearer until I could see it: a carriage pulled by a sleek bay and a dappled gray.

My hand gripped the bar more tightly. I recognized those horses.

The carriage rolled to a stop, and the driver hopped down, then opened the door. Phineas stepped out, and I blinked, certain I was imagining things. But there he was.

He turned back toward the carriage, conversing with someone through the open door. I narrowed my eyes as if that might help me see. The tip of a straw bonnet peeked out from the doorway, suddenly turning up to reveal Rebecca's face. She was looking up, searching the façade of the building.

My heart sped to a gallop, as though spurred by a cat o' nine tails. Her gaze came to my window, and I leaned forward as far as the bars would allow. Could she see me? But the bars were too thick, and she turned her head away again, nodding at something Phineas said, and retreating back into the carriage. While my heart seemed intent on jumping through the bars, I was grateful Phineas had insisted she stay inside. This was no place for a woman. Or any human, really.

It was all I could do to keep from positioning myself at the door to listen for whatever might be happening downstairs. Soon enough, though, footsteps traipsed up those wretched, uneven stairs. The key grated in the lock, and the door opened.

"Ye've a visitor, sir," said the bailiff's dog. He cocked an eyebrow at me. "Another one."

It was clear that, with his expression, he meant to communicate to me not to make a muddle of this opportunity to get him the money he was owed.

Phineas stepped into the room, and it struck me how very out of place he was here, even more so than the Admiral. Phineas would never accrue a debt he couldn't pay—unless, perhaps, it was for books. But he was far too responsible, far too reasonable for that, and I grimaced to know that he would likely never have known such a place if not for me.

"Phin, what are you doing here?"

He glanced at the bailiff's dog, as though waiting for him to leave before he answered. But the dog merely stretched his mouth wide, giving us a glimpse at every missing and blackened tooth he possessed. Then, he entered the room and closed the door, making it clear he was going nowhere.

Phineas turned back to me. "I have come to pay your debts."

"Phin . . ."

"Rebecca and I have come up with the necessary money." He turned back to the bailiff's dog. "Are you the one capable of receiving payment and setting my brother at liberty?"

The man nodded, his beady eyes gleaming at us. "That I am, good sir."

Phineas gave a nod and reached into his coat. I stopped him with a hand. I couldn't let Rebecca and Phineas pay my debt.

He met my gaze calmly. "Let me at least retrieve something from my pocket."

I let go of his hand, and he pulled out a small, folded piece of paper, which he handed to me. Before I could take it, the bailiff's dog snatched it away and opened it.

He glanced at it, then up at me, cocking a thick, bushy brow. "From a lady, it is. *My dearest Valentine,*" he read in a falsetto tone, putting a hand to his heart, "*I always swore I would repay you for that hideous vase. Yours, Rebecca. P.S. Far beyond the day I stick my spoon in the wall . . .*"

The man's face contorted in confusion as he read the last part. I snatched it from his hands, looking at the beautiful, flowing script for myself. *Far beyond the day I stick my spoon in the wall . . .* The words flooded me with warmth that ached. She was reaffirming the loyalty of her feelings.

I stared at the note a moment longer, then looked up at Phineas, who was watching me.

"I cannot let you pay my debt, Phin."

"You cannot *keep* me from paying it, either," he said with a smile that shifted his glasses up a bit. "I imagine this man will gladly take it."

"That I will," replied the bailiff's dog cheerfully.

Eyes on me, Phineas reached into his pocket again and pulled out three bank notes. I clenched my jaw but refrained from interfering. The bailiff's dog counted the notes—all three of them—while licking his lips. I didn't even mind how disgusting it was, for this meant I could leave. Not only that, but I would be leaving with Rebecca. I would give her back her money, of course, and Phin's, too, the moment my prize money was in my possession. But for now, I could do more outside the sponging house to take care of my debts than I could do from within.

"Is there some paper which needs signing?" Phineas asked. "Something official we must do before my brother can leave?"

The bailiff's dog looked up from the money, his eyebrows raised. "Aye, there would be." The way he emphasized *would* produced a niggling of dismay in my stomach.

"Meaning . . .?" Phineas asked.

"Well, sir," he said, "ye've paid fifteen pounds, which is what yer brother was originally brought in for. But since then, he's accrued a few more debts, I'm afeared, not to mention the new complaints laid against him by other creditors. As of today, I believe the total owin' is in the region of a hundred and eighteen pounds."

My stomach dropped, my hopes dashed to the dirty, warped floorboards.

Phineas stalked up to the man and grabbed him by the shirt. "You are a scoundrel," he said through clenched teeth.

I blinked in surprise. I had never seen Phineas do anything so combative or threatening.

The man smiled back at him genially—if such a word could be used for someone with such appalling dentition. "Take care, sir. The bailiff is downstairs, and I doubt ye'd wish to make gaol yer destination. 'Tis not as nice as debtor's prison."

I stepped forward, putting a hand on Phineas's shoulder. "Leave it be, Phin."

Phineas held the man's shirt another moment, then dropped his hand, leaving the dog's clothing disheveled. The man brushed at his shirt carelessly. "And that concludes this lovely visit."

Phineas looked at me, adjusting his glasses, apology and defeat in his eyes.

"Thank you, Phin. And thank Rebecca for me."

"We will find a way to get you out of here, Valentine."

T argued and argued with the bailiff's dogs, doing everything I could to convince them that they would have nothing more than what they had already received. At least in debtor's prison, I could earn my keep. But my arguments were to no avail. Phineas's visit had encouraged them to expect more. No doubt they thought he would soon return with the required money in hand. I did not share their expectations. Neither did I wish for Phineas or Rebecca to make such an attempt.

It was later in that interminable day that one of the bailiff's dogs brought me a note. His manner was markedly less jovial than it had been during Phineas's visit. The seal of the letter had been broken, and I needed only one guess regarding those responsible. Whatever the note said, I would not be the first to know its contents. And apparently, those contents were not pleasing.

"Ye'll be goin' to the prison come mornin'," the bailiff's dog said. He shut the door before I could respond.

I stared at the closed door for a moment. This would be my

last night in this wretched place, and that couldn't but relieve me. But what to expect from this letter had my stomach turning.

Resting my back against the nearest wall, I pulled the paper open, my eyes darting to the signature. Yates. I frowned.

Donovan,

I tried to come speak with you in person, but once it was discovered I had no money on my person, I was refused entrance. Hence this letter. I wish I could be the bearer of good news, but alas, the case is otherwise. It pains me to write this to you, but as I know you are one for plain speaking, I shan't beat around the bush.

I received word from Jones. The case has finally concluded, which means the prize money can be distributed amongst our crew. He informed me of the final amounts each of us can expect. They are all greatly depleted due to the length of the battle in the Admiralty Court. Lieutenants who were aboard at the time of capture will each receive one hundred pounds.

My vision flickered for a moment, and I blinked, forcing my gaze to focus on that last sentence.

Lieutenants who were aboard at the time of the capture will each receive one hundred pounds.

Those final three words rang in my ears like a death knell, over and over. One hundred pounds. It was a mere fraction of what we had expected. It would not come close to covering my debts, of which those keeping me here were only a part.

My breath started to come quickly, and I turned back to the letter, hoping for some ray of light amidst the bad news.

I am terribly sorry, Donovan. I suspected the final amount would be less than anticipated, but this is an unimaginable disappointment, to you more than anyone, I know.

Unfortunately, it is not the only bad news I bear. Lord Newham died. I know this will come as another disappointment to you.

Through all this, I hope you know you may count on me in whatever ways I can be of service. I will do my level best to have you out of there.

Ever your friend and captain,

Yates

My back slipped down the wall, and I let my body fall to the floor with a thud, the hand holding Yates's note making a thump as I let it fall to the floor. I shut my eyes, dropping my head back as the despair began to set in.

What hope had I now?

Chapter Thirty-Three

REBECCA

My foot tapped impatiently on the floor of the breakfast room rug. The bites I had taken out of my toast were small, distracted ones. It had been days since I had had my last cup of chocolate. I knew my abstention was silly—it was not as though it helped Valentine in any way—but I refrained all the same.

This morning's breakfast was different in other ways, though, too. It was nearly ten o'clock, far later than I generally ate in the mornings. Duke had spent the entire evening after dinner enclosed with Admiral Donovan in the study. In the hopes of hearing the result of the *tête-à-tête*, I had stayed awake later than usual, until Diana had persuaded me to retire.

"All shall be well," she said. "I will make sure of it."

Given all she had done to assist Valentine and me, I obliged. Thanks to her and Phineas, bless their souls, Duke had been persuaded that Valentine's changes were not just a figment of my infatuated imagination. That had not sufficed for him to offer his blessing for a match, however.

His remaining concerns had been for Valentine's ability to properly care for me. It was for the purpose of ascertaining the particulars of Valentine's financial situation that he had spoken with the Admiral.

The door to the breakfast room opened, and I shot up from my seat.

Duke paused in the doorway. "You needn't stand when I enter, dearest sister," he said with a glimmer of amusement in his smile. "Very respectful but very unnecessary."

"How did the meeting go?" I asked, ignoring his quip.

Duke went to the sideboard and picked up a plate. He sent me a sidelong glance, his eyes moving to my hands gripping the back of the chair as I waited for a response. "I have the power to make your life miserable by pretending not to know what you are referring to, but I shan't." He took two pieces of bread and set them on his plate. "All in all, it went fairly well." He looked at me again. "Valentine's debts are substantial, Rebecca. There is no escaping that."

I nodded.

"But," he said, "there is a silver lining to that black cloud. The late Mrs. Donovan set aside money of her own for Valentine. It seems that, given their tumultuous history, she was concerned over the potential for a falling out between the Admiral and her son, and she wished to ensure Valentine was not left without some means of supporting himself in that event. A shrewd woman, in fact. Admiral Donovan has been keeping that money from Valentine, convinced his wife would not want it squandered. It took a great deal of tact on my side, but I finally managed to convince him that it was not only unkind but unlawful for him to keep the money from Valentine."

I ran over to my brother and wrapped my arms about him. I must have taken him by surprise, for he did not react immediately.

"Thank you, Duke," I said into his waistcoat.

He wrapped his free arm about my back and pulled me gently to him for a moment.

"You are a bang-up brother," I said.

He grasped me by the shoulders, putting enough distance between us that he could look at me properly. "What did you say?"

"A bang-up brother," I repeated. "It means—"

"I know what it means. What I want to know is how you come to say it."

I raised my brows enigmatically. "I have learned a great deal since you last saw me."

"I assume I have Valentine to thank for that."

"You mustn't blame him," I said hurriedly. "He was merely answering my questions—under the threat that I should go in search of the answers elsewhere."

He gave a sigh. "We can discuss that later." His expression grew serious. "Even with his mother's money freed up for his use, Valentine's finances are in a sad state. He has no source of income to speak of and no profession to generate such an income, for he is set against the Navy."

I ceased smiling, trying to ensure Duke saw that I understood the gravity of the situation. "And with my dowry?"

"The interest from your dowry would certainly help. But, Rebecca, I want to be certain that *you* are certain about this. I would not be doing my duty as your guardian if I did not warn you. You will be living in straitened circumstances. Indefinitely. And if I did not trust Diana and Phineas—if I did not believe they had your own interests in mind as much as Valentine's—I would not feel comfortable giving my blessing."

"You are only trying to protect me," I replied. "I understand, and I love you for that. But this *is* what I want. And once you have had a chance to speak with Valentine, I think you will feel more at peace."

He nodded. "As soon as I have breakfasted, I shall go to the sponging house and bring him back with me."

I wrapped my arms about him again, and he embraced me in return. "I only wish for your happiness and well-being, Rebecca. I hope I am doing the right thing."

I stepped back and looked at him. "I promise I shall be happy and that you shan't regret it."

He released me and walked to a chair at the table. "I am already regretting leaving Valentine in the sponging house this long. I thought a night or two would not harm him, but from Phineas's description, it sounds as though I was mistaken."

I gave a shudder. Phineas had clearly spared me the more gruesome details of his venture inside, but I had learned enough to fill in the gaps. Duke had been less than pleased when he learned of our expedition to the sponging house.

"I shan't allow you to come this time," he said. "You may have your reunion with him when we return."

"Of course," I replied, running my hands down my skirts nervously. I would be seeing Valentine within the next hour or two, and the mere thought sent a kaleidoscope of butterflies flapping at the walls of my stomach. "Does Admiral Donovan know of your intent?" I did not imagine that would be a happy reunion, and I did not wish for anything to taint Valentine's return.

"Yes," Duke replied, taking a bite from his toast. He chewed for a few moments, looking thoughtful. "He and Phineas left for Kent earlier this morning."

"Oh." I had heard a bit of commotion downstairs earlier, but I had only been half-aware of it, late as I had allowed myself to sleep. Perhaps I was becoming more a creature of town than I thought. Or perhaps not having the prospect of breakfasting with Valentine had rid me of the wish to rise early.

"I think it for the best," he said.

Behind me, the door opened. Duke was bringing a teacup to

his mouth, but he stilled with it hovering midway between the table and his mouth, staring.

Frowning, I turned and immediately stilled.

Valentine looked back at me from the doorway, a hint of caution in his gaze.

"Valentine," Duke said with surprise.

I couldn't even speak. I could only stare in bafflement.

"No doubt you are wondering why it took me so long to come," Valentine said, his gaze flitting to me again and again. "I didn't feel it right to offer my thanks in the state I was in, so I went to Yates's first to . . . well, to clean up."

"Your thanks?" Duke asked, looking as confused as I felt.

Valentine frowned. "If you think me the sort of man to neglect expressing my gratitude for paying to free me from that hellish place, I wonder that you did so at all."

"But I did *not* pay to free you," Duke replied. "Not yet, at least. I meant to do so momentarily."

Now all three of us were bewildered. Valentine looked to me, a question in his eyes.

I shook my head. "It was not me." My heart was jumping in my chest, as though trying to break through to him.

"Then who?" Valentine asked.

Duke looked just as puzzled. "The bailiff did not tell you who was responsible?"

Valentine shook his head. "He said it was none of his business—or mine—so long as the money was paid. I assumed it had been you or Diana."

Duke shook his head. "In an hour, that would have been true."

"Perhaps it was Yates," Valentine said, only to shake his head immediately after. "It couldn't have been. His finances are in utter disarray."

Duke regarded him thoughtfully, then lifted his shoulders in a shrug. "I suppose you must simply be grateful to whoever *is* responsible and be content knowing that, unless they choose to tell you, you shall never know their identity."

Still perplexed, Valentine nodded. His gaze moved to me again. It was all I could do to stay in my chair instead of standing up and running over to him.

Our gazes held, and the muscle in his jaw tightened. I knew that look: determination.

"I know you do not look kindly upon my suit, Russell, and I am not fool enough to blame you for it. No one would." He took a slow step toward Duke, who still sat at the table, listening to Valentine intently. "In no realm of thought am I worthy of your sister, and the only thing that pushes me to even speak of a marriage between us is the strength of my feelings for her and my determination to make myself worthy of the feelings she has expressed for me." He took in a breath. "I wish to provide the type of life for Rebecca which she deserves, and my current position does not allow for that." His gaze flitted to me for a moment, then back to Duke. "I have given consideration to the matter and decided that the surest way of achieving this is to try my hand at making my fortune abroad." He glanced at me again, uncertainty in his eyes.

I could only meet his gaze with my own surprised one. What, precisely, was he saying?

"It will take two years at the very least, I imagine," he continued, "to make something of myself. I do not ask Rebecca to wait; I love her too well to do that. But—"

Duke put up a hand. He had been sipping his tea, but he set down the cup. "Allow me to stop you there. I will not pretend that hearing you state such intentions does not set my mind at ease, for it does, which is why I let you keep speaking. But I can see the horror growing in Rebecca's eyes. If I allowed you to go off to India or Jamaica or some such place *without* her, she would never forgive me for it." He looked at me, eyes twinkling.

I gave a shaky laugh, for he was right. My body had been

filling with panic. It was a strange panic, though, tempered by wonder that Valentine would be willing to do such things for *me* . . .

"I am not certain I understand," Valentine said.

Duke rose from his seat. "I am willing to give my blessing to you and Rebecca. And, because I am a selfish man, I beg you not to take my sister away from me now that I can finally be near her. Your father has agreed to provide you with the inheritance your mother left you. That, along with Rebecca's dowry, should give you enough money to purchase a modest property upon which you can make an equally modest living." He smiled slightly. "Nothing that allows for a continuation of your past habits at the card table, obviously, but enough to live upon with a bit of economizing. Or a fair bit of economizing. There is a fitting property but fifteen miles from Birchleigh Hall, and I happen to know the owner wishes to sell."

Valentine blinked, and I had the strongest urge to take his hand in mine as he learned of these changes.

Duke smiled at the dazed silence. "And as I have been deprived of setting you at liberty from that devil's lair you were just in, I shall make a present to you of the money I had set aside for the purpose. Consider it an early wedding gift." He winked at me.

Valentine looked back and forth between me and my brother, clearly struggling to understand. I, on the other hand, was feeling suddenly and inordinately shy, anxious to know how he was feeling.

"I imagine," Duke continued with a hint of amusement, "that I am very much unwanted here at the moment, so I shall leave you two to your reunion." He came to me first, and I stood to receive his embrace. He pulled me in tightly and whispered in my ear, "Be happy, dear Rebecca."

My throat thick, I nodded, for it was all I could do.

He released me and walked over to Valentine. "Brothers

twice over, then, I think."

Valentine let out a strange, breathy laugh that showed just how dumbfounded he still was. Duke pulled him into his arms, speaking more softly, though not enough that I couldn't hear. "I shan't hesitate to call you out if you hurt her, brother or no." Duke released him and walked to the door, and, sending me a little smile, he left the room.

I fiddled with the skirts of my dress, unsure if Valentine's utter overwhelm was the good sort or . . . something else. Perhaps this had all happened too quickly for him and he was rethinking things.

"Are you"—I swallowed—"happy?"

Valentine was staring at me, and his eyebrows pulled together. "Happy?" He walked toward me, and I stayed in place, anxious to know the state of his mind and heart. "I thought I had lost everything, Rebecca. Thought that I might go off to some forsaken place and return only to find you had married someone else." He scrubbed a hand over his jaw. "And now . . ." He stopped in front of me, his gaze searching my face. He touched a soft finger to one of the curls at my temple, sending shivers all the way to my toes as he stared into my eyes. "Happy does not even begin to describe it."

Taking my face between his hands, he pressed his lips to mine. My entire body shuddered, and I steadied myself with my hands on his arms, feeling their strength as they held us together.

Kissing Valentine the first time had been impossible rapture, but this . . . this was euphoria, for it came on the heels of a separation neither of us had been certain would end, and with the new knowledge that our future together was secure.

I surrendered to the euphoria, to the push and pull, the give and take of kissing Valentine. For no sooner did the pressure of his lips lessen on mine than I pursued him, not ready to let go. And each time, he responded by pulling me more tightly to him, by kissing me with more ardor, as though it was only evidence that I wished for more which had been keeping him from offering it.

We pulled apart, slowly, reluctantly, and I looked up at him, at those deep, dark eyes, full of everything I wanted.

"Are we to become leg-shackled, then?"

He laughed, pulling me in for an embrace as heady as had been our kiss.

"Did I say it wrong?" I asked into his shoulder.

"No, my love," he replied, his breath ruffling my hair. "You said it perfectly."

There was a knock on the door, and we broke apart in time for Duke to appear again. From the way his eyes shifted between us, it was clear he was aware what had been happening.

"Forgive the interruption," he said, "but this just came for you, Valentine." He held up a letter.

Taking my hand in his, Valentine walked us over to receive it.

"Do you recognize the name?" Duke asked.

Valentine was frowning again, and he shook his head. "Solicitors of some sort, it seems." He glanced up at Duke with a grimace. "Not good news, I imagine." I surrendered his hand to allow him to break the seal and unfold the missive, feeling nervous again that something would take away the precious happiness I had managed to grasp, just as it had happened the first time.

"What does it say?" I asked.

"That I am to present myself at the offices of Booth and Cottle tomorrow on a matter of business."

"Do not let it concern you," said Duke, though I could see in the set of the jaw that he was anything but confident himself. "Whatever it is, we will manage."

Valentine glanced down at me, and I smiled back up at him reassuringly. We *would* manage. Together, we would face and manage anything.

Chapter Thirty-Four

REBECCA

Valentine and I enjoyed breakfast together the next morning, and I decided that the only thing that could enhance my enjoyment of a cup of smiling chocolate was holding Valentine's hand beneath the table while both of us did so. It was easier to eat and drink with the use of both hands, of course, but love was all about sacrifice, wasn't it?

I could sense his unease as he prepared to make his way to the solicitors' offices. I tried to reassure him in every way I knew how that, just as Duke said, we would face whatever the news was and overcome it.

Once he left, I was too nervous to read or sew. I needed something to occupy me more fully. If Valentine came home disappointed, I wanted to be prepared for it. I meant to brighten his spirits somehow.

After a moment of hesitation, I made my way toward the stairs that led belowstairs. The cook, Mrs. Pimm, and the kitchen maid, Anne, both blinked at me when I appeared in the doorway of the kitchen.

"I would like to make brioche buns," I stated.

The two women looked at one another, then Mrs. Pimm

looked back to me. "Very well, miss. We'll start on them right away."

"I wish to help you," I clarified. When my declaration was met with silence, I added, "If it is not too much of a nuisance."

If I had thought their brows incapable of raising more, I was quickly proven wrong. Mrs. Primm's disappeared entirely under her cap.

"Not a nuisance, no," she said. "If you're willin' to learn, miss, we'd be happy to teach you."

———

The smell of butter and bread filled every corner of the kitchen as I watched the buns turn golden at the oven. Dorothea had lent me one of her aprons, which was generously sprinkled with flour and bits of dough.

"You know they're done," said the cook, "when they start to turn golden on the tops. If they begin to go brown, you've waited too long."

"Now, then?"

"Yes, miss," she replied patiently.

We transferred the hot buns to the long, wooden table, and I hoped Valentine would be home soon enough to have one while it was still warm. He had been gone two entire hours already, and my nerves simmered under the surface. What if creditors of his had banded together? What if he had been arrested *again*?

Dorothea appeared in the doorway. She looked to Anne and Mrs. Pimm. "The mistress needs us upstairs."

"Oh," said Mrs. Pimm, blinking. "Very well." She untied the strings of her apron, and Anne followed suit. The cook glanced at the brioche buns with a little frown. "Those should be moved to a basket."

"I can do that," I said.

She smiled at me and wiped the sweat from her brow with

the sleeve of her dress. "Thank you, miss. I reckon we'll be back down shortly."

The three of them disappeared through the door, leaving me to the kitchen by myself. I took one of the baskets hanging on the wall and set it beside the pan, carefully transferring the buns one by one, wondering how I would occupy myself once my task was done.

There was a knock on the window, and I startled, whirling around.

Valentine stood outside, looking back at me with that charming, crooked smile he reserved specially for me. And then, he started singing.

O Mistress mine, where are you roaming?
O stay and hear, your true love's coming.

He set his hands to the window and pushed up on the sash. It didn't budge, and he looked at me again.

Trip no further pretty sweeting.
Journeys end in lovers' meeting,
Every wise man's son doth know.

Unable to keep from smiling, I went over and used the iron handles on the bottom of the sash, pulling up on them as Valentine did the same. The window gave way easily, making me guess that his failed effort to open it without my help had been pretended.

I put out a hand to him, helping him climb through the window. "The door is open, you know. And you are still singing the wrong tune."

He scrunched his nose at the comment as he slipped down onto the floor and brushed off his coat and pantaloons. Then, without a moment's hesitation, he pulled me into his arms, singing as we waltzed.

What is love, 'tis not hereafter,
Present mirth, hath present laughter:

I couldn't stop from laughing as we tried to avoid the tables and odds and ends that littered the kitchen on a normal mid-morning. Whatever I had expected on Valentine's return, this had certainly not been it.

"I take it the news you received at the solicitors' office was *not* unwelcome?"

He paused our dancing, both of his hands around my waist and his eyes alight in a way I had never seen. After gazing at me for a moment, he continued singing.

What's to come, is still unsure.
In delay there lies no plenty,
Then come kiss me sweet and twenty:
Youth's a stuff will not endure.

He pulled me against him and kissed me, running his hand down my back so that my legs turned useless. Surrendering to this intoxicatingly energetic mood of his, I responded to the kiss by placing my hands on his chest and deepening it.

"You are fortunate I am here alone," I said when we pulled away, looking around to ensure the maids hadn't returned.

"Fortunate, am I?" he asked, pulling me in for another kiss. "Crafty, rather. Dorothea told me I could find you here when I came in the front door. It was I who told her to call Cook and the other maid upstairs."

He reached for one of the buns behind me, and I smacked his hand.

"You shan't have one until you tell me what happened at the solicitors' office."

He abandoned his efforts to snatch a bun and looked at me, losing some of his lightheartedness. "It was the strangest thing. Do you know whose solicitors Booth and Cottle are?"

I shook my head.

"Lord Newham's. He included me in his will."

I stared.

He nodded. "I was as surprised as you were." He reached

around me for a bun, but I grabbed his hand before he could take one.

"And?" I said.

He threaded his hand through mine and raised incredulous brows. "He had no children, you know, so the title goes to a cousin. But"—he rubbed his chin with a hand, then met my gaze. "He left me one of his unentailed estates. And a thousand pounds."

My mouth opened, and I stared at him, entirely mute.

He shook his head in disbelief. "I asked Cottle three times if there was not some sort of error, but he showed it to me himself—the clause in the will. Newham changed it just two days before his death."

"How very generous of him," I said, feeling remorse at the way I had spoken to him. But perhaps it had been needed. A sudden idea occurred to me. "Was it he who paid for your release?"

Valentine shook his head. "It couldn't have been. He died three days ago." His brow furrowed.

"What is it?"

He shook his head. "It is just that . . . well, I know how to bear with scorn and antipathy, for I have done so all my life. But all this kindness, this generosity, this joy . . ." He set a hand to my jaw, brushing his thumb across my cheek. "I am at a loss for what to make of it, what to *do* with it."

I smiled, running my hand through his hair as a surge of love for him coursed through me. "There is only one thing to do with it: extend the same kindness, generosity, and joy to others."

He nodded, then pressed his lips to mine softly, tenderly.

I pulled away and looked at him, smiling. "And"—I twisted my body to allow me to reach for a bun—"you are to eat brioche."

His mouth drew up in a half-smile, and he accepted it from

me. He looked at it for a moment, then to me. "Did you make these?"

"With a great deal of help."

"For me?"

"I thought to cheer you up from the bad news you were receiving. Now that I know the truth, though . . ."

He brought the bun to his mouth, and I snatched it out of his hand. His empty hand hovered in the air, his mouth still open and ready to take a bite.

"You took *my* brioche the first time I met you. Today I have my revenge." I took a bite from the bun, and crumbs spilled down between us.

"I took it because I wanted to give it to you."

I cocked a brow at him. "You make as little sense now as you did that night, but today you have not been foxing. Have you?"

He chuckled, shaking his head and reaching for the bun, which I hid behind my back. His arms followed mine, wrapping around me and bringing our bodies against each other and our faces near enough for our noses to touch. I was obliged to bend back in an attempt to avoid him, but he pursued me still, just as I had hoped he would.

"What I mean," he said, his lips a breath away from mine, "is that I forbade myself from giving it to you. I had only just met you, but already I wished to please you, to give in to your wishes." He brushed the tip of his nose against mine, his efforts to take the bun weakening. "Little did I know, that was the last and only time I would ever manage to say no to you."

Unable to resist a moment longer, I brought my lips to his, and the brioche bun fell to the ground behind me, forgotten.

Epilogue

VALENTINE

SEPTEMBER 1816, NORTHUMBERLAND, ENGLAND

The parish church of Eastbury was surrounded by trees on the cusp of autumn, with yellow-tipped leaves fluttering in the morning breeze. I readjusted Mr. Philpotts's arm resting on mine as I helped him amble toward the church. His rheumatism was rearing its head, as he had been recounting to me for the past five minutes, but he was determined not to let it keep him from the wedding.

Mr. Finner, too, was in attendance, and Phineas had offered to provide him with any assistance he might need. Finner had waved away the suggestion. He was proud of his robust health, for he was beset by neither gout nor rheumatism. It was his grandson's recent antics which continued to plague him. Young Finner was apparently dangling after Haymarket ware. *A vulgar and entirely unsuitable woman.* That was what Rebecca had delightedly inscribed in her notebook upon my explaining the meaning of the phrase to her.

Just now, Rebecca was assisting her grandfather down from the carriage, but she glanced at me once his gouty feet were safely on the ground. The corners of her eyes wrinkled as she smiled at me, and my heart was off to the races. Even if the morning light hadn't settled on her in a warm glow just now, she would have looked like an angel. The soft pink gown she wore brought out the blush in her cheeks, which was visible now more than ever as I stared unapologetically at her, taking in the sight of my soon-to-be wife.

Mr. Philpott smacked my arm to bring me out of my neglectful admiration, for we had reached the stairs—the greatest obstacle in our path.

I hadn't imagined my own wedding would be attended primarily by elderly men, but then again, I couldn't truthfully say I had *ever* imagined my own wedding. As Mr. Philpott detailed his most recent attack of ill-health, though, I could confidently say that the reality eclipsed any possible vision I might have had. What better than anecdotes of old age to make one appreciate one's own youth and good fortune? *My* good fortune was blindingly brilliant—and following just behind me with her grandfather.

Once Mr. Philpott was settled in one of the seats beside Mr. Finner, both of them complaining of the dampness of the church, I stepped aside to allow Rebecca and her grandfather to pass, standing beside Phineas in the path between the pews.

"When do you leave?" I asked.

"The day after tomorrow," Phineas replied.

I looked over at him. He would fit in well at the university, but I would miss him. "The first Cambridge man in the family. What an accomplishment."

"Not the accomplishment Father was hoping for," he said as Diana slipped up beside us.

"I am still trying to convince Phin to go to London for the Season instead," she said. "I am convinced he would take the *ton* by storm if he could be convinced to put down his books long enough to hold a proper conversation with a young woman."

I put an arm around Phineas's shoulders. "He would rather study love than enjoy it himself. Isn't that right?"

"Close enough," Phineas replied distractedly, staring ahead at the vicar. At Cambridge, he would obtain a degree allowing him to take orders. No doubt he was observing everything today with a keen eye and a mind to what his future would hold.

"Don't be absurd," Diana replied. "Neither you nor I thought ourselves the type to fall in love, Val. And yet here we are. Why would Phineas be any different? Besides, I demand another aunt for this child."

I watched Phineas, waiting for understanding to pierce his distraction.

"There it is," I said as comprehension and then surprise lit his eyes behind his large spectacles. He looked at me, then at Diana, who was smiling wickedly.

"You are in the family way?" Phineas asked.

"For a man of such intellect," I said, "you can be terribly slow at times."

Diana looked at me, narrowing her eyes. "Did Duke tell you? I specifically forbade him from doing so."

I shook my head. "I have had my own suspicions since seeing the many dessert plates you filled in Brighton over the past month and the abundance of napping you have engaged in."

Diana flicked my ear. "You are abominable. How *did* you manage to persuade a treasure like Rebecca to have you?"

My gaze drifted to Rebecca, who was listening intently to her entourage of elderly men speaking about heaven only knew what. "No doubt you believe you are the reason for it." I cocked an eyebrow at Diana.

She looked pleased at my acknowledgement of her involvement. "It only took seeing you together once to deduce that you would be the perfect match." She put out her cheek and tapped it with a finger, waiting expectantly.

I shot a long-suffering look at Phineas, then obliged by kissing her. "Temper your self-congratulations, Di. If it had been up to you, I would be rotting in debtor's prison even today."

She drew back in mock offense. "How dare you! Who do you think paved the way for Father to pay your bail?"

Phineas stiffened, and Diana's eyes widened slightly. "That is to say, I—"

"The Admiral paid my bail?" I interrupted her rudely, looking back and forth between her and Phineas.

Diana pulled her lips between her teeth, as if to keep herself from talking more.

"Phin?" I fixed my gaze on my brother, willing him to look at me. He was silent, looking anywhere and everywhere else. That was answer enough.

Diana seemed to have recovered from her guilt, though, for she was the one to fill the silence. "Well, I never agreed with keeping it from you, so I am glad I misspoke. It *was* Father who paid."

I looked to the door, where the Admiral stood in conversation with Duke. It had occurred to me once or twice that he might have done so, but I had dismissed the notion each time. He had provided my direction to my creditors, after all. Without him, I would never have been in the sponging house at all. He had also told me he washed his hands of me.

But I had been wrong to reject the idea of his involvement in my release, just as I had been wrong in assuming he would not come to the wedding. Northumberland was not an easy drive from Kent—not by any stretch of the imagination—but he had come all the same.

"I think the encounter with Lord Newham affected him in an unexpected way," Phineas explained, following my gaze. "And the death even more so. I gather, too, that your determination to flout him and to marry Rebecca secretly impressed him. He is trying to be better, Valentine. But it is not easy for a man of such pride."

I gave a curt nod, my eyes still fixed on him. I was a man of pride as well, and I was not sure I was ready to mend things with the Admiral. If it happened at all, it would be a long and slow effort on both our parts. I would not hold my breath for it, but I would try to be open to the possibility. And Rebecca would help me, sure as anything. She was coming to like the Admiral, and, of course, I could see his affection for *her* growing, against his will as it might be. That was Rebecca's way, though. She was impossible not to love. If anyone knew that, it was I. That the Admiral should be growing fond of her somehow made the prospect of forgiving him a bit less unpalatable.

Another carriage slowed outside, and Rebecca and I went to greet the newcomers together. They were members of the parish I was not acquainted with, and after exchanging greetings and well-wishes, they moved up the path toward the church door.

Rebecca turned to me. "I believe that is everyone we are expecting."

I took her hand, suddenly eager to be married and call her mine. It would take time for me to believe my good fortune— and that it was here to stay for as long as I was willing to work to make it so. "Are all the aged and infirm in the parish inside, then? Or should we wait a few more minutes to ensure we haven't missed anyone?"

Rebecca smiled and reached her hand up to pull my lips to hers.

I would never accustom myself to kissing Rebecca, to the all-consuming experience of it. It commanded every one of my senses, each one of my faculties, and I devoted myself to the task heartily. I did not deserve Rebecca Russell yet; I was not certain I ever truly would. But I would endeavor to do so all my life.

She pulled away, looking up at me with warm cheeks and red

lips as she took the lapels of my coat in hand. "Promise you will never stop kissing me that way."

I brushed my lips against hers. "I will kiss you every way under the sun and at every opportunity you allow me to."

She looked content—and almost impish. "Then you shall be fulfilling at least one item on the list."

I raised a brow. "The list?"

Her smile grew more mischievous, and she pulled a paper from her stays.

I took it from her and unfolded it, my eyes darting to the top. *The Husband List,* it read.

She lifted a shoulder. "I thought you could use a few suggestions for how to be a convincing husband."

"Undoubtedly," I said, turning my focus back to the paper and wondering what items I would find she had concocted this time. My eyes widened as I perused the list. I looked up at Rebecca, whose expression was an enchanting mixture of saucy and nervous.

"You have learned a great deal in that notebook of yours, it would seem."

Her cheeks turned a deeper shade of pink. "You mustn't let that paper out of your sight, Valentine. In fact, I believe it will be best if we burn it. Grandfather would die of an apoplexy if he saw it."

I folded it up with a smile, then, my eyes on hers, tucked it back into her stays. "Then you must keep it safe, for I shall never let you burn it." I pulled her into me, bringing my lips to her ear and whispering, "I agree wholeheartedly to every single item on your list." I pressed a soft kiss into the hollow of her neck and felt her shiver, then grasp my coat in her hands. "I hope you will allow me to venture outside of the list, though, for I noticed it is not at all exhaustive. And I mean to love you in every way imaginable."

She tightened her hold on me, not speaking for a moment. I

felt her lashes close against my cheek and heard the soft inhale. I recognized what she was doing: savoring this moment with all her senses, just as she had taught me to do. Finally, her voice came softly in my ear. "You may write a list for me, as well, you know."

I thought for a moment before responding. "You *are* my list. And an exhaustive one."

"Exhaustive or exhausting?"

"Both," I said with a smile. "I couldn't possibly ask for more."

She gave a little sigh and sought my lips with hers.

A throat cleared loudly somewhere beyond us, and we pulled apart. Duke stood near the door, watching us with an impassable expression.

"It is almost as though he does it on purpose," I murmured to Rebecca.

"Shall we just carry on without you, then?" The ghost of a smile touched Duke's mouth, and he turned back into the church without waiting for a response. He would be the one giving Rebecca's hand to me when the time came in the ceremony. I couldn't think of a man I would rather have as a brother twice over.

Rebecca began to move forward, but I stopped her with a hand on her wrist. She looked a question at me.

Slowly, I put out my arm, inviting her to take it. Her mouth broke into a smile in recognition of my gesture. Moving back beside me, she placed her hand on my arm, and I pulled her in snugly toward me.

"How was that?" I asked as we began our walk to the church —our last moments unmarried.

"I believe," she said, "that the student has become the master."

I looked over at her, for her eyes were trained on me. "What? Why are you looking at me in that way?"

"I am just admiring your profile now. It is so young and free of wrinkles. But it shan't always be."

"True. And *you* shall be the one tasked with caring for me when I become wrinkly. Bedridden with gout. Determined to speak to anyone who will listen of the woes of old age."

She smiled broadly at me. "It is a good thing, then, that I have so much practice."

THE END

Continue the Donovans' journey with Phineas's story.

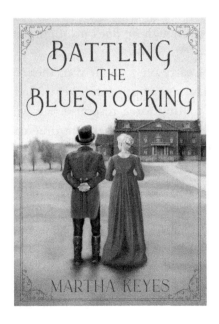

Other Titles by Martha Keyes

The Donovans

Unrequited (Book .5)

The Art of Victory (Book 1)

A Confirmed Rake (Book 2)

Battling the Bluestocking (Book 3)

Sheppards in Love

Kissing for Keeps (Book 1)

Tales from the Highlands Series

The Widow and the Highlander (Book 1)

The Enemy and Miss Innes (Book 2)

The Innkeeper and the Fugitive (Book 3)

The Gentleman and the Maid (Book 4)

Families of Dorset Series

Wyndcross: A Regency Romance (Book 1)

Isabel: A Regency Romance (Book 2)

Cecilia: A Regency Romance (Book 3)

Hazelhurst: A Regency Romance (Book 4)

Romance Retold Series

Redeeming Miss Marcotte (Book 1)

A Conspiratorial Courting (Book 2)

A Matchmaking Mismatch (Book 3)

Standalone Titles

Host for the Holidays (Christmas Escape Series)

A Suitable Arrangement (Castles & Courtship Series)

Goodwill for the Gentleman (Belles of Christmas Book 2)

The Christmas Foundling (Belles of Christmas: Frost Fair Book 5)

The Highwayman's Letter (Sons of Somerset Book 5)

Of Lands High and Low

A Seaside Summer (Timeless Regency Collection)

The Road through Rushbury (Seasons of Change Book 1)

Eleanor: A Regency Romance

Acknowledgments

I wrote the entirety of this book while our family has been living abroad, which has been an interesting experience. My husband has taken on the lion's share of the work to make this a reality: childcare, cooking, cleaning, letting me escape for research expeditions. He is unbelievably supportive.

My kids are patient with my constant preoccupation, even though they don't understand how somehow my books are never finished.

To my critique group—Kasey, Jess, Deborah—you are my people, and your friendship is the best part of this gig by far!

To my beta readers—Mom, Britney, Heidi, Brooke, Becky— thank you for reading the first version of this and for making it better than it ever would have been without your careful eyes and feedback. To Brooke especially, whose actual dreams about the story helped me decide how to finish it.

Thank you to my editor, Julia Allen, for her wonderful work and for cleaning up the messes I made.

Thank you to my Review Team for your help and support in an often nervewracking business.

And thank you, finally and most importantly, to God, for blessing me with everything I have.

About the Author

Whitney Award-winning Martha Keyes was born, raised, and educated in Utah—a home she loves dearly but also dearly loves to escape to travel the world. She received a BA in French Studies and a Master of Public Health, both from Brigham Young University.

Her route to becoming an author has been full of twists and turns, but she's finally settled into something she loves. Research, daydreaming, and snacking have become full-time jobs, and she couldn't be happier about it. When she isn't writing, she is honing her photography skills, looking for travel deals, and spending time with her family. She is currently traveling the world full time with her husband and twin boys.

Printed in Great Britain
by Amazon

40226304R00182